SAMANTHA

AMONG THE BRETHREN.

BY

"JOSIAH ALLEN'S WIFE"

(MARIETTA HOLLEY).

WITH ILLUSTRATIONS.

New York

FUNK & WAGNALLS COMPANY

LONDON AND TORONTO

1892

PREFACE.

AGAIN it come to pass, in the fulness of time, that my companion, Josiah Allen, see me walk up and take my ink stand off of the manteltry piece, and carry it with a calm and majestick gait to the corner of the settin' room table devoted by me to literary pursuits. And he sez to me:

" What are you goin' to tackle now, Samantha ?"

And sez I, with quite a good deal of dignity, "The Cause of Eternal Justice, Josiah Allen."

" Anythin' else ?" sez he, lookin' sort o' oneasy at me. (That man realizes his shortcomin's, I believe, a good deal of the time, he duz.)

"Yes," sez I, " I lay out in petickuler to tackle the Meetin' House. She is in the wrong on't, and I want to set her right."

Josiah looked sort o' relieved like, but he sez out,

in a kind of a pert way, es he set there a-shellin'
corn for the hens:

"A Meetin' House hadn't ort to be called she—it
is a he."

And sez I, "How do you know?"

And he sez, "Because it stands to reason it is.
And I'd like to know what you have got to say
about him any way?"

Sez I, "That 'him' don't sound right, Josiah
Allen. It sounds more right and nateral to call it
'she.' Why," sez I, "hain't we always hearn about
the Mother Church, and don't the Bible tell about
the Church bein' arrayed like a bride for her husband?
I never in my life hearn it called a 'he' before."

"Oh, wall, there has always got to be a first
time. And I say it sounds better. But what
have you got to say about the Meetin' House, any.
way?"

"I have got this to say, Josiah Allen. The Meetin' House hain't a-actin' right about wimmen. The
Founder of the Church wuz born of woman. It wuz
on a woman's heart that His head wuz pillowed first
and last. While others slept she watched over His
baby slumbers and His last sleep. A woman wuz

His last thought and care. Before dawn she wuz at the door of the tomb, lookin' for His comin'. So she has stood ever sense—waitin', watchin', hopin', workin' for the comin' of Christ. Workin', waitin' for His comin' into the hearts of tempted wimmen and tempted men—fallen men and fallen wimmen —workin', waitin', toilin', nursin' the baby good in the hearts of a sinful world—weepin' pale-faced over its crucefixion—lookin' for its reserection. Oh how she has worked all through the ages!"

" Oh shaw !" sez Josiah, " some wimmen don't care about anythin' but crazy work and back combs."

I felt took down, for I had been riz up, quite considerble, but I sez, reasonable :

" Yes, there are such wimmen, Josiah, but think of the sweet and saintly souls that have given all their lives, and hopes, and thoughts to the Meetin' House —think of the throngs to-day that crowd the aisles of the Sanctuary—there are five wimmen to one man, I believe, in all the meetin' houses to-day a-workin' in His name. True Daughters of the King, no matter what their creed may be—Catholic or Protestant.

" And while wimmen have done all this work for

the Meetin' House, the Meetin' House ort to be honorable and do well by her."

" Wall, hain't *he* ?" sez Josiah.

" No, *she* hain't," sez I.

" Wall, what petickuler fault do you find ? What has *he* done lately to rile you up ?"

Sez I, " *She* wuz in the wrong on't in not lettin' wimmen set on the Conference."

"Wall, I say *he* wuz right," sez Josiah. " *He* knew, and I knew, that wimmen wuzn't strong enough to set."

" Why," sez I, " it don't take so much strength to set as it duz to stand up. And after workin' as hard as wimmen have for the Meetin' House, she ort to have the priveledge of settin'. And I am goin' to write out jest what I think about it."

" Wall," sez Josiah, as he started for the barn with the hen feed, " don't be too severe with the Meetin' House."

And then, after he went out, he opened the door agin and stuck his head in and sez :

" Don't be too hard on *him*."

And then he shet the door quick, before I could say a word.

But good land ! I didn't care. I knew I could say what I wanted to with my faithful pen—and I am bound to say it.

> JOSIAH ALLEN'S WIFE,
> Bonny View,
> near Adams, New York.

Oct. 14th, 1890.

CONTENTS.

xiv CONTENTS.

SAMANTHA AMONG THE BRETHREN.

BY JOSIAH ALLEN'S WIFE.

CHAPTER I.

WHEN I first heard that wimmen wuz goin' to make a effort to set on a Conference, it wuz on a Wednesday, as I remember well. For my companion, Josiah Allen, had drove over to Loontown in a Democrat and in a great hurry, to meet two men who wanted him to go into a speculation with 'em.

And it wuz kinder curious to meditate on it, that they wuz all deacons, every one on 'em. Three on 'em wuz Baptis'es, and two on 'em had jined our meetin' house, deacons, and the old name clung to 'em—we spoze because they wuz such good, stiddy men, and looked up to.

Take 'em all together there wuz five deacons. The two foreign deacons from 'way beyond Jonesville, Deacon Keeler and Deacon Huffer, and our own three Jonesvillians—Deacon Henzy, Deacon Sypher, and my own particular Deacon, Josiah Allen.

It wuz a wild and hazardous skeme that them two foreign deacons wuz a-proposin', and I wuz strongly in favor of givin' 'em a negative answer; but Josiah wuz fairly crazy with the idee, and so wuz Deacon Henzy and Deacon Sypher (their wives told me how they felt).

The idee was to build a buzz saw mill on the creek that runs through Jonesville, and have branches of it extend into Zoar, Loontown, and other more adjacent townships (the same creek runs through 'em all).

As near as I could get it into my head, there wuz to be a buzz saw mill apiece for the five deacons—each one of 'em to overlook their own particular buzz saw—but the money comin' from all

"A WILD AND HAZARDOUS SKEME."

on 'em to be divided up equal among the five deacons.

They thought there wuz lots of money in the idee. But I wuz very set against it from the first. It seemed to me that to have buzz saws a-per-meatin' the atmosphere, as you may say, for so wide a space, would make too much of a confusion and noise, to say nothin' of the jarin' that would take place and ensue. I felt more and more, as I medi-tated on the subject, that a buzz saw, although es-timable in itself, yet it wuz not a spear in which a religious deacon could withdraw from the world, and ponder on the great questions pertainin' to his own and the world's salvation.

I felt it wuz not a spear that he could revolve 'round in and keep that apartness from this world and nearness to the other, that I felt that deacons ought to cultivate.

But my idees wuz frowned at by every man in Jonesville, when I ventured to promulgate 'em. They all said, " The better the man, the better the deed."

They said, " The better the man wuz, the better the buzz saw he would be likely to run."

The fact wuz, they needed some buzz saw mills bad, and wuz very glad to have these deacons lay holt of 'em.

TALKING OVER THE BUZZ-SAW.

But I threw out this question at 'em, and stood by it—"If bein' set apart as a deacon didn't mean anything? If there wuzn't any deacon-work that they ought to be expected to do—and if it wuz right for 'em to go into any world's work so wild and hazardous and engrossin', as this enterprise ?"

And again they sez to me in stern, decided axents, "The better the man, the better the deed. We need buzz saws."

And then they would turn their backs to me and stalk away very high-headed.

And I felt that I wuz a gettin' fearfully onpopular all through Jonesville, by my questions. I see that the hull community wuz so sot on havin' them five deacons embark onto these buzz saws that they would not brook any interference, least of all from a female woman.

But I had a feelin' that Josiah Allen wuz, as you may say, my lawful prey. I felt that I had a right to question my own pardner for the good of his own soul, and my piece of mind.

And I sez to him in solemn axents:

"Josiah Allen, what time will you get when you are fairly started on your buzz saw, for domestic life, or social, or for religious duties ?"

And Josiah sez, " Dumb 'em ! I guess a man is a goin' to make money when he has got a chance."

And I asked him plain if he had got so low, and if I had lived with him twenty years for this, to hear him in the end dumb religious duties.

And Josiah acted skairt and conscience smut for most half a minute, and said, " he didn't dumb 'em."

" What wuz you dumbin'?" sez I, coldly.

" I wuz dumbin' the idee," sez he, " that a man can't make money when he has a chance to."

But I sez, a haulin' up this strong argument agin—

" Every one of you men, who are a layin' holt of this enterprise and a-embarkin' onto this buzz saw are married men, and are deacons in a meetin' house. Now this work you are a-talkin' of takin' up will devour all of your time, every minute of it, that you can spare from your farms.

" And to say nothin' of your wives and children not havin' any chance of havin' any comfort out of your society. What will become of the interests of Zion at home and abroad, of foreign and do- mestic missions, prayer meetin's, missionary soci- eties, temperance meetin's and good works gener- ally ?"

And then again I thought, and it don't seem as

if I can be mistaken, I most know that I heerd
Josiah Allen mutter in a low voice,

"Dumb good works!"

"I HEERD JOSIAH MUTTER, 'DUMB GOOD WORKS!'"

But I wouldn't want this told of, for I may be
mistook. I didn't fairly ketch the words, and I
spoke out agin, in dretful meanin' and harrowin'
axcnts, and sez,

" What will become of all this gospel work?"

And Josiah had by this time got over his skare and conscience smite (men can't keep smut for more'n several minutes anyway, their consciences are so elastic; good land! rubber cord can't compare with 'em), and he had collected his mind all together, and he spoke out low and clear, and in a tone as if he wuz fairly surprised I should make the remark:

" Why, the gospel work will get along jest as it always has, the wimmen will 'tend to it."

And I own I was kinder lost and by the side of myself when I asked the question—and very anxious to break up the enterprise or I shouldn't have put the question to him.

For I well knew jest as he did that wimmen wuz most always the ones to go ahead in church and charitable enterprises. And especially now, for there wuz a hardness arozen amongst the male men of the meetin' house, and they wouldn't do a thing they could help (but of this more anon and bimeby).

There wuz two or three old males in the meetin' house, too old to get mad and excited easy, that held firm, and two very pious old male brothers, but

poor, very poor, had to be supported by the meetin'
house, and lame. They stood firm, or as firm as
they could on such legs as theirs wuz, inflammatory
rheumatiz and white swellin's and such.

But all the rest had got their feelin's hurt, and got
mad, etc., and wouldn't do a thing to help the meetin'
house along.

Well, I tried every lawful, and mebby a little on-
lawful way to break this enterprise of theirs up—
and, as I heern afterwards, so did Sister Henzy.

Sister Sypher is so wrapped up in Deacon Sypher
that she would embrace a buzz saw mill or any other
enterprise he could bring to bear onto her.

"She would be perfectly willin' to be trompled
on," so she often sez, "if Deacon Sypher wuz to
do the tromplin'."

Some sez he duz.

Wall, in spite of all my efforts, and in spite of all
Sister Henzy's efforts, our deacons seemed to jest
flourish on this skeme of theirn. And when we see
it wuz goin' to be a sure thing, even Sister Sypher
begin to feel bad.

She told Albina Widrig, and Albina told Miss
Henn, and Miss Henn told me, that "what to do

she didn't know, it would deprive her of so much of the deacon's society." It wuz goin' to devour so much of his time that she wuz afraid she couldn't stand it. She told Albina in confidence (and Albina wouldn't want it told of, nor Miss Henn, nor I wouldn't) that she had often been obleeged to go out into the lot between breakfast and dinner to see the deacon, not bein' able to stand it without lookin' on his face till dinner time.

And when she was laid up with a lame foot it wuz known that the deacon left his plowin' and went up to the house, or as fur as the door step, four or five times in the course of a mornin's work, it wuz spozed because she wuz fearful of forgettin' how he looked before noon.

She is a dretful admirin' woman.

She acts dretful reverential and admirin' towards men—always calls her husband "the Deacon," as if he was the one lonely deacon who was perambulatin' the globe at this present time. And it is spozed that when she dreams about him she dreams of him as "the Deacon," and not as Samuel (his given name is Samuel).

But we don't know that for certain. We only

"THE INITIALS STOOD FOR 'MISS DEACON SYPHER.'"

spoze it. For the land of dreams is a place where you can't slip on your sun-bonnet and foller neighbor wimmen to see what they are a-doin' or what they are a-sayin' from hour to hour.

No, the best calculator on gettin' neighborhood news can't even look into that land, much less foller a neighborin' female into it.

No, their barks have got to be moored outside of them mysterious shores.

But, as I said, this had been spozen.

But it is known from actual eyesight that she marks all her sheets, and napkins, and piller-cases, and such, "M. D. S." And I asked her one day what the M. stood for, for I 'spozed, of course, the D. S. stood for Drusilla Sypher.

And she told me with a real lot of dignity that the initials stood for "Miss Deacon Sypher."

Wall, the Jonesville men have been in the habit of holdin' her up as a pattern to their wives for some time, and the Jonesville wimmen hain't hated her so bad as you would spoze they all would under the circumstances, on account, we all think, of her bein' such a good-hearted little creeter. We all like Drusilly and can't help it.

Wall, even she felt bad and deprested on account of her Deacon's goin' into the buzz saw-mill business.

But she didn't say nothin', only wept out at one side, and wiped up every time he came in sight.

They say that she hain't never failed once of a-smilin' on the Deacon every time he came home. And once or twice he has got as mad as a hen at her for smilin'. Once, when he came home with a sore thumb—he had jest smashed it in the barn door—and she stood a-smilin' at him on the door step, there are them that say the Deacon called her a "infernal fool."

But I never have believed it. I don't believe he would demean himself so low.

But he yelled out awful at her, I do 'spoze, for his pain wuz intense, and she stood stun still, a-smilin' at him, jest accordin' to the story books. And he sez :

"Stand there like a —— fool, will you ! Get me a *rag !*"

I guess he did say as much as that.

But they say she kept on a-smilin' for some time

—couldn't seem to stop, she had got so hardened into that way.

And once, when her face wuz all swelled up with the toothache, she smiled at him accordin' to rule

"ONCE, WHEN HER FACE WUZ ALL SWELLED UP, SHE SMILED AT HIM."

when he got home, and they say the effect wuz fearful, both on her looks and the Deacon's acts. They say he was mad again, and called her some names.

But as a general thing they get along first rate, I guess, or as well as married folks in general, and he makes a good deal of her.

I guess they get along without any more than the usual amount of difficulties between husbands and wives, and mebby with less. I know this, anyway, that she just about worships the Deacon.

Wall, as I say, it was the very day that these three deacons went to Loontown to meet Deacon Keeler and Deacon Huffer, to have a conference together as to the interests of the buzz saw mill that I first heard the news that wimmen wuz goin' to make a effort to set on the Methodist Conference, and the way I heerd on't wuz as follows:

Josiah Allen brought home to me that night a paper that one of the foreign deacons, Deacon Keeler, had lent him. It contained a article that wuz wrote by Deacon Keeler's son, Casper Keeler —a witherin' article about wimmen's settin' on the Conference. It made all sorts of fun of the projeck.

We found out afterwards that Casper Keeler furnished nearly all the capital for the buzz saw mill enterprise at his father's urgent request.

His father, Deacon Keeler, didn't have a cent of money of his own; it fell onto Casper from his mother and aunt. They had kept a big millinery store in the town of Lyme, and a branch store in Loontown, and wuz great workers, and had laid up a big property. And when they died, the aunt, bein' a maiden woman at the time, the money naturally fell onto Casper. He wuz a only child, and they had brung him up tender, and fairly worshipped him.

They left him all the money, but left a anuety to be paid yearly to his father, Deacon Keeler, enough to support him.

The Deacon and his wife had always lived happy together—she loved to work, and he loved to have her work, so they had similar tastes, and wuz very congenial—and when she died he had the widest crape on his hat that wuz ever seen in the town of Lyme. (The crape was some she had left in the shop.)

He mourned deep, both in his crape and his feelin's, there hain't a doubt of that.

Wall, Miss Keelerses will provided money special for Casper to be educated high. So he went to school and to college, from the time he was born, almost. So he knew plenty of big words, and used 'em fairly lavish in this piece. There wuz words in it of from six to seven syllables. Why, I hadn't no idee till I see 'em with my own eye, that there wuz any such words in the English language, and words of from four to six syllables wuz common in it.

His father, Deacon Keeler, wouldn't give the paper to my companion, he thought so much of it, but he offered to lend it to him, because he said he felt that the ideas it promulgated wuz so sound and deep they ought to be disseminated abroad.

The ideas wuz, " that wimmen hadn't no business to set on the Conference. She wuz too weak to set on it. It wuz too high a place for her too ventur' on, or to set on with any ease. There wuzn't no more than room up there for what men would love to set on it. Wimmen's place wuz in the sacred precinks of home. She wuz a tender, fragile plant, that needed guardin' and guidin' and kep by man's great strength and tender care from havin' any cares and labors whatsoever and wheresoever and howsumever."

Josiah said it wuz a masterly dockument. And

it wuz writ well. It painted in wild, glarin' colors
the fear that men had that wimmen would strain
themselves to do anything at all in the line of work
—or would weaken her hull constitution, and lame
her moral faculties, and ruin herself by tryin' to set
up on a Conference, or any other high and tottlin'
eminence.

The piece wuz divided into three different parts,
with a headin' in big letters over each one.

The *first* wuz, wimmen to have no labors and
cares WHATSOEVER;

Secondly, NONE WHERESOEVER;

Thirdly, NONE HOWSUMEVER.

The writer then proceeded to say that he would
show first, *what* cares and labors men wuz willin'
and anxious to ward offen women.   And he proved
right out in the end that there wuzn't a thing that
they wanted wimmen to do—not a single thing.

Then he proceeded to tell *where* men wuz willin'
to keep their labors and cares offen wimmen.   And
he proved it right out that it wuz every *where*.   In
the home, the little sheltered, love-guarded home of
the farmer, the mechanic and the artizen (makin'
special mention of the buzz sawyers).   And also in

the palace walls and the throne. There and every *where* men would fain shelter wimmen from every care, and every labor, even the lightest and slight-est.

Then lastly came the *howsumever*. He pro-ceeded to show *how* this could be done. And he proved it right out (or thought he did) that the first great requisit' to accomplish all this, wuz to keep wimmen in her place. Keep her from settin' on the Conference, and all other tottlin' eminences, fitted only for man's stalwart strength.

And the end of the article wuz so sort of tragick and skairful that Josiah wept when he read it. He pictured it out in such strong colors, the danger there wuz of puttin' wimmen, or allowin' her to put herself in such a high and percipitous place, such a skairful and dangerous posture as settin' up on a Conference.

"To have her set up on it," sez the writer, in conclusion, "would endanger her life, her spiritual, her mental and her moral growth. It would shake the permanency of the sacred home relations to its downfall. It would hasten anarchy, and he thought sizm."

"JOSIAH WEPT WHEN HE READ IT."

Why, Josiah Allen handled that paper as if it wuz pure gold. I know he asked me anxiously as he handed it to me to read, " if my hands wuz perfectly clean," and we had some words about it.

And till he could pass it on to Deacon Sypher to read he kep it in the Bible. He put it right over in Galatians, for I looked to see—Second Galatians.

And he wrapped it up in a soft handkerchief when he carried it over to Deacon Sypherses. And Deacon Sypher treasured it like a pearl of great price (so I spoze) till he could pass it on to Deacon Henzy.

And Deacon Henzy was to carry it with care to a old male Deacon in Zoar, bed rid.

Wall, as I say, that is the very first I had read about their bein' any idee promulgated of wimmens settin' up on the Conference.

And I, in spite of Josiah Allen's excitement, wuz in favor on't from the very first.

Yes, I wuz awfully in favor of it, and all I went through durin' the next and ensuin' weeks didn't put the idee out of my head. No, far from it. It seemed as if the severer my sufferin's wuz, the much more this idee flourished in my soul. Just as a heavy plow will meller up the soil so white lilies can take root, or any other kind of sweet posies.

And oh! my heart! wuz not my sufferin's with Lodema Trumble, a hard plow and a harrowin' one, and one that turned up deep furrows?

But of this, more anon and bimeby.

CHAPTER II.

ALL, it wuz on the very next day—on a Thursday as I remember well, for I wuz a-thinkin' why didn't Lodema's letter come the next day—Fridays bein' considered onlucky—and it being a day for punishments, hangin's, and so forth.

But it didn't, it came on a Thursday. And my companion had been to Jonesville and brung me back two letters; he brung 'em in, leavin' the old mair standin' at the gate, and handed me the letters, ten pounds of granulated sugar, a pound of tea, and the request I should have supper on the table by the time that he got back from Deacon Henzy's.

(On that old buzz-saw business agin, so I spozed, but wouldn't ask.)

Wall, I told him supper wuz begun any way, and he had better hurry back. But he wuz belated by

reason of Deacon Henzy's bein' away, so I set there
for some time alone.

Wall, I wuz goin' to have some scolloped oysters
for supper, so the first thing I did wuz to put 'em
into the oven—they wuż all ready, I had scolloped
'em before Josiah come, and got 'em all ready for
the oven—and then I set down and read my
letters.

Wall, the first one I opened wuz from Lodema
Trumble, Josiah's cousin on his own side. And
her letter brought the sad and harrowin' intelligence
that she was a-comin' to make us a good long visit.
The letter had been delayed. She was a-comin'
that very night, or the next day. Wall, I sithed
deep. I love company dearly, but—oh my soul, is
there not a difference, a difference in visitors?

Wall, suffice it to say, I sithed deep, and opened
the other letter, thinkin' it would kind o' take my
mind off.

And for all the world! I couldn't hardly believe
my eyes. But it wuz! It wuz from Serena Fogg.
It wuz from the Authoress of "Wedlock's Peaceful
Repose."

I hadn't heard a word from her for upwards of

four years. And the letter brung me startlin' intelligence.

. It opened with the unexpected information that
she wuz married. She had been married three
years and a half to a butcher out to the Ohio.

And I declare my first thought wuz as I read it,
" Wall, she has wrote dretful flowery on wedlock,
and its perfect, onbroken calm, and peaceful repose,
and now she has had a realizin' sense of what it
really is."

But when I read a little further, I see what the
letter wuz writ for. I see why, at this late day, she
had started up and writ me a letter. I see it wuz
writ on duty.

She said she had found out that I wuz in the
right on't and she wuzn't. She said that when in
the past she had disputed me right up and down,
and insisted that wedlock wuz a state of perfect
serenity, never broken in upon by any cares or
vexations whatsomever, she wuz in the wrong on't.

She said she had insisted that when anybody had
moored their barks into that haven of wedded life,
that they wuz forever safe from any rude buffetin's
from the world's waves; that they wuz exempt

from any toil, any danger, any sorrow, any trials
whatsomever.   And she had found she was mistook.

She said I told her it wuz a first-rate state, and
a satisfactory one for wimmen ; but still it had its
trials, and she had found it so.   She said that I
insisted its serenity wuz sometimes broken in upon,
and she had found it so.   The last day at my house
had tottled her faith, and her own married experience had finished the work.   Her husband wuz a
worthy man, and she almost worshipped him.   But
he had a temper, and he raved round considerable
when meals wuzn't ready on time, and she havin'
had two pairs of twins durin' her union (she comes
from a family on her mother's side, so I had hearn
before, where twins wuz contagious), she couldn't
always be on the exact minute.   She had to work
awful hard ; this broke in on her serenity.

Her husband devotedly loved her, so she said ;
but still, she said, his bootjack had been throwed
voyalent where corns wuz hit onexpected.

Their souls wuz mated firm as they could be in
deathless ties of affection and confidence, yet doors
had been slammed and oaths emitted, when clothin'
rent and buttons tarried not with him.

"FOUR TWINS BROKE IN ALSO ON HER WAVELESS CALM."

Strange actions and demeanors had been dis-
played in hours of high-headedness and impatience,
which had skaired her almost to death before
gettin' accustomed to 'em.

The four twins broke in also on her waveless
calm. They wuz lovely cherubs, and the four apples
of her eyes. But they did yell at times, they
kicked, they tore round and acted; they made
work—lots of work. And one out of each pair
snored. It broke up each span, as you may say.
The snorin' filled each room devoted to 'em.

He snored, loud. A good man and a noble
man he wuz, so she repeated it, but she found out
too late—too late, that he snored. The house wuz
small; she could *not* escape from snores, turn she
where she would. She got tired out with her work
days, and couldn't rest nights. Her husband, as he
wuz doin' such a flourishin' business, had opened a
cattle-yard near the house. She wuz proud of his
growin' trade, but the bellerin' of the cattle disturbed her fearfully. Also the calves bleating and
the lambs callin' on their dams.

It wuz a long letter, filled with words like these,
and it ended up by saying that for years now she

had wanted to write and tell me that I had been
in the right on't and she in the wrong.   I had been

THE LECTURE.

megum and she hadn't.   And she ended by sayin',
" God bless me and adoo."

The fire crackled softly on the clean hearth.
The teakettle sung a song of welcome and cheer.
The oysters sent out an agreeable atmosphere.

The snowy table, set out in pretty china and glass-ware, looked invitin', and I set there comfortable and happy and so peaceful in my frame, that the events of the past, in which Serena Fogg had flour-ished, seemed but as yesterday.

I thought it all over, that pleasant evenin' in the past, when Josiah Allen had come in unexpected, and brung the intelligence to me that there wuz goin' to be a lectur' give that evenin' by a young female at the Jonesville school-house, and beset me to go.

And I give my consent. Then my mind trav-elled down that pleasant road, moongilded, to the school-house. It stopped on the door-step while Josiah hitched the mair.

We found the school-house crowded full, fur a female lecturer wuz a rarity, and she wuz a pretty girl, as pretty a girl as I ever see in my life.

And it wuz a pretty lecture, too, dretful pretty. The name of the lecture wuz, "Wedlock's Peaceful and Perfect Repose."

A pretty name, I think, and it wuz a beautiful lecture, very, and extremely flowery. It affected some of the hearers awfully; they wuz all carried

away with it. Josiah Allen wept like a child durin'
the rehearsin' of it. I myself didn't weep, but I
enjoyed it, some of it, first rate.

I can't begin to tell it all as she did, 'specially
after this length of time, in such a lovely, flowery
way, but I can probably give a few of the heads
of it.

It hain't no ways likely that I can give the heads
half the stylish, eloquent look that she did as she
held 'em up, but I can jest give the bare heads.

She said that there had been a effort made in
some directions to try to speak against the holy
state of matrimony. The papers had been full of
the subject, " Is Marriage a Failure, or is it not ?"

She had even read these dreadful words—" Marriage is a Failure." She hated these words, she de-
spised 'em. And while some wicked people spoke
against this holy institution, she felt it to be her
duty, as well as privilege, to speak in its praise.

I liked it first rate, I can tell you, when she went
on like that. For no living soul can uphold marriage with a better grace that can she whose name
vuz once Smith.

I *love* Josiah Allen, I am *glad* that I married him.

But at the same time, my almost devoted love doesn't make me blind. I can see on every side of a subject, and although, as I said heretofore, and prior, I love Josiah Allen, I also love megumness, and I could not fully agree with every word she said.

But she went on perfectly beautiful—I didn't wonder it brought the school-house down—about the holy calm and perfect rest of marriage, and how that calm wuz never invaded by any rude cares.

How man watched over the woman he loved; how he shielded her from every rude care; kept labor and sorrow far, far from her; how woman's life wuz like a oneasy, roarin', rushin' river, that swept along discontented and onsatisfied, moanin' and lonesome, until it swept into the calm sea of Repose—melted into union with the grand ocian of Rest, marriage.

And then, oh! how calm and holy and sheltered wuz that state! How peaceful, how onruffled by any rude changes! Happiness, Peace, Calm! Oh, how sweet, how deep wuz the ocian of True Love in which happy, united souls bathed in blissful repose!

It was dretful pretty talk, and middlin' affectin'.

"He had on a new vest."

There wasn't a dry eye in Josiah Allen's head, and I didn't make no objection to his givin' vent to his feelin's, only when I see him bust out a-weepin' I jest slipped my pocket-handkerchief 'round his neck and pinned it behind. (His handkerchief wuz in constant use, a cryin' and weepin' as he wuz.) And I knew that salt water spots black satin awfully. He had on a new vest.

Submit Tewksbury cried and wept, and wept and cried, caused by remembrances, it wuz spozed. Of which, more anon, and bimeby.

And Drusilly Sypher, Deacon Sypherses wife, almost had a spazzum, caused by admiration and bein' so highly tickled.

I myself didn't shed any tears, as I have said heretofore. And what kep' me calmer wuz, I *knew*, I knew from the bottom of my heart, that she went too fur, she wuzn't megum enough.

And then she went on to draw up metafors, and haul in illustrations, comparin' married life and single—jest as likely metafors as I ever see, and as good illustrations as wuz ever brung up, only they every one of 'em had this fault—when she got to drawin' 'em, she drawed 'em too fur. And though she brought the school-house down, she didn't con-vince me.

Once she compared single life to a lonely goose travellin' alone acrost the country, 'cross lots, lone-

"I MYSELF DIDN'T SHED ANY TEARS."

some and despairin', travellin' along over a thorny way, and desolate, weighed down by melancholy and gloomy forebodin's, and takin' a occasional rest by standin' up on one cold foot and puttin' its weery

head under its wing, with one round eye lookin' out
for dangers that menaced it, and lookin', also, perhaps, for a possible mate, for the comin' gander—
restless, wobblin', oneasy, miserable.

Why, she brought the school-house down, and got
the audience all wrought up with pity, and sympathy.
Oh, how Submit Tewksbury did weep; she wept
aloud (she had been disappointed, but of this more
bimeby).

And then she went on and compared that lonesome voyager to two blissful wedded ones.   A pair
of white swans floatin' down the waveless calm,
bathed in silvery light, floatin' down a shinin' stream
that wuz never broken by rough waves, bathed in a
sunshine that wuz never darkened by a cloud.

And then she went on to bring up lots of other
things to compare the two states to—flowery things
and sweet, and eloquent.

She compared single life to quantities of things,
strange, weird, melancholy things, and curius. Why,
they wuz so powerful that every one of 'em brought
the school-house down.

And then she compared married life to two apple
blossoms hangin' together on one leafy bough on

the perfumed June air, floatin' back and forth under the peaceful benediction of summer skies.

And she compared it to two white lambs' gambolin' on the velvety hill-side. To two strains of music meltin' into one dulcet harmony, perfect, divine harmony, with no discordant notes.

Josiah hunched me, he wanted me to cry there, at that place, but I wouldn't. He did, he cried like an infant babe, and I looked close and searchin' to see if my handkerchief covered up all his vest.

He didn't seem to take no notice of his clothes at all, he wuz a-weepin' so—why, the whole school-house wept, wept like a babe.

But I didn't. I see it wuz a eloquent and powerful effort. I see it was beautiful as anything could be, but it lacked that one thing I have mentioned prior and before this time. It lacked me-gumness.

I knew they wuz all impressive and beautful illustrations, I couldn't deny it, and I didn't want to deny it. But I knew in my heart that the lonely goose that she had talked so eloquent about, I knew that though its path might be tegus the most of the time, yet occasionally it stepped upon velvet grass

and blossomin' daisies. And though the happy
wedded swans floated considerable easy a good deal
of the time, yet occasionally they had their wings
rumpled by storms, thunder storms, sudden squalls,
and et cetery, et cetery.

And I knew the divine harmony of wedded love,
though it is the sweetest that earth affords, I knew
that, and my Josiah knew it—-the very sweetest and
happiest strains that earthly lips can sing.

Yet I knew that it wuz both heavenly sweet, and
divinely sad, blended discord and harmony. I knew
there wuz minor chords in it, as well as major, I
knew that we must await love's full harmony in
heaven. There shall we sing it with the pure melody of the immortals, my Josiah and me. But I
am a eppisodin', and to continue and resoom.

Wall, we wuz invited to meet the young female
after the lecture wuz over, to be introduced to her
and talk it over.

She wuz the Methodist minister's wive's cousin,
and the minister's wife told me she wuz dretful
anxious to get my opinion on the lecture. I spoze
she wanted to get the opinion of one of the first
wimmen of the day. For though I am fur from

bein' the one that ort to mention it, I have heard of such things bein' said about me all round Jonesville, and as far as Loontown and Shackville. And so, I spoze, she wanted to get hold of my opinion.

Wall, I wuz introduced to her, and I shook hands with her, and kissed her on both cheeks, for she is a sweet girl and I liked her looks.

I could see that she was very, VERY sentimental, but she had a sweet, confidin', innocent look to her, and I give her a good kissin' and I meant it. When I like a person, I *do* like 'em, and visy-versey.

But at the same time my likin' for a person mustn't be strong enough to overthrow my principles. And when she asked me in her sweet axents, "How I liked her lecture, and if I could see any faults in it?" I leaned up against Duty, and told her, "I liked it first-rate, but I couldn't agree with every word of it."

Here Josiah Allen give me a look sharp enough to take my head clear off, if looks could behead anybody. But they can't.

And I kept right on, calm and serene, and sez I, "It wuz very full of beautiful idees, as full of 'em

as a rose-bush is full of sweetness in June, but,"
says I, "if I speak at all I must tell the truth, and
I must say that while your lecture is as sweet and
beautiful a effort as I ever see tackled, full of beau·
tiful thoughts, and eloquence, still I must say that
in my opinion it lacked one thing, it wuzn't mean
enough."

"Mean enough?" sez she. "What do you
mean?"

"Why," sez I, "I mean, mean temperature, you
know, middleinness, megumness, and whatever you
may call it; you go too fur."

She said with a modest look "that she guessed
she didn't, she guessed she didn't go too far."

And Josiah Allen spoke up, cross as a bear, and,
sez he, "I know she didn't. She didn't say a word
that wuzn't gospel truth."

Sez I, "Married life is the happiest life in my
opinion; that is, when it is happy. Some hain't
happy, but at the same time the happiest of 'em
hain't *all* happiness."

"It is," sez Josiah (cross and surly), "it is,
too."

And Serena Fogg said, gently, that she thought I

"YOU GO TOO FUR."

wuz mistaken, "she thought it wuz." And Josiah
jined right in with her and said:

" He *knew* it wuz, and he would take his oath
to it."

But I went right on, and, sez I, " Mebby it is in
one sense the most peaceful; that is, when the
affections are firm set and stabled it makes 'em
more peaceful than when they are a-traipsin' round
and a-wanderin'. But," sez I, " marriage hain't *all*
peace."

Sez Josiah: " It is, and I'll swear to it."

Sez I, goin' right on, cool and serene, " The
sunshine of true love gilds the pathway with the
brightest radiance we know anything about, but it
hain't all radiance."

" Yes, it is," sez Josiah, firmly, " it is, every mite
of it."

And Serena Fogg sez, tenderly and amiably,
" Yes, I think Mr. Allen is right; I think it
is."

" Wall," sez I, in meanin' axcents, awful
meanin', " when you are married you will change
your opinion, you mark my word."

And she said, gently, but persistently, " That she

guessed she shouldn't ; she guessed she was in the right of it."

Sez I, " You think when anybody is married they have got beyond all earthly trials, and nothin' but perfect peace and rest remains ?"

And she sez, gently, " Yes, mem!"

" Why," sez I, " I am married, and have been for upwards of twenty years, and I think I ought to know somethin' about it ; and how can it be called a state of perfect rest, when some days I have to pass through as many changes as a comet, and each change a tegus one. I have to wabble round and be a little of everything, and change sudden, too.

" I have to be a cook, a step-mother, a house-maid, a church woman, a wet nurse (lots of times I have to wade out in the damp grass to take care of wet chickens and goslins). I have to be a tai-loress, a dairy-maid, a literary soarer, a visitor, a fruit-canner, a adviser, a soother, a dressmaker, a hostess, a milliner, a gardener, a painter, a surgeon, a doctor, a carpenter, a woman, and more'n forty other things.

" Marriage is a first-rate state. and agreeable a

good deal of the time; but it haint a state of perfect peace and rest, and you'll find out it haint if
you are ever married."

But Miss Fogg said, mildly, "that she thought I
wuz mistaken—she thought it wuz."

"You do?" sez I.

"Yes, mem," sez she.

I got up, and sez I, "Come, Josiah, I guess we
had better be a-goin'." I thought it wouldn't do
no good to argue any more with her, and Josiah
started off after the mair. He had hitched it on
the barn floor.

She didn't seem willin' to have me go; she
seemed to cling to me. She seemed to be a good,
affectionate little creetur. And she said she would
give anything almost if she could rehearse the hull
lecture over to me, and have me criticise it. Sez
she:

"I have heard so much about you, and what a
happy home you have."

"Yes," sez I, "it is as happy as the average of
happy homes, any way."

And sez she, "I have heard that you and your
husband wuz just devoted to each other."

And I told her "that our love for each other wuz like two rocks that couldn't be moved."

And she said, "On these very accounts she fairly hankered after my advice and criticism. She said she hadn't never lived in any house where there wuz a livin' man, her father havin' died several months before she was born; and she hadn't had the experience that I had, and she presumed that I could give her several little idees that she hadn't thought on."

And I told her calmly "that I presumed I could."

It seemed that her father died two months after marriage, right in the midst of the mellow light of the honeymoon, before he had had time to drop the exstatic sweetness of courtship and 'newly-married bliss and come down into the ordinary, every-day, good and bad demeanors of men.

And she had always lived with her mother (who naturally worshipped and mentally knelt before the memory of her lost husband) and three sentimental maiden aunts. And they had drawed all their knowledge of manhood from Moore's poems and Solomon's Songs. So Serena Fogg's idees of men and married life wuz about as thin and as well suited to stand the wear and tear of actual experience as a gauze dress would be to face a Greenland winter in.

And so, after considerable urgin' on her part (for I kinder hung back and hated to tackle the job, but not knowin' but that it wuz duty's call), I finally consented, and it wuz arranged this way:

She wuz to come down to our house some day, early in the mornin', and stay all day, and she wuz to stand up in front of me and rehearse the lecture over to me, and I wuz to set and hear it, and when she came to a place where I didn't agree with her I wuz to lift up my right hand and she wuz to stop rehearsin', and we wuz to argue with each other back and forth and try to convince each other.

And when we got it all arranged Josiah and I set out for home. I calm in my frame, though dreadin' the job some.

CHAPTER III.

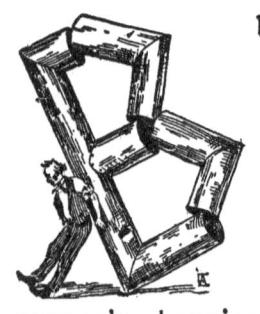UT Josiah Allen wuz jest crazy over that lecture—crazy as a loon. He raved about it all the way home, and he would repeat over lots of it to me. About "how a man's love was the firm anchor that held a woman's happiness stiddy; how his calm and peaceful influence held her mind in a serene calm —a waveless repose; how tender men wuz of the fair sect, how they watched over 'em and held 'em in their hearts."

"Oh," sez he, "it went beyond anything I ever heard of. I always knew that men wuz good and pious, but I never realized how dumb pious they wuz till to-night."

" She said," sez I, in considerable dry axents—not so dry as I keep by me, but pretty dry—" No true man would let a woman perform any manuel labor."

"Wall, he won't. There ain't no need of your liftin' your little finger in emanuel labor."

" Manuel, Josiah."

"Wall, I said so, didn't I? Hain't I always noldin' you back from work?"

"Yes," sez I. "You often speak of it, Josiah. You are as good," sez I, firmly, "full as good as the common run of men, and I think a little better. But there are things that have to be done. A married woman that has a house and family to see to and don't keep a hired girl, can't get along without some work and care."

"Wall I say," sez he, "that there hain't no need of you havin' a care, not a single care. Not as long as I live—if it wuzn't for me, you might have some cares, and most probable would, but not while I live."

I didn't say nothin' back, for I don't want to hurt his feelin's, and won't, not if I can help it. And he broke out again anon, or nearly anon—

"Oh, what a lecture that wuz. Did you notice when she wuz goin' on perfectly beautiful, about the waveless sea of married life—did you notice how it took the school house down? And I wuz perfectly

"OH, WHAT A LECTURE THAT WUZ."

mortified to see you didn't weep or even clap your hands."

"Wall," sez I, firmly, "when I weep or when I clap, I weep and clap on the side of truth. And I can't see things as she duz. I have been a-sailin' on that sea she depictured for over twenty years, and have never wanted to leave it for any other waters. But, as I told her, and tell you now, it hain't always a smooth sea, it has its ups and downs, jest like any other human states."

Sez I, soarin' up a very little ways, not fur, for it wuz too cold, and I was too tired, "There hain't but one sea, Josiah Allen, that is calm forever, and one day we will float upon it, you and me. It is the sea by which angels walk and look down into its crystal depths, and behold their blessed faces. It is the sea on whose banks the fadeless lilies blow— and that mirrors the soft, cloudless sky of the Happy Morning. It is the sea of Eternal Repose, that rude blasts can never blow up into billows But our sea—the sea of married life—is not like that, it is ofttimes billowy and rough."

"I say it hain't," sez he, for he was jest carried away with the lecture, and enthused.

"We have had a happy time together, Josiah
Allen, for over twenty years, but has our sea of life
always been perfectly smooth?"

"Yes, it has; smooth as glass."

"Hain't there never been a cloud in our sky?"

"No, there hain't; not a dumb cloud."

Sez I, sternly, "There has in mine. Your wicked and profane swearin' has cast many and many
a cloud over my sky, and I'd try to curb in my
tongue if I was in your place."

"'Dumb' hain't swearin'," sez he. And then he
didn't say nothin' more till anon, or nearly at that
time, he broke out agin, and sez he:

"Never, never did I hear or see such eloquence
till to-night. I'll have that girl down to our house
to stay a week, if I'm a living Josiah Allen."

"All right," sez I, cheerfully. "I'd love to have
her stay a week or ten days, and I'll invite her, too,
when she comes down to rehearse her lecture."

Wall we got home middlin' tired, and the subject
kinder dropped down, and Josiah had lots of work
come on the next day, and so did I, and company.
And it run along for over a week before she come.
And when she did come, it wuz in a dreadful bad

time.   It seems as if she couldn't have come in a much worse time.

It wuz early one mornin', not more than nine o'clock, if it wuz that.   There had come on a cold snap of weather unexpected, and Josiah wuz a-bringin' in the cook stove from the summer kitchen, when she come.

Josiah Allen is a good man.   He is my choice out of a world full of men, but I can't conceal it from myself that his words at such a time are always voy-alent, and his demeanor is not the demeanor that I would wish to have showed off to the public.

He wuz at the worst place, too.   He had got the stove wedged into the entry-way door, and couldn't get it either way.   He had acted awkward with it, and I told him so, and he see it when it wuz too late.

He had got it fixed in such a way that he couldn't get into the kitchen himself without gettin' over the stove, and I, in the course of duty, thought it wuz right to tell him that if he had heerd to me he wouldn't have been in such a fix.   Oh! the voya-lence and frenzy of his demeanor as he stood there a-hollerin'.

I wuz out in the wood-house shed a-bilin' my
cider apple sass in the big cauldron kettle, but I
heard the racket, and as I come a-runnin' in I
thought I heard a little rappin' at the settin'-room
door, but I didn't notice it much, I wuz that agi-
tated to see the way the stove and Josiah wuz set
and wedged in.

There the stove wuz, wedged firm into the door-
way, perfectly sot there. There wuz sut all over the
floor, and there stood Josiah Allen, on the wood-
house side, with his coat off, his shirt all covered with
black, and streaks of black all over his face. And
oh! how wild and almost frenzied his attitude wuz.
as he stood there as if he couldn't move nor be
moved no more than the stove could. And oh I
the voyalence of the language he hurled at me
acrost that stove.

"Why," sez I, "you must come in here, Josiah
Allen, and pull it from this side."

And then he hollered at me, and asked me :

" How in thunder he was a goin' to *get* in." And
then he wanted to know " if I wanted him squshed
into jelly by comin' in by the side of it—or if I
thought he wuz a crane, that he could step over it.

or a stream of water that he could run under it, or
what else do you think?" He hollered wildly.

"Wall," sez I, "you hadn't ort to got it fixed in
that shape. I told you what end to move first," sez
I. "You have moved it in side-ways. It would go
in all right if you had started it the other way."

"Oh, yes! It would have been all right. You
love to see me, Samantha, with a stove in my arms.
You love it dearly. I believe you would be perfectly happy if you could see me a luggin' round
stoves every day. But I'll tell you one thing, if this
dumb stove is ever moved either way out of this
door—if I ever get it into a room agin, it never shall
be stirred agin so much as a hair's breadth—not
while I have got the breath of life in me."

Sez I, "Hush! I hear somebody a-knockin' at
the door."

"I won't hush. It is nothin' but dumb foolish-
ness a movin' round stoves, and if anybody don't
believe it let 'em look at me—and let 'em look at
that stove set right here in the door as firm as a rock."

Sez I agin in a whisper, "Do be still, and I'll let
'em in, I don't want them to ketch you a talkin' so
and a-actin'."

"WON'T YOU BE STILL?"

"Wall, I want 'em to ketch me, that is jest what I want 'em to do. If it is a man he'll say every word I say is Gospel truth, and if it is a woman it will make her perfectly happy to see me a-swelterin' in the job—seven times a year do I have to move this stove back and forth—and I say it is high time I said a word. So you can let 'em in just as quick as you are a mind to."

Sez I, a whisperin' and puttin' my finger on my lip :

"Won't you be still ?"

"No, I won't be still !" he yelled out louder than ever. "And you may go through all the motions you want to and you can't stop me. All you have got to do is to walk round and let folks in, happy as a king. Nothin' under the heavens ever made a woman so happy as to have some man a-breakin' his back a-luggin' round a stove."

I see he wouldn't stop, so I had to go and open the door, and there stood Serena Fogg, there stood the author of "Wedlock's Peaceful Repose." I felt like a fool. For I knew she had heard every word, I see she had by her looks. She looked skairt, and as surprised and sort o' awe-stricken as if she had

seen a ghost.   I took her into the parlor, and took
her things, and I excused myself by tellin' her that
I should have to be out in the kitchen a-tendin' to
things for a spell, and went back to Josiah.

And I whispered to him, sez I : " Miss Fogg has
come, and she has heard every word you have said,
Josiah Allen.   And what will she think now about
Wedlock's Peaceful Repose ?"

But he had got that wild and reckless in his demeanor and acts, that he went right on with his
hollerin', and, sez he, " She won't find much repose
here to-day, and I'll tell her that.   This house has
got to be all tore to pieces to get that stove started."

Sez I, " There won't be nothin' to do only to
take off one side of the door casin'.   And I believe
it can be done without that."

" Oh, you believe ! you believe !   You'd better
take holt and lug and lift for two hours as I have,
and then see."

Sez I, " You hain't been here more'n ten minutes, if you have that.   And there," sez I, liftin'
up one end a little, " see what anybody can do who
is calm.   There I have stirred it, and now you can
move it right along."

" Oh, *you* did it ! I moved it myself."

I didn't contend, knowin' it wuz men's natural nater to say that.

Wall, at last Josiah got the stove in, but then

"AND HE SAID I HAD RUBBED 'EM OUT."

the stove-pipe wouldn't go together, it wouldn't seem to fit. He had marked the joints with chalk, and the marks had rubbed off, and he said I had rubbed 'em out."

I wuz just as innocent as a babe, but I didn't dispute him much, for I see a little crack open in the parlor door, and I knew the author of " Wedlock's Peaceful Repose" was a-listenin'.

But when he told me for the third time that I rubbed 'em out on purpose to make him trouble, and that I had made a practice of rubbin' 'em out for years and years—why, then I *had* to correct him on the subject, and we had a little dialogue.

I spoze Serena Fogg heard it. But human nater can't bear only just so much, especially when it has stoves a dirtien up the floor, and apple sass on its mind, and unexpected company, and no cookin' and a threshin' machine a-comin'.

CHAPTER IV.

 NEVER knew a word about the threshin' machine a-comin' till about half an hour before. Josiah Allen wuzn't to blame. It come just as onexpected onto him as it did onto me.

Solomon Gowdey wuz a-goin' to have 'em first, which would have left me ample time to cook up for 'em. But he wuz took down bed sick, so they had to come right onto us with no warnin' previous and beforehand.

They wuz a drivin' up just as Josiah got the stove-pipe up. They had to go right by the side of the house, right by the parlor winders, to get to the side of the barn where they wanted to thresh; and just as they wuz a-goin' by one of the horses got down, and of all the yellin' I ever heard that was the cap sheaf.

Steve Yerden is rough on his horses, dretful

rough. He yells at 'em enough to raise the ruff.
His threshin' machine is one of the kind where the
horses walk up and look over the top. It is kinder
skairful any way, and it made it as bad agin when
you expected to see the horse fall out every
minute.

Wall, that very horse fell out of the machine
three times that day. It wuz a sick horse, I believe, and hadn't ort to have been worked. But
three times it fell, and each time the yellin' wuz
such that it skairt the author of " Peaceful Repose,"
and me, almost to death.

The machine wuz in plain sight of the house, and
every time we see the horse's head come a mountin'
up on top of the machine, we expected that over
it would go. But though it didn't fall out only
three times, as I said, it kep' us all nerved up and
uneasy the hull of the time expectin' it. And
Steve Yerden kep' a-yellin' at his horses all the
time; there wuzn't no comfort to be took within
a mile of him.

I wuz awful sorry it happened so, on her account.

Wall, I had to get dinner for nine men, and cook
it all from the very beginnin'. If you'll believe it,

"It didn't fall out only three times."

I had to begin back to bread. I hadn't any bread in the house, but I had it a-risin', and I got two loaves out by dinner time. But I had to stir round lively, I can tell you, to make pies and cookies and fried cakes, and cook meat, and vegetables of all kinds.

The author of "Wedlock's Peaceful Repose" came out into the kitchen. I told her she might, if she wanted to, for I see I wuzn't goin' to have a minute's time to go into the parlor and visit with her.

She looked pretty sober and thoughtful, and I didn't know as she liked it, to think I couldn't do as I promised to do, accordin' to agreement, to hear her lecture, and lift my hand up when I differed from her.

But, good land! I couldn't help it. I couldn't get a minute's time to lift my hand up. I could have heard the lecture, but I couldn't spare my hands.

And then Josiah would come a-rushin' in after one thing and another, actin' as was natural, accordin' to the nater of man, more like a wild man than a Christian Methodist. For he was so wrought up and excited by havin' so much on his hands to do, and the onexpectedness of it, that he couldn't help actin' jest as he did act. I don't believe he could. And then Steve Yerden is enough to distract a leather-man, any way.

"To find a piece of old rope to tie up the harness."

Twice I had to drop everything and find cloths to do up the horse's legs, where it had grazed 'em a-fallin' out of the machine. And once I took my hands out of the pie-crust to find a piece of old rope

to tie up the harness. It seemed as if I left off every
five minutes to wait on Josiah Allen, to find somethin' that he wanted and couldn't find, or else to do
somethin' for him that he couldn't do.

Truly, it was a wild and harrowin' time, and tegus.
But I kept a firm holt of my principles, and didn't
groan—not when anybody could hear me. I won't
deny that I did, out in the buttery by myself, give
vent to a groan or two, and a few sithes. But immegiately, or a very little after, I was calm again.

Wall, worse things wuz a-comin' onto me, though
I didn't know it. I owed a tin peddler; had been
owin' him for four weeks. I owed him twenty-five
pounds of paper rags, for a new strainer. I had been
expectin' him for over three weeks every day. But
in all the three hundred and sixty-five days of the
year, there wuzn't another day that would satisfy
him; he had got to come on jest that day, jest as I
wuz fryin' my nut cakes for dinner.

I tried to put him off till another day. But no !
He said it wuz his last trip, and he must have his
rags. And so I had to put by my work, and lug
down my rag-bag. His steel-yards wuz broke, so he
had to weigh 'em in the house. It wuz a tegus job,

for he wuz one of the perticuler kind, and had to look 'em all over before he weighed 'em, and pick out every little piece of brown paper, or full cloth—everything, he said, that wouldn't make up into the nicest kind of writin' paper.

And my steel-yards wuz out of gear any way, so they wouldn't weigh but five pounds at a time, and he wuz dretful perticuler to have 'em just right by the notch.

And he would call on me to come and see just how the steel-yards stood every time. (He wuz as honest as the day; I hain't a doubt of it.)

But it wuz tegus, fearful tegus, and excitin'. Excitin', but not exhileratin', to have the floor all covered with rags of different shapes and sizes, no two of a kind. It wuz a curius time before he come, and a wild time, but what must have been the wildness, and the curosity when there wuz, to put a small estimate on it, nearly a billion of crazy lookin' rags scattered round on the floor.

But I kep' calm; I have got giant self-control, and I used every mite of it, every atom of control I had by me, and kep' calm. I see I must—for I see that Miss Fogg looked bad; yes, I see that the

"SHE LOOKED CURIUS, CURIUSER THAN THE FLOOR LOOKED."

author of " Wedlock's Peaceful Repose" wuz pretty
much used up. She looked curius, curiuser than
the floor looked, and that is goin' to the complete
end of curosity, and metafor.

Wall, I tussled along and got dinner ready. The
tin peddler had to stay to dinner, of course. I
couldn't turn him out jest at dinner time. And
sometimes I almost think that he delayed matters
and touzled 'round amongst them rags jest a purpose to belate himself, so he would have to stay to
dinner.

I am called a good cook. It is known 'way out
beyend Loontown and Zoar—it is talked about, I
spoze. Wall, he stayed to dinner. But he only
made fourteen; there wuz only thirteen besides him,
so I got along. And I had a good dinner and
enough of it.

I had to wait on the table, of course—that is, the
tea and coffee. And I felt that a cup of good,
strong tea would be a paneky. I wuz that wore out
and flustrated that I felt that I needed a paneky to
soothe.

And I got the rest all waited on and wuz jest a
liftin' my cup to my lips, the cup that cheers every-

body but don't inebriate 'em—good, strong Japan
tea with cream in it. Oh, how good it smelt. But
I hadn't fairly got it to my mouth when I wuz
called off sudden, before I had drinked a drop, for
the case demanded help at once.

Miss Peedick had unexpected company come in,
jest as they wuz a-settin' down to the dinner-table,
and she hadn't hardly anything for dinner, and the
company wuz very genteel—a minister and a Justice of the Peace—so she wanted to borrow a loaf
of bread and a pie.

She is a good neighbor and is one that will put
herself out for a neighborin' female, and I went into
the buttery, almost on the run, to get 'em for her,
for her girl said she wanted to get 'em into the
house and onto the table before Mr. Peedick come
in with 'em from the horse barn, for they knew that
Mr. Peedick would lead 'em out to dinner the very
second they got into the house, and Miss Peedick
didn't want her husband to know that she had borrowed vittles, for he would be sure to let the cat out
of the bag, right at the table, by speakin' about 'em
and comparin' 'em with hern.

I see the necessity for urgent haste, and the

trouble wuz that I hurried too much.   In takin'
down a pie in my awful hurry, I tipped over a pan
of milk right onto my dress.   It wuz up high and I

"I SEE THE NECESSITY FOR URGENT HASTE."

wuz right under the shelf, so that about three tea-
cupsful went down into my neck.   But the most
went onto my dress, about five quarts, I should judge

besides that that wuz tricklin' down my backbone.

Wall, I started Serintha Ann Peedick off with her ma's pie and bread, and then wiped up the floor as well as I could, and then I had to go and change my clothes. I had to change 'em clear through to my wrapper, for I wuz wet as sop— as wet as if I had been takin' a milk swim.

CHAPTER V.

WALL, the author of " Wedlock's Peaceful Repose" wuz a-waitin' for me to the table; the men had all got through and gone out. She sot right by me, and she had missed me, I could see. Her eyes looked bigger than ever, and more sad like.

She said " she was dretful sorry for me," and I believed her.

She asked me in a awe-stricken tone, " if I had such trials every day ?"

And I told her " No, I didn't." I told her that things would run along smooth and agreeable for days and days, but that when things got to happenin', they would happen right along for weeks at a time, sometimes, dretful curius. A hull batch of diffi-culties would rain down on anybody to once. Sez I, " You know Mr. Shakespeare says that ' Sorrows never come a-spyin' along as single fighters, but they come in hull battles of 'em,' or words to that effect."

Sez I, in reasonable axents, " Mebby I shall have a hull lot of good things happen to me right along, one after another, some dretful agreeable days, and easy."

Sez she in the same sad axents, and wonderin', " Did you ever have another day in your hull life as hard as this you are a-passin' through?"

" Oh, yes," sez I, "lots of 'em—some worse ones, and," sez I, " the day has only jest begun yet, I presume I shall have lots and lots of new things happen to me before night.   Because it is jest as I tell you, when things get to happenin' there hain't no tellin' when they will ever stop."

Miss Fogg groaned, a low, deep groan, and that is every word she said, only after a little while she spoke up, and sez :

" You hain't eaten a bit of dinner; it all got cold while you wuz a changin' your dress."

" Oh, wall," sez I, " I can get along some way. And I must hurry up and get the table cleared off any way, and get to my work agin', for I have got to do a lot of cookin' this afternoon.   It takes a

sight of pies and cakes and such to satisfy twelve or
a dozen men."

So I went to work vigorously agin. But well
might I tell Miss Fogg "that the day had only jest
begun, and there wuz time for lots of things to
happen before night," for I had only jest got well to
work on the ingregiences of my pies when Submit
Tewksbury sent over "to see if I could let her have
them sturchien seeds I had promised her—she
wanted 'em to run up the inside of her bedroom
winder, and shade her through the winter. She wuz
jest a-settin' out her winter stock of flower roots
and seeds, and wanted 'em immegiatly, and to once,
that is, if it was perfectly convenient," so the boy
said.

Submit is a good creeter, and she wouldn't have
put that burden on me on such a time for nothin',
not if she had known my tribulations; but she
didn't, and I felt that one trial more wouldn't,
as the poet hath well said, "either make or break
me."

So I went to huntin' for the seeds. Wall, it wuz
a good half-hour before I could find 'em, for of
course it wuz natural nater, accordin' to the total

deprivity of things, that I should find 'em in the
bottom of the last bag of seeds that I over-
hauled.

But Submit had been disappointed, and I didn't
want to make her burdens any heavier, so I sent
her the sturchien seeds.

But it wuz a trial I do admit to look over more
than forty bags of garden and flower seeds in such
a time as that. But I sent 'em. I sent Submit
the sturchien seeds, and then I laid to work again
fast as I possibly could.

But I sez to the author of " Peaceful Repose," I
sez to her, sez I :

" I feel bad to think I hain't gettin' no time to
hear you rehearse your lecture, but you can see jest
how it is; you see I hain't had a minute's time to-
day.   Mebby I will get a few minutes' time before
night; I will try to," sez I.

" Oh," sez she, " it hain't no matter about that; I
—I—I somehow—I don't feel like rehearsin' it as
it was." Sez she, " I guess I shall make some
changes in it before I rehearse it agin."

Sez I, " You lay out to make a more mean thing
of it, more megum."

"Yes," sez she, in faint axents, "I am a-thinkin' of it."

"Wall," sez I cheerfully, as I started for the but-

"As I started for the buttery."

tery with a pile of cups in one hand, the castor and pickle dish in the other, and a pile of napkins under my arm, "I believe I shall like it as well again if you do, any way," sez I, as I kicked away the cat that wuz a-clawin' my dress, and opened the door with my foot, both hands bein' full.

" Any way, there will be as much agin truth in it."

Wall, I went to work voyalently, and in two hours' time I had got my work quelled down some. But I had to strain nearly every nerve in the effort.

And I am afraid I didn't use the colporter just exactly right, who come when I wuz right in the midst of puttin' the ingregiences into my tea cakes. I didn't enter so deep into the argument about the Revised New Testament as I should in easier and calmer times. I conversed considerable, I argued some with him, but I didn't get so engaged as meb-by I had ort to. He acted disappointed, and he didn't stay and talk more'n an hour and three quarters.

He generally spends half a day with us. He is a master hand to talk; he'll make your brain fairly spin round he talks so fast and handles such large, curius words. He talked every minute, only when I wuz a-answerin' his questions.

Wall, he had jest gone, the front gate had just clicked onto him, when Miss Philander Dagget came in at the back door. She had her press-board in

"THERE WUZ SOMETHIN' WRONG ABOUT 'EM."

her hand, and a coat over her arm, and I see in a minute that I had got another trial onto me. I see I had got to set her right.

I set her a chair, and she took off her sun-bonnet and hung it over the back of her chair, and set down, and then she asked me if I could spend time to put in the sleeves of her husband's coat. She said "there wuz somethin' wrong about em', but she didn't know what."

She said "she wouldn't have bothered me that day when I had so much round, but Philander had got to go to a funeral the next day, as one of the barriers, and he must have his coat."

Wall, I wrung my hands out of the dish-water they was in at the time, and took the coat and looked at it, and the minute I set my eyes on it I see what ailed it.   I see she had got the sleeves sot in so the elbows come right in front of his arms, and if he had wore it in that condition to the funeral or anywhere else he would have had to fold up his arms right acrost his back ; there wuzn't no other possible way.

And then I turned tailoress and helped her out of her trouble.   I sot the sleeves in proper, and fix-ed the collar.   She had got it sot on as a ruffle.   I

drawed it down smooth where it ort to be and pinned it—and she went home feelin' first rate.

I am very neighborly, and helpful, and am called

"SHE IS APT TO GET THINGS WRONG."

so. Jonesville would miss me if any thing should
happen.

I have often helped that woman a sight. She is a
good, willin' creeter, but she is apt to get things
wrong, dretful apt. She made her little boy's pantaloons once wrong side before, so it would seem

that he would have to set down from the front side, or else stand up.

And twice she got her husband's pantaloons sewed up so there wuz no way to get into em' only to crawl up into 'em through the bottom of the legs. But I have always made a practice of rippin' and tearin' and bastin', and settin' her right, and I did now.

Wall, she hadn't hardly got out of the back door, when Josiah Allen came in in awful distress, he had got a thorn in his foot, he had put on an old pair of boots, and there wuz a hole in the side of one of 'em, and the thorn had got in through the hole. It pained him dretfully, and he wuz jest as crazy as a loon for the time bein'. And he hollered the first thing that "he wanted some of Hall's salve." And I told him "there wuzn't a mite in the house."

And he hollered up and says, "There would be some if there wuz any sense in the head of the house."

I glanced up mechanically at his bald head, but didn't say nothin', for I see it wouldn't do. And he hollered out agin, "Why hain't there any Hall's salve ?"

"HE WANTED SOME OF HALL'S SALVE."

Sez I, " Because old Hall has been dead for years and years, and hain't made any salve."

" Wall, he wouldn't have been dead if he had had any care took of him," he yelled out.

" Why," sez I, " he wuz killed by lightnin'; struck down entirely onexpected five years ago last summer."

" Oh, argue and dispute with a dying man. Gracious Peter! what will become of me !" he groaned out, a-holdin' his foot in his hand.

Sez I, "Let me put some Pond's Extract on it, Josiah."

" Pond's Extract !" he yelled, and then he called that good remedy words I wuz ashamed to hear him utter.

And he jumped round and pranced and kicked just as it is the nater of man to act under bodily injury of that sort. And then he ordered me to take a pin and get the thorn out, and then acted mad as a hen at me all the time I wuz a-doin' it; acted jest as if I wuz a-prickin' him a-purpose.

He talked voyalent and mad. I tried to hush him down; I told him the author of " Wedlock's Peaceful Repose" would hear him, and he hollered back " he didn't care a cent who heard him. He wuz killed, and he shouldn't live to trouble anybody long if that pain kept up."

His acts and words wuz exceedingly skairful to anybody who didn't understand the nater of a man. But I wuzn't moved by 'em so much as the width of a horse hair. Good land! I knew that jest as soon as the pain subsided he would be good as gold, so I kep' on, cool and collected, and got the thorn out, and did up the suffering toe in Pond's Extract, and I hadn't only jest got it done, when, for all the world! if I didn't see a double team stop in front of the house, and I peeked through the winder and see as it wuz the livery stable man from Jonesville, and he had brung down the last straws to be lifted onto the camel's back—a hull lot of onexpected company. A hull load of 'em.

There wuz the Baptist minister and his wife and their three children, and the minister's wife's sister-in-law from the West, who wuz there a-visitin', and the editor of the *Augur'ses* wife (she wuz related to the visitor from the West by marriage) and three of the twins. And old Miss Minkley, she wuz acquainted with the visitor's mother, used to go to school with her. And Drusilly Sypher, she wuz the visitor from the West's bosom friend, or used to be.

Wall, they had all come down to spend the afternoon and visit with each other, and with me and Josiah, and stay to supper.

CHAPTER VI.

HE author of "Peaceful Repose" sez to me, and she looked pale and skairt; she had heard every word Josiah had said, and she wuz dretful skairt and shocked (not knowin' the ways of men, and not understandin', as I said prior and before, that in two hours' time he would be jest as good as the very best kind of pie, affectionate, and even spoony, if I would allow spoons, which I will not the most of the time). Wall, she proposed, Miss Fogg did, that she should ride back with the livery man. And though I urged her to stay till night, I couldn't urge her as hard as I would otherwise, for by that time the head of the procession of visitors had reached the door-step, and I had to meet 'em with smiles.

I smiled some, I thought I must. But they wuz curius smiles, very, strange-lookin' smiles, sort o' gloomy ones, and mournful lookin'.

"She proposed that she should ride back with the livery man."

I have got lots of different smiles that I keep by me for different occasions, every woman has, and this wuz one of my most mournfulest and curiusest ones.

Wall, the author of "Wedlock's Peaceful and Perfect Repose" insisted on goin', and she went. And I sez to her as she went down the steps, "That if she would come up some other day when I didn't have quite so much work round, I would be as good as my word to her about hearin' her re-hearse the lecture."

But she said, as she hurried out to the gate, lookin' pale an' wan (as wan agin as she did when she came, if not wanner):

"That she should make *changes* in it before she ever rehearsed it agin—*deep changes.*"

And I should dare to persume to say that she did. Though, as I say, she went off most awful sudden, and I hadn't seen nor heard from her sence till I got this letter.

*   *   *   *   *   *   *

Wall, jest as I got through with the authoresses letter, and Lodema Trumble's, Josiah Allen came. And I hurried up the supper. I got it all on the table while I wuz a steepin' my tea (it wuz good tea). And we sot down to the table happy as a king and his queen. I don't s'pose queens make a practice of steepin' tea, but mebby they would be better

"MY PARDNER ENJOYS GOOD VITTLES."

off if they did—and have better appetites and better tea. Any way we felt well, and the supper tasted good. And though Josiah squirmed some when I told him Lodema wuz approachin' and would be there that very night or the next day—still the cloud

wore away and melted off in the glowin' mellowness
of the hot tea and cream, the delicious oysters and
other good things.

My pardner, though, as he often says, is not a
epicack, still he duz enjoy good vittles dretful well,
and appreciates 'em.   And I make a stiddy practice
of doin' the best I can by him in this direction.

And if more females would foller on and cipher
out this simple rule, and get the correct answer to
ít, the cramp in the right hands of divorce lawyers
would almost entirely disappear.

For truly it seems that *no* human man *could be*
more worrysome, and curius, and hard to get along
with than Josiah Allen is at times; still, by stiddy
keepin' of my table set out with good vittles from
day to day, and year to year, the golden cord of affection has bound him to me by ties that can't never
be broken into.

He worships me !   And the better vittles I get,
the more he thinks on me.   For love, however true
and deep it is, is still a tumultous sea ; it has its high
tides, and its low ones, its whirlpools, and its calms.

He loves me a good deal better some days than
he does others ; I see it in his mean.   And mark

you! mark it well, female reader, these days are the
ones that I cook up sights and sights of good food,
and with a cheerful countenance and clean apron,
set it before him in a bright room, on a snowy table-
cloth !

Great—great is the mystery of men's love.

I have often and often repeated this simple fact
and truth that underlies married life, and believe me,
dear married sisters, too much cannot be said about
it, by those whose hearts beat for the good of female
and male humanity—and it *cannot* be too closely
followed up and practised by female pardners.

But I am a-eppisodin'; and to resoom.

Wall, Lodema Trumble arrove the next mornin'
bright and early—I mean the mornin' wuz bright,
not Lodema—oh no, fur from it ; Lodema is never
bright and cheerful—she is the opposite and reverse
always.

She is a old maiden. I do think it sounds so
much more respectful to call 'em so ruther than " old
maid" (but I had to tutor Josiah dretful sharp before
I could get him into it).

I guess Lodema is one of the regular sort. There
is different kinds of old maidens, some that could

marry if they would, and some that would but
couldn't. And I ruther mistrust she is one of the
"would-but-couldnt's," though I wouldn't dast to let
her know I said so, not for the world.

Josiah never could bear the sight of her, and he
sort o' blamed her for bein' a old maiden. But I
put a stop to that sudden, for sez I:

" She hain't to blame, Josiah."

And she wuzn't. I hain't a doubt of it.

Wall, how long she calculated to stay this time
we didn't know. But we had our fears and forebodin's about it; for she wuz in the habit of makin'
awful long visits. Why, sometimes she would de-
scend right down onto us sudden and onexpected,
and stay fourteen weeks right along—jest like a
famine or a pestilence, or any other simely that you
are a mind to bring up that is tuckerin' and
stiddy.

And she wuz disagreeable, I'll confess, and she
wuz tuckerin', but I done well by her, and stood between her and Josiah all I could. He loved to
put on her, and she loved to impose on him. I
don't stand up for either on 'em, but they wuz at
regular swords' pints all the time a'most. And it

come fearful tuff on me, fearful tuff, for I had to stand the brunt on it.

But she is a disagreeable creeter, and no mistake. She is one of them that can't find one soli-

"BUT SHE IS A DISAGREEABLE CREETER."

tary thing, or one solitary person in this wide world to suit 'em. If the weather is cold she is pinin' for hot weather, and if the weather is hot she is pantin' for zero.

If it is a pleasant day the sun hurts her eyes,

and if it is cloudy she groans aloud and says " she can't see."

And no human bein' wuz ever known to suit her. She gets up early in the mornin' and puts on her specs, and goes out (as it were) a-huntin' up faults in folks. And she finds 'em, finds lots of 'em. And then she spends the rest of the day a-drivin' 'em ahead of her, and groanin' at 'em.

You know this world bein' such a big place and so many different sort o' things in it that you can generally find in it the perticuler sort of game you set out to hunt in the mornin'.

If you set out to hunt beauty and goodness, if you take good aim and are perseverin'—if you jest track 'em and foller 'em stiddy from mornin' till night, and don't get led away a-follerin' up some other game, such as meanness and selfishness and other such worthless head o' cattle—why, at night you will come in with a sight of good game. You will be a noble and happy hunter.

At the same time, if you hunt all day for faults you will come in at night with sights of pelts. You will find what you hunt for, track 'em right along and chase 'em down.

"BUT FIT WITH THEIR TONGUES, FEARFUL."

Wall, Lodema never got led away from her perticuler chase. She just hunted faults from mornin'
till night, and done well at it. She brought in
sights of skins.

But oh ! wuzn't it disagreeable in the extreme to
Samantha, who had always tried to bend her bow
and bring down Beauty, to have her familiar huntin'
grounds turned into so different a warpath. It wuz
disagreeable ! It wuz ! It wuz !

And then, havin' to stand between her and Josiah
too, wuz fearful wearin' on me. I had always stood
there in the past, and now in this visit it wuz jest
the same; all the hull time, till about the middle
of the fifth week, I had to stand between their two
tongues—they didn't fight with their hands, but fit
with their tongues, fearful.

CHAPTER VII.

—UT along about the middle of the fifth week I see a change. Lodema had been uncommon exasperatin', and I expected she would set Josiah to goin', and I groaned in spirit, to think what a job wuz ahead of me, to part their two tongues—when all of a sudden I see a curius change come over my pardner's face.

I remember jest the date that the change in his mean wuz visible, and made known to me—for it wuz the very mornin' that we got the invitation to old Mr. and Miss Pressley's silver weddin'. And that wuz the fifteenth day of the month along about the middle of the forenoon.

And it wuz not half an hour after Elnathen Pressley came to the door and give us the invitations, that I see the change in his mean.

And when I asked him about it afterwards, what

that strange and curius look meant, he never hung
back a mite from tellin' me, but sez right out plain :

"Mebby, Samantha, I hain't done exactly as I
ort to by cousin Lodema, and I have made up
my mind to make her a happy surprise before she
goes away."

"Wall," sez I, "so do."

I thought he wuz goin' to get her a new dress
She had been a-hintin' to him dretful strong to that
effect. She wanted a parmetty, or a balzereen, or a
circassien, which wuz in voge in her young days.
But I wuz in hopes he would get her a cashmere,
and told him so, plain.

But I couldn't get him to tell what the surprise
wuz. He only sez, sez he :

"I am goin' to make her a happy surprise."

And the thought that he wuz a-goin' to branch
out and make a change, wuz considerable of a
comfort to me. And I needed comfort—yes, in
deed I did—I needed it bad. For not one single
thing did I do for her that I done right, though I
tried my best to do well by her.

But she found fault with my vittles from mornin'
till night, though I am called a excellent cook all

over Jonesville, and all round the adjoining country, out as far as Loontown, and Zoar. It has come straight back to me by them that wouldn't lie. But it hain't made me vain.

But I never cooked a thing that suited Lodema, not a single thing. Most of my vittles wuz too fresh, and then if I braced up and salted 'em extra so as to be sure to please her, why then they wuz briny, and hurt her mouth.

Why, if you'll believe it, I give her a shawl, made her a present of it; it had even checks black and white, jest as many threads in the black stripes as there wuz in the white, for I counted 'em.

And she told me, after she had looked it all over, and said it wuz kinder thin and slazy, and checkered shawls had gone out of fashion, and the black look-ed some as if it would fade with washin', and the white wuzn't over clear, and the colors wuzn't no ways becomin' to her complexion, and etcetery, et-cetery.

"But," sez she, after she had got all through with the rest of her complaints—"if the white stripes wuz where the black wuz, and the black where the white wuz, she should like it quite well."

And there it wuz, even check, two and two.

Wall, that wuz a sample of her doin's. If any-body had a Roman nose she wanted a Greecy one.

"IF THE WHITE STRIPES WUZ WHERE THE BLACK WUZ."

And if the nose wuz Greece, why then she wanted Rome.

Why, Josiah sez to me along about the third week, he said (to ourselves, in private), " that if Lo-dema went to Heaven she would be dissatisfied with it, and think it wuz livelier, and more goin' on down to the other place." And he said she would get the angels all stirred up a findin' fault with their feathers.

I told him " I would not hear such talk."

" Wall," sez he, " don't you believe it?"

And I kinder turned him off, and wouldn't tell, and told him it wuz wicked to talk so.

" Wall," sez Josiah, " you dassent say she wouldn't."

And I dassent, though I wouldn't own it up to him, I dassent.

And if she kinder got out of other occupations for a minute durin' them first weeks she would be a quarrelin' with Josiah Allen about age.

I s'pose she and Josiah wuzn't far from the same age, for they wuz children together. But she wanted to make out she wuz young.

And she would tell Josiah that " he seemed jest like a father to her, and always had." And some-times when she felt the most curius, she would call him " Father," and "Pa," and " Papa." And it would mad Josiah Allen so that I would have all I could do to quell him down.

Now I didn't feel so, I didn't mind it so much.

Why, there would be days, when she felt the curiusest, that she would call me " Mother," and " Ma," and
foller me round with foot-stools and things, when I
went to set down, and would kinder worry over my
fallin' off the back step, and would offer to help me
up the suller stairs, and so forth, and watchin' over
what I et, and tellin' me folks of my age ort to be
careful, and not over-eat.

And Josiah asked me to ask her " How she felt
about that time ?"   For she wuz from three to four
years older than I wuz.

But I wouldn't contend with her, and the foot-
stools come kinder handy, I had jest as lieve have
'em under my feet as not, and ruther.   And as for rich
vittles not agreein' with me, and my not over-eatin',
I broke that up by fallin' right in with her, and not
cookin' such good things—that quelled her down,
and gaulded Josiah too.

But, as I said, it riled Josiah the worst of anything to have Lodema call him father, for he wants
to make out that he is kinder young himself.

And sez he to her one day, about the third week,
when she was a-goin' on about how good and
fatherly he looked, and how much he seemed like a

parent to her, and always had, sez he: "I wonder if I seemed like a father to you when we wuz a-kickin' at each other in the same cradle?" Sez he: "We both used to nuss out of the same bottle, any way, for I have heard my mother say so lots of times. There wuzn't ten days' difference in our ages. You wuz ten days the oldest as I have always made out."

She screamed right out, "Why, Josiah Allen, where is your conscience to talk in that way—and your heart?"

"In here, where everybody's is," sez Josiah, strikin' himself with his right hand—he meant to strike against his left breast, but struck too low, kinder on his stomach.

And sez I, "That is what I have always thought, Josiah Allen. I have always had better luck reachin' your conscience through your stomach than in any other way. And now," sez I coldly, "do you go out and bring in a pail of water."

I used to get beat out and sick of their scufflin's and disagreein's, and broke 'em up whenever I could.

But oh! oh! how she did quarrel with Josiah Allen and that buzz saw scheme of his'n. How light she made of that enterprise, how she demeaned the

buzz, and run the saws—till I felt that bad as I
hated the enterprise myself, I felt that a variety of
loud buzz saws would be a welcome relief from her
tongue—from their two tongues; for as fur down

LODEMA AND JOSIAH IN YOUTH.

as she would run them buzz saws, jest so fur would
Josiah Allen praise 'em up.

She never agreed with Josiah Allen but in jest
one thing while she was under his ruff.   I happened
to mention one day how extremely anxious I wuz
to have females set on the Conference; and then,

wantin' to dispute me, and also bein' set on that side, she run down the project, and called it all to nort— and when too late she see that she had got over on Josiah Allen's side of the fence.

But it had one good effect. When that man see she wuz there, he waded off, way out of sight of the project, and wouldn't mention it—it madded him so to be on the same side of the fence she wuz —so that it seemed to happen all for the best.

Why, I took her as a dispensation from the first, and drawed all sorts of morels from her, and sights of 'em—sights.

But oh, it wuz tuff on me, fearful tuff.

And when she calculated and laid out to make out her visit and go, wuz more than we could tell.

CHAPTER VIII.

OR two weeks had passed away like a nite mair of the nite— and three weeks, and four weeks —and she didn't seem to be no nigher goin' than she did when she came.

And I would not make a move towards gettin' rid of her, not if I had dropped down in my tracts, because she wuz one of the relatives on his side.

But I wuz completely fagged out; it did seem, as I told Tirzah Ann one day in confidence, "that I never knew the meanin' of the word "fag" before.

And Tirzah Ann told me (she couldn't bear her) that if she wuz in my place, she would start her off. Sez she:

"She has plenty of brothers and sisters, and a home of her own, and why should she come here to torment you and father;" and sez she, "I'll talk to her, mother, I'd jest as leve as not."

Sez I, "Tirzah Ann, if you say a word to her, I'll—I'll never put confidence in you agin;" sez I, "Life is full of tribulations, and we must expect to bear our crosses;" sez I, "The old martyrs went through more than Lodema."

Sez Tirzah Ann, "I believe Lodema would have wore out John Rogers."

And I don't know but she would, but I didn't encourage her by ownin' it up that she would; but I declare for't, I believe she would have been more tegus than the nine children, and the one at the breast, any way.

Wall, as I said, it wuz durin' the fifth week that Josiah Allen turned right round, and used her first rate.

And when she would talk before folks about how much filial affection she had for him, and about his always havin' been jest like a parent to her, and everything of the kind—he never talked back a mite, but looked clever, and told me in confidence, "That he had turned over a new leaf, and he wuz goin' to surprise her—give her a happy surprise."

And he seemed, instead of lovin' to rile her up,

as he had, to jest put his hull mind on the idee of the joyful surprise.

Wall, I am always afraid (with reason) of Josiah Allen's enterprizes. But do all I could, he wouldn't tell me one word about what he wuz goin' to do, only he kep it up, kep a-sayin' that,

"It wuz somethin' I couldn't help approvin' of, and it wuz somethin' that would happify me, and be a solid comfort to her, and a great gain and honor."

So (though I trembled some for the result) I had to let it go on, for she wuz one of the relations on his own side, and I knew it wouldn't do for me to interfere too much, and meddle.

Why, he did come right out one day and give hints to me to that effect.

Sez I, "Why do you go on and be so secret about it? Why don't you tell your companion all about it, what you are a-goin' to do, and advise with her?"

And he sez, "I guess I know what I am about. She is one of the relations on my side, and I guess I have got a few rights left, and a little spunk."

"Yes," sez I, sadly, "you have got the spunk."

"Wall," sez he, "I guess I can spunk up, and do

somethin' for one of my own relations, without any interference or any advice from any of the Smith family, or anybody else."

Sez I, " I don't want to stop your doin' all you can for Lodema, but why not tell what you are a-goin' to do ?"

" It will be time enough when the time comes," sez he. " You will find it out in the course of next week."

Wall, it run along to the middle of the next week. And one day I had jest sot down to tie off a comforter.

It wuz unbleached cheese cloth that I had bought and colored with tea leaves. It wuz a sort of a light mice color, a pretty soft gray, and I wuz goin' to tie it in with little balls of red zephyr woosted, and work it in buttonhole stitch round the edge with the same.

It wuz fur our bed, Josiah's and mine, and it wuz goin' to be soft and warm and very pretty, though I say it, that shouldn't.

It wuzn't quite so pretty as them that hain't colored. I had 'em for my spare beds, cream color tied with pale blue and pink, that wuz perfectly

"I HAD JEST SOT DOWN TO TIE OFF A COMFORTER."

beautiful and very dressy ; but I thought for every-
day use a colored one would be better.

Wall, I had brought it out and wuz jest a-goin'
to put it onto the frames (some new-fashioned ones
I had borrowed from Tirzah Ann for the occasion).

And Cousin Lodema had jest observed, "that
the new-fashioned frames with legs wuzn't good for
nothin', and she didn't like the color of gray, it
looked too melancholy, and would be apt to de-
press our feelin's too much, and would be tryin' to
our complexions."

And I told her "that I didn't spoze there would
be a very great congregation in our bedroom, as a
general thing in the dead of night, to see whether
it wuz becomin' to Josiah and me or not. And, it
bein' as dark as Egypt, our complexions wouldn't
make a very bad show any way."

"Wall," she said, "to tie it with red wuzn't at all
appropriate, it wuz too dressy a color for folks of
our age, Josiah's and mine." "Why," sez she, "even
I, at *my* age, would skurcely care to sleep under one
so gay. And she wouldn't have a cheese cloth
comforter any way."

She sort o' stopped to ketch breath, and Josiah sez:

"Oh, wall, Lodema, a cheese cloth comforter is better than none, and I should think you would be jest the one to like any sort of a frame on legs."

But I wunk at him, a real severe and warnin' wink, and he stopped short off, for all the world as if he had forgot bein' on his good behavior; he stopped short off, and went right to behavin', and sez he to me:

"Don't put on your comforter to-day, Samantha, for Tirzah Ann and Whitfield and the babe are a-comin' over here bimeby, and Maggie is a-comin', and Thomas Jefferson."

"Wall," sez I, "that is a good reason why I should keep on with it; the girls can help me if I don't get it off before they get here."

And then he sez, "Miss Minkley is a-comin', too, and the Elder."

"Why'ee," sez I, "Josiah Allen, why didn't you tell me before, so I could have baked up somethin' nice? What a man you are to keep things; how long have you known it?"

" Oh, a week or so !"

" A week !" sez I ; "Josiah Allen, where is your conscience ? if you have got a conscience."

" In the same old place," sez he, kinder hittin' himself in the pit of his stomach.

" Wall, I should think as much," sez I.

And Lodema sez, sez she : "A man that won't tell things is of all creeters that walks the earth the most disagreeable. And I should think the girls, Maggie and Tirzah Ann, would want to stay to home and clean house such a day as this is. And I should think a Elder would want to stay to home so's to be on hand in case of anybody happenin' to be exercised in their minds, and wantin to talk to him on religious subjects. And if I wuz a Elder's wife, I should stay to home with him ; I should think it wuz my duty and my privilege. And if I wuz a married woman, I would have enough baked up in the house all the time, so's not to be afraid of company."

But I didn't answer back. I jest sot away my frames, and went out and stirred up a cake ; I had one kind by me, besides cookies and jell tarts.

But I felt real worked up to think I hadn't heard

Wall, I hadn't more'n got that cake fairly into the oven when the children come, and Elder Minkley and his wife. And I thought they looked queer, and I thought the Elder begun to tell me somethin', and I thought I see Josiah wink at him. But I wouldn't want to take my oath whether he wunk or not, but I *thought* he wunk.

I wuz jest a turnin' this over in my mind, and a carryin' away their things, when I glanced out of the settin' room winder, and lo, and behold! there wuz Abi Adsit a comin' up to the front door, and right behind her wuz her Pa and Ma Adsit, and Deacon Henzy and his wife, and Miss Henn and Metilda, and Lute Pitkins and his wife, and Miss Petengill, and Deacon Sypher and Drusilly, and Submit Tewksbury—a hull string of 'em as long as a procession.

Sez I, and I spoke it right out before I thought— sez I—

"Why'ee!" sez I. "For the land's sake!" sez I, "has there been a funeral, or anything? And are these the mourners?" sez I. "Are they stoppin' here to warm?"

For it wuz a cold day—and I repeated the words

to myself mechanically as it wuz, as I see 'em file
up the path.

"They be mourners, hain't they?"

"No," sez Josiah, who had come in and wuz a
standin' by the side of me, as I spoke out to myself
unbeknown to me—sez he in a proud axent—

"No, they hain't mourners, they are Happyfiers;
they are Highlariers; they have come to our party.
We are givin' a party, Samantha. We are havin' a
diamond weddin' here for Lodema."

"A diamond weddin'!" I repeated mechanically.

"Yes, this is my happy surprise for Lodema."

I looked at Lodema Trumble. She looked
strange. She had sunk back in her chair. I
thought she wuz a-goin' to faint, and she told somebody the next day, "that she did almost lose her
conscientiousness."

"Why," sez I, "she hain't married."

"Wall, she ort to be, if she hain't," sez he. "I
say it is high time for her to have some sort of a
weddin'. Everybody is a havin' 'em—tin, and silver
and wooden, and basswood, and glass, and etc.—
and I thought it wuz a perfect shame that Lodema
shouldn't have none of no kind—and I thought I'd

"WE ARE GIVIN' A PARTY, SAMANTHA."

lay to, and surprise her with one. Every other man seemed to be a-holdin' off, not willin' seemin'ly that she should have one, and I jest thought I would happify her with one."

" Wall, why didn't you make her a silver one, or a tin ?" sez I.

"Or a paper one !" screamed Lodema, who had riz up out of her almost faintin' condition. " That would have been much more appropriate," sez she.

" Wall, I thought a diamond one would be more profitable to her. For I asked 'em all to bring dia-monds, if they brought anything. And then I thought it would be more suitable to her age."

" Why !" she screamed out. " They have to be married seventy-five years before they can have one."

" Yes," sez he dreemily, " I thought that would be about the right figure."

Lodema wuz too mad to find fault or complain or anything, She jest marched up-stairs and didn't come down agin that night. And the young folks had a splendid good time, and the old ones, too.

Tirzah Ann and Maggie had brought some re-freshments with 'em, and so had some of the other wimmen, and, with what I had, there wuz enough, and more than enough, to refresh ourselves with.

Wall, the very next mornin' Lodema marched down like a grenideer, and ordered Josiah to take her to the train. And she eat breakfast with her things on, and went away immegiately after, and hain't been back here sense.

And I wuz truly glad to see her go, but wuz sorry she went in such a way, and I tell Josiah he wuz to blame,

But he acts as innocent as you pleese. And he goes all over the arguments agin every time I take him to do about it. He sez "she wuz old enough to have a weddin' of some kind."

And of course I can't dispute that, when he faces me right down, and sez :

" Hain't she old enough ?"

And I'll say, kinder short—

" Why, I spoze so !"

" Wall," sez he, " wouldn't it have been profitable to her if they had brought diamonds? Wouldn't it have been both surprisin' and profitable?" And sez he, "I told 'em expressly to bring diamonds if they had more than they wanted. I charged old

Bobbet and Lute Pitkins specially on the subject.
I didn't want 'em to scrimp themselves; but," sez I,
"if you have got more diamonds than you want,
Lute, bring over a few to Lodema."

"IF YOU HAVE GOT MORE DIAMONDS THAN YOU WANT."

"Yes," sez I, coldly, "he wuz dretful likely to
have diamonds more then he wanted, workin' out
by day's work to support his family. You know
there wuzn't a soul you invited that owned a diamond."

"How did I know what they owned? I never have prowled round into their bureau draws and things, tryin' to find out what they had; they might have had quarts of 'em, and I not know it."

Sez I, "You did it to make fun of Lodema and get rid of her. And it only makes it worse to try to smooth it over." Sez I, "I'd be honorable about it if I wuz in your place, and own up."

"Own up? What have I got to own up? I shall always say if my orders wuz carried out, it would have been a profitable affair for Lodema, and it would—profitable and surprisin'."

And that is all I can get him to say about it, from that day to this.

CHAPTER IX.

UT truly the labors that descended onto my shoulders immegiately after Lodema's departure wuz hard enough to fill up my hull mind, and tax every one of my energies.

Yes, my labors and the labors of the other female Jonesvillians wuz deep and arjuous in the extreme (of which more and anon bimeby).

I had been the female appinted in a private and becomin' female way, to go to Loontown to see the meetin' house there that we heard they had fixed over in a cheap but commojous way. And for reasons (of which more and anon) we wanted to inquire into the expense, the looks on't, etc., etc.

So I persuaded Josiah Allen to take me over to Loontown on this pressin' business, and he gin his consent to go on the condition that we should stop for a visit to Cephas Bodley'ses. Josiah sets store by 'em.

You see they are relations of ourn and have been for some time, entirely unbeknown to us, and they'd come more'n a year ago a huntin' of us up. They said they " thought relations ought to be hunted up and hanged together." They said " the idea of huntin' us up had come to 'em after readin' my books." They told me so, and I said, " Wall !"   I didn't add nor diminish to that one " wall," for I didn't want to act too backward, nor too forward. I jest kep' kinder neutral, and said, " Wall !"

You see Cephas'ses father's sister-in-law wuz step-mother to my aunt's second cousin on my father's side. And Cephas said that " he had felt more and more, as years went by, that it wuz a burnin' shame for relations to not know and love each other." He said " he felt that he loved Josiah and me dearly."

I didn't say right out whether it wuz reciprokated or not. I kinder said, " Wall !" agin.

And I told Josiah, in perfect confidence and the wood-house chamber, " that I had seen nearer relations than Mr. Bodley'ses folks wuz to us."

Howsumever, I done well by 'em. Josiah killed a fat turkey, and I baked it, and done other things for their comfort, and we had quite a good time.

"Cephas said it wuz a burnin' shame for relations to not know and love each other."

Cephas wuz ruther flowery and enthusiastick, and his mouth and voice wuz ruther large, but he meant well, I should judge, and we had quite a good time.

She wuz very freckled, and a second-day Baptist by perswasion, and wuz piecin' up a crazy bedquilt. She went a-visitin' a good deal, and got pieces of the women's dresses where she visited for blocks. So it wuz quite a savin' bedquilt, and very good-lookin', considerin'.

But to resoom and continue on. Cephas'ses folks made us promise on our two sacred honors, Josiah's honor and mine, that we would pay back the visit, for, as Cephas said, "for relatives to live so clost to each other, and not to visit back and forth, wuz a burnin' shame and a disgrace." And Josiah promised that we would go right away after sugerin'.

We wouldn't promise on the New Testament, as Cephas wanted us to (he is dretful enthusias-tick); but we gin good plain promises that we would go, and laid out to keep our two words.

Wall, we got there onexpected, as they had come onto us. And we found 'em plunged into trouble. Their only child, a girl, who had mar-ried a young lawyer of Loontown, had jest lost

her husband with the typus, and they wuz a-makin'
preparations for the funeral when we got there.
She and her husband had come on a visit, and
he wuz took down bed-sick there and died.

I told 'em I felt like death to think I had descended down onto 'em at such a time.

But Cephas said he wuz jest dispatchin' a mes-
senger for us when we arrove, for, he said, "in a
time of trouble, then wuz the time, if ever, that
a man wanted his near relations clost to him."

And he said "we had took a load offen him
by appearin' jest as we did, for there would have
been some delay in gettin' us there, if the mes-
senger had been dispatched."

He said "that mornin' he had felt so bad that
he wanted to die—it seemed as if there wuzn't
nothin' left for him to live for; but now he felt that
he had sunthin' to live for, now his relatives wuz
gathered round him."

Josiah shed tears to hear Cephas go on. I myself didn't weep none, but I wuz glad if we could
be any comfort to 'em, and told 'em so.

And I told Sally Ann, that wuz Cephas'ses wife,
that I would do anything I could to help 'em.

And she said everything wuz a-bein' done that wuz necessary. She didn't know of but one thing that wuz likely to be overlooked and neglected, and that wuz the crazy bedquilt. She said "she would love to have that finished to throw over a lounge in the settin'-room, that wuz frayed out on the edges, and if I felt like it, it *would* be a great relief to her to have me take it right offen her hands and finish it."

So I took out my thimble and needle (I always carry such necessaries with me, in a huzzy made ex-pressly for that purpose), and I sot down and went to piecin' up. There wuz seventeen blocks to piece up, each one crazy as a loon to look at, and it wuz all to set together.

She had the pieces, for she had been off on a vis-itin' tower the week before, and collected of 'em.

So I sot in quiet and the big chair in the settin'-room, and pieced up, and see the preparations goin' on round us.

I found that Cephas'ses folks lived in a house big and showy-lookin', but not so solid and firm as I had seen.

It wuz one of the houses, outside and inside,

where more pains had been took with the porticos and ornaments than with the underpinnin'.

It had a showy and kind of a shaky look. And I found that that extended to Cephas'ses business ar-

"So I sot in quiet and the big chair."

rangements. Amongst the other ornaments of his buildin's wuz mortgages, quite a lot of 'em, and of almost every variety. He had gin his only child, S. Annie (she wuz named after her mother, Sally Ann, but spelt it this way), he had gin S. Annie a showy education, a showy weddin', and a showy settin'-out. But she had had the good luck to marry a sensible man, though poor.

He took S. Annie and the brackets, the piano and hangin' lamps and baskets and crystal bead lambrequins, her father had gin her, moved 'em all into a good, sensible, small house, and went to work to get a practice and a livin'. He was a lawyer by perswasion.

Wall, he worked hard, day and night, for three little children come to 'em pretty fast, and S. Annie consumed a good deal in trimmin's and cheap lace to ornament 'em; she wuz her father's own girl for ornament. But he worked so hard, and had so many irons in the fire, and kep' 'em all so hot, that he got a good livin' for 'em, and begun to lay up money towards buyin' 'em a house—a home.

He talked a sight, so folks said that knew him well, about his consumin' desire and aim to get his wife and children into a little home of their own, into a safe little haven, where they could live if he wuz called away. They say that that wuz on his mind day and night, and wuz what nerved his hand so in the fray, and made him so successful.

Wall, he had laid up about nine hundred dollars towards a home, every dollar on it earned by hard work and consecrated by this deathless hope and affection. The house he had got his mind on only cost about a thousand dollars. Loontown property is cheap.

Wall, he had laid up nine hundred, and wuz a-beginnin' to save on the last hundred, for he wouldn't run in debt a cent any way, when he wuz took voyalent sick there to Cephas'ses; he and S. Annie had come home for a visit of a day or two, and he bein' so run down, and weak with his hard day work and his night work, that he suckumbed to his sickness, and passed away the day before I got there.

Wall, S. Annie wuz jest overcome with grief the day I got there, but the day follerin' she begun to take some interest and help her father in makin' preparations for the funeral.

The body wuz embalmed, accordin' to Cephas'ses and S. Annie's wish, and the funeral wuz to be on the Sunday follerin', and on that Cephas and S. Annie now bent their energies.

To begin with, S. Annie had a hull suit of clear

crape made for herself, with a veil that touched the
ground; she also had three other suits commenced,
for more common wear, trimmed heavy with crape,
one of which she ordered for sure the next week, for
she said, "she couldn't stir out of the house in any
other color but black."

I knew jest how dear crape wuz, and I tackled
her on the subject, and sez I—

" Do you know, S. Annie, these dresses of your'n
will cost a sight ?"

"Cost?" sez she, a-bustin' out a-cryin 'What do
I care about cost? I will do everything I can to
respect his memory. I do it in remembrance of him."

Sez I, gently, " S. Annie, you wouldn't forget
him if you wuz dressed in white. And as for respect, such a life as his, from all I hear of it, don't
need crape to throw respect on it ; it commands respect, and gets it from everybody."

" But," sez Cephas, " it would look dretful odd
to the neighbors if she didn't dress in black." Sez
he in a skairful tone, and in his intense way—

" I would ruther resk my life than to have her fail
in duty in this way; it would make talk. And,"
sez he, " what is life worth when folks talk ?"

"WHAT IS LIFE WORTH WHEN FOLKS TALK?"

I turned around the crazed block and tackled it
in a new place (more luny than ever it seemed to
me), and sez I, mekanickly—

"It is pretty hard work to keep folks from talkin';
to keep 'em from sayin' somethin'."

But I see from their looks it wouldn't do to say
anything more, so I had to set still and see it go on.

At that time of year flowers wuz dretful high, but
S. Annie and Cephas had made up their minds
that they must have several flower-pieces from the
city nighest to Loontown.

One wuz a-goin' to be a gate ajar, and one wuz to
be a gate wide open, and one wuz to be a big book.
Cephas asked what book I thought would be pref-
erable to represent. And I mentioned the Bible.

But Cephas sez, "No, he didn't think he would
have a Bible; he didn't think it would be appropriate, seein' the deceased wuz a lawyer." He said
"he hadn't quite made up his mind what book to
have. But anyway it wuz to be in flowers—beautiful flowers." Another piece wuz to be his name in
white flowers on a purple background of pansies.
His name wuz Wellington Napoleon Bonaparte
Hardiman. And I sez to Cephas—

"To save expense, you will probable have the moneygram W. N. B. H.?"

"Oh, no," sez he.

Sez I, "Then the initials of his given names, and the last name in full."

"Oh, no," he said; "it wuz S. Annie's wish, and hisen, that the hull name should be put on. They thought it would show more respect."

I sez, "Where Wellington is now, that hain't a goin' to make any difference, and," sez I, "Cephas, flowers are dretful high this time of year, and it is a long name."

But Cephas said agin that he didn't care for expense, so long as respect wuz done to the memory of the deceased. He said that he and S. Annie both felt that it wuz their wish to have the funeral go ahead of any other that had ever took place in Loontown or Jonesville. He said that S. Annie felt that it wuz all that wuz left her now in life, the memory of such a funeral as he deserved.

Sez I, "There is his children left for her to live for," sez I—"three little bits of his own life, for her to nourish, and cherish, and look out for."

"Yes," sez Cephas, "and she will do that nobly,

and I will help her. They are all goin' to the funeral, too, in deep-black dresses." He said "they
wuz too little to realize it now, but in later and ma-
turer years it would be a comfort to 'em to know
they had took part in such a funeral as that wuz
goin' to be, and wuz dressed in black."

"Wall," sez I (in a quiet, onassumin' way I
would gin little hints of my mind on the subject),
"I am afraid that will be about all the comforts of
life the poor little children will ever have," sez I.
"It will be if you buy many more flower-pieces and
crape dresses."

Cephas said " it wouldn't take much crape for the
children's dresses, they wuz so little, only the baby's ;
that would have to be long."

Sez I, "The baby would look better in white,
and it will take sights of crape for a long baby
dress."

"Yes, but S. Annie can use it afterwards for veils.
She is very economical; she takes it from me.
And she feels jest as I do, that the baby must
wear it in respect to her father's memory."

Sez I, "The baby don't know crape from a
clothes-pin."

"No," sez Cephas, "but in after years the thought of the respect she showed will sustain her."

"Wall," sez I, "I guess she won't have much besides thoughts to live on, if things go on in this way."

I would give little hints in this way, but they wuzn't took. Things went right on as if I hadn't spoke. And I couldn't contend, for truly, as a bad little boy said once on a similar occasion, "it wuzn't my funeral," so I had to set and work on that insane bedquilt and see it go on. But I sithed constant and frequent, and when I wuz all alone in the room I indulged in a few low groans.

CHAPTER X.

WO dressmakers wuz in the house, to stay all the time till the dresses wuz done; and clerks would come around, anon, if not oftener, with packages of mournin' goods, and mournin' jewelry, and mournin' handkerchiefs, and mournin' stockings, and mournin' stockin'-supporters, and mournin' safety-pins, and etc., etc., etc., etc., etc.

Every one of 'em, I knew, a-wrenchin' boards offen the sides of that house that Wellington had worked so hard to get for his wife and little ones.

Wall, the day of the funeral come. It wuz a wet, drizzly day, but Cephas wuz up early, to see that everything wuz as he wanted it to be.

As fur as I wuz concerned, I had done my duty, for the crazy bedquilt wuz done; and though brains might totter as they looked at it, I felt that it wuzn't my fault. Sally Ann spread it out with complacency over the lounge, and thanked me, with tears in her eyes, for my noble deed.

Along quite early in the mornin', before the show commenced, I went in to see Wellington.

He lay there calm and peaceful, with a look on his face as if he had got away at last from a atmosphere of show and sham, and had got into the great Reality of life.

It wuz a good face, and the worryment and care that folks told me had been on it for years had all faded away. But the look of determination, and resolve, and bravery,—that wuz ploughed too deep in his face to be smoothed out, even by the mighty hand that had lain on it. The resolved look, the brave look with which he had met the warfare of life, toiled for victory over want, toiled to place his dear and helpless ones in a position of safety,—that look wuz on his face yet, as if the deathless hope and endeavor had gone on into eternity with him.

And by the side of him, on a table, wuz the big high flower-pieces, beginnin' already to wilt and decay.

Wall, it's bein' such an uncommon bad day, there

wuzn't many to the funeral. But we rode to the meetin'-house in Loontown in a state and splendor that I never expect to again. Cephas had hired eleven mournin' coaches, and the day bein' so bad, and so few a-turnin' out to the funeral, that in order to occupy all the coaches—and Cephas thought it would look better and more popular to have 'em all occupied—we divided up, and Josiah went in one, alone, and lonesome as a dog, as he said afterwards to me. And I sot up straight and oncomfortable in another one on 'em, stark alone.

Cephas had one to himself, and his wife another one, and two old maids, sisters of Cephas'ses who always made a point of attendin' funerals, they each one of 'em had one. S. Annie and her children, of course, had the first one, and then the minister had one, and one of the trustees in the neighborhood had another; so we lengthened out into quite a crowd, all a-follerin' the shiny hearse, and the casket all covered with showy plated nails. I thought of it in jest that way, for Wellington, I knew, the real Wellington, wuzn't there. No, he wuz fur away—as fur as the Real is from the Unreal.

Wall, we filed into the Loontown meetin'-house in pretty good shape. The same meetin'-house I had been sent to reconoiter. But Cephas hadn't no black handkerchief, and he looked worried about it. He had shed tears a-tellin' me about it, what a oversight it wuz, while I wuz a fixin' on his mournin' weed. He took it into his head to have a deeper weed at the last minute, so I fixed it on. He had the weed come up to the top of his hat and lap over. I never see so tall a weed. But it suited Cephas; he said "he thought it showed deep re spect."

"Wall," sez I, "it is a deep weed, anyway—the deepest I ever see." And he said as I wuz a sewin' it on, he a-holdin' his hat for me, "that Wellington deserved it; he deserved it all."

But, as I say, he shed tears to think that his handkerchief wuzn't black-bordered He said "it wuz a fearful oversight; it would probably make talk."

"But," I sez, "mebby it won't be noticed."

"Yes, it will," sez he. "It will be noticed." And sez he, "I don't care about myself, but I am afraid it will reflect onto Wellington. I am

"As a procession we wuz middlin' long, but ruther thin."

afraid they will think it shows a lack of respect for
him. For Wellington's sake I feel cut down about
it."

And I sez, " I guess where Wellington is now,
the color of a handkerchief-border hain't a-goin' to
make much difference to him either way."

And I don't spoze it wuz noticed much, for
there wuzn't more'n ten or a dozen folks there
when we went in. We went in in Injin file mostly
by Cephas'ses request, so's to make more show.
And as a procession we wuz middlin' long, but
ruther thin.

The sermon wuz not so very good as to quality,
but abundant as to quantity. It wuz, as nigh as I
could calkerlate, about a hour and three-quarters
long. Josiah whispered to me along about the last
that " we had been there over seven hours, and his
legs wuz paralyzed."

And I whispered back that " seven hours would
take us into the night, and to stretch his feet out
and pinch 'em," which he did.

But it wuz long and tegus. My feet got to
sleep twice, and I had hard work to wake 'em up
agin. The sermon meant to be about Wellington,

I s'pose ; he did talk a sight about him, and then he kinder branched off onto politics, and then the Inter-State bill ; he kinder favored it, I thought.

Wall, we all got drippin' wet a-goin' home, for Cephas insisted on our gettin' out at the grave, for he had hired some uncommon high singers (high every way, in price and in notes) to sing at the grave.

And so we disembarked in the drippin' rain, on the wet grass, and formed a procession agin. And Cephas had a long exercise right there in the rain.   But the singin' wuz kinder jerky and curius, and they had got their pay beforehand, so they hurried it through.   And one man, the tenor, who wuz dretful afraid of takin' cold, hurried through his part and got through first, and started on a run for the carriage.   The others stood their grounds till the piece wuz finished, but they put on some dretful curius quavers.   I believe they had had chills ; it sounded like it.

Take it altogether, I don't believe anybody got much satisfaction out of it, only Cephas. S. Annie sp'ilt her dress and bonnet entirely—they wuz wilted all down ; and she ordered another suit jest like it before she slept.

Wall, the next mornin' early two men come with plans for monuments. Cephas had telegrafted to 'em to come with plans and bid for the job of furnishin' the monument.

And after a good deal of talk on both sides, Cephas and S. Annie selected one that wuz very high and p'inted.

The men stayed to dinner, and I said to Cephas out to one side—

"Cephas, that monument is a-goin' to cost a sight."

"Wall," sez he, "we can't raise too high a one. Wellington deserved it all."

Sez I, "Won't that and all these funeral expenses take about all the money he left?"

"Oh, no!" sez he. "He had insured his life for a large amount, and it all goes to his wife and children. He deserves a monument if a man ever did."

"But," sez I, "don't you believe that Wellington would ruther have S. Annie and the children settled down in a good little home with sumthin' left to take care of 'em, than to have all this money spent in perfectly useless things?"

" *Useless !*" sez Cephas, turnin' red. "Why," sez he, " if you wuzn't a near relation I should resent that speech bitterly."

" Wall," sez I, " what do all these flowers, and empty carriages, and silver-plated nails, and crape, and so forth—what does it all amount to ?"

" Respect and honor to his memory," sez Cephas, proudly.

Sez I, " Such a life as Wellington's had them ; no-body could take 'em away nor deminish 'em. Such a brave, honest life is crowned with honor and respect any way. It don't need no crape, nor flowers, nor monuments to win 'em. And, at the same time," sez I dreamily, " if a man is mean, no amount of crape, or flower-pieces, or flowery ser-mons, or obituries, is a-goin' to cover up that mean-ness. A life has to be lived out-doors as it were ; it can't be hid. A string of mournin' carriages, no matter how long, hain't a-goin' to carry a dishonor-able life into honor, and no grave, no matter how low and humble it is, is a-goin' to cover up a honorable life.

" Such a life as Wellington's don't need no monu-ment to carry up the story of his virtues into the

heavens; it is known there already. And them
that mourn his loss don't need cold marble words
to recall his goodness and faithfulness. The heart
where the shadow of his eternal absence has fell
don't need crape to make it darker.

"Wellington wouldn't be forgot if S. Annie wore
pure white from day to day. No, nobody that knew
Wellington, from all I have hearn of him, needs
crape to remind 'em that he wuz once here and now
is gone.

"Howsomever, as fur as that is concerned, I always
feel that mourners must do as they are a mind to
about crape, with fear and tremblin'—that is, if they
are well off, and *can* do as they are a mind to ; and
the same with monuments, flowers, empty coaches,
etc. But in this case, Cephas Bodley, I wouldn't be
a doin' my duty if I didn't speak my mind. When
I look at these little helpless souls that are left in a
cold world with nothin' to stand between them and
want but the small means their pa worked so hard
for and left for the express purpose of takin' care of
'em, it seems to me a foolish thing, and a cruel thing,
to spend all that money on what is entirely onnec·
essary."

"Onnecessary!" sez Cephas, angrily. "Agin I say, Josiah Allen's wife, that if it wuzn't for our close relationship I should turn on you. A worm will turn," sez he, "if it is too hardly trampled on."

"I hain't trampled on you," sez I, "nor hain't had no idea on't. I wuz only statin' the solemn facts and truth of the matter. And you will see it some time, Cephas Bodley, if you don't now."

Sez Cephas, "The worm has turned, Josiah Allen's wife! Yes, I feel that I have got to look now to more distant relations for comfort. Yes, the worm has been stomped on too heavy."

He looked cold, cold as a iceickle almost. And I see that jest the few words I had spoke, jest the slight hints I had gin, hadn't been took as they should have been took. So I said no more. For agin the remark of that little bad boy came up in my mind and restrained me from sayin' any more.

Truly, as the young male child observed, "it wuzn't my funeral."

We went home almost immegiately afterwards, my heart nearly a-bleedin' for the little children, poor little creeters, and Cephas actin' cold and distant to the last.

And we hain't seen 'em sence. But news has
come from them, and come straight. Josiah heerd
to Jonesville all about it. And though it is hitchin'
the democrat buggy on front of the mare—to tell
the end of the funeral here—yet I may as well tell
it now and be done with it.

The miller at Loontown wuz down to the Jonesville mill to get the loan of some bags, and Josiah
happened to be there to mill that day, and heerd all
about it.

Cephas had got the monument, and the ornaments on it cost fur more than he expected. There
wuz a wreath a-runnin' round it clear from the bottom
to the top, and verses a kinder runnin' up it at the
same time. And it cost fearful. Poetry a-runnin'
up, they say, costs fur more than it duz on a level.

Any way, the two thousand dollars that wuz insured on Wellington's life wuzn't quite enough to
pay for it. But the sale of his law library and the
best of the housen' stuff paid it. The nine hundred
he left went, every mite of it, to pay the funeral expenses and mournin' for the family.

And as bad luck always follers on in a procession, them mortgages of Cephas'ses all run out sort o'

CARRIED TO THE COUNTY POOR HOUSE.

together. His creditors sold him out, and when his property wuz all disposed of it left him over four-teen hundred dollars in debt.

The creditors acted perfectly greedy, so they say —took everything they could; and one of the meanest ones took that insane bedquilt that I fin-ished. That *wuz* mean. They say Sally Ann crumpled right down when that wuz took. Some say that they got hold of that tall weed of Cephas'ses, and some dispute it; some say that he wore it on the last ride he took in Loontown.

But, howsomever, Cephas wuz took sick, Sally Ann wuzn't able to do anything for their support, S. Annie wuz took down with the typhus, and so it happened the very day the monument wuz brought to the Loontown cemetery, Cephas Bodley's folks wuz carried to the county house, S. Annie, the chil-dren and all.

And it happened dretful curius, but the town hired that very team that drawed the monument there, to take the family back.

It wuz a good team.

The monument wuzn't set up, for they lacked money to pay for the underpinnin'! (Wuz n't it curius, Cephas Bodley never would think of the underpinnin' to anything?) But it lay there by the side of the road, a great white shape.

And they say the children wuz skairt, and cried when they went by it—cried and wept.

But I believe it wuz because they wuz cold and hungry that made 'em cry. I don't believe it wuz the monument.

CHAPTER XI.

 FEW days follerin' on and ensuin' after this eppisode, Submit Tewksbury wuz a takin' supper with me. She had come home with me from the meetin' house where we had been to work all day.

I had urged her to stay, for she lived a mile further on the road, and had got to walk home afoot.

And she hain't any too well off, Submit hain't— she has to work hard for every mite of food she eats, and clothes she wears, and fuel and lights, etc., etc.

So I keep her to dinners and suppers all I can, specially when we are engaged in meetin' house work, for as poor as Submit is, she will insist on doin' for the meetin' house jest as much as any other female woman in Jonesville.

She is quite small boneded, and middlin' good lookin' for a women of her years. She has got big

dark eyes, very soft and mellow lookin' in expres-
sion—and a look deep down into 'em, as if she had
been waitin' for something, for some time.   Her

SUBMIT TEWKSBURY.

hair is gettin' quite gray now, but its original color
was auburn, and she has got quite a lot of it—
kinder crinkly round her forward.   Her complexion is pale.

She is a very good lookin' woman yet, might marry any day of the week now, I hain't no doubt of it. She is a single woman, but is well thought on in Jonesville, and the southern part of Zoar, where she has relatives on her mother's side.

She has had chances to my certain knowledge (widowers and such).

But if all the men in the world should come and stand in rows in front of her gate with gilded crowns in their hands all ready to crown her, and septers all ready for her to grasp holt of, and wield over the world, she would refuse every one of 'em.

She has had a disappointment, Submit has. And she looked at the world so long through tears, that the world got to lookin' sort o' dim like and shadowy to her, and the whole men race looked to her fur off and misty, as folks will when you look at 'em through a rain.

She couldn't marry one of them shadows of men, if she tried, and she hain't never tried. No, her heart always has been, and is now, fur away, a-travellin' through unknown regions, unknown, and yet more real to her than Jonesville or Zoar, a-follerin' the one man in the world who is a reality to her.

Submit wuz engaged to a young Methodist minister by the name of Samuel Danker.   I remember
him well.   A good lookin' young fellow at the time,
with blue eyes and light hair, ruther long and curly,
and kinder wavin' back from his forward, and a deep
spiritual look in his eyes.   In fact, his eyes looked
right through the fashions and follys of the civilized
world, into the depths of ignorance, rivers of ruin
and despair, that wuz a-washin' over a human race,
black jungles where naked sin and natural depravi-
ties crouched hungry for victims.

Samuel Danker felt that he had got to go into
heathen lands as a missionary.   He wuz engaged
to Submit, and loved her dearly, and he urged her
to go too.

But Submit had a invalid father on her hands,
a bed rid grandfather, and three young brothers, too
young to earn a thing, and they all on 'em together
hadn't a cent of money to their names.   They had
twenty-five acres of middlin' poor land, and a old
house.

Wall, Submit felt that she couldn't leave these
helpless ones and go to more foreign heathen lands.
So, with a achin' heart, she let Samuel Danker go

from her, for he felt a call, loud, and she couldn't counsel him to shet up his ears, or put cotton into 'em. Submit Tewksbury had always loved and worked for the Methodist meetin' house (she jined it on probation when she wuz thirteen). But although she always had been extremely liberal in givin', and had made a practice of contributin' every cent she could spare to the meetin' house, it wuz spozed that Samuel Danker wuz the biggest offerin' she had ever give to it.

Fur it wuz known that he went to her the night before he sot sail, took supper with her, and told her she should decide the matter for him, whether he went or whether he staid.

It wuz spozed his love for Submit wuz so great that it made him waver when the time come that he must leave her to her lot of toil and sacrifice and loneliness.

But Submit loved the Methodist meetin' house to that extent, she leaned so hard on the arm of Duty, that she nerved up her courage anew, refused to accept the sacrifice of his renunciation, bid him go to his great work, and quit himself like a man— told him she would always love him, pray for him,

be constant to him.   And she felt that the Master
they both wanted to serve would some day bring
him back to her.

So he sailed away to his heathens—and Submit
stayed to home with her five helpless males and her
achin' heart.   And if I had to tell which made her
the most trouble, I couldn't to save my life.

She knew the secret of her achin' heart, and the
long dark nights she kep awake with it.   The neigh-
bers couldn't understand that exactly, for there
hain't no language been discovered yet that will
give voice to the silent crys of a breakin' heart, a
tender heart, a constant heart, cryin' out acrost the
grayness of dreary days acrost the blackness of
lonely nights.

But we could see her troubles with the peevish
paralasys of age, with the tremendus follys of un-
disciplined youth.

But Submit took care of the hull caboodle of 'em ;
worked out some by days' works, to get more necessaries for 'em than the poor little farm would bring
in ; nursed the sick on their sick-beds and on their
death-beds, till she see 'em into Heaven—or that is
where we spoze they went to, bein' deservin' old

males both on 'em, her father and her grandfather,
and in full connectin with the Methodist Episcopel
meetin' house.

She took care of her young brothers, patient with
'em always, ready to mend bad rents in their clothin'
and their behavior—tryin' to prop up their habits
and their morals, givin' 'em all the schoolin' she
could, givin' 'em all a good trade, all but the young-
est, him she kep with her always till the Lord took
him (scarlet fever), took him to learn the mysterius trade of the immortals.

Submit had a hard fit of sickness after that. And
when she got up agin, there wuz round her
pale forward a good many white hairs that
wuz orburn before the little boy went away from
her.

Sense that, the other boys have married, and Submit has lived alone in the old farm-house, lettin'
the farm out on shares. It is all run down; she
don't get much from it; it don't yield much but
trouble and burdocks, but as little as she gets, she
always will, as I say, do her full share, and more
than her share, for the meetin' house.

Some think it is on account of her inherient

"He took supper with her for the last time."

goodness, and some think it is on account of Samuel Danker.

We all spose she hain't forgot Samuel. And they
do say that every year when the day comes round,
that he took supper with her for the last time, she
puts a plate on for him—the very one he eat on last
—a pink edged chiny plate, with gilt sprigs, the
last one left of her mother's first set of chiny.

That is what they *say*, I hain't never seen the
plate.

It is now about twenty years sense Samuel Danker went to heathen lands. And as it wuz a man-
eatin' tribe he went to preach to, and as he hain't
been heern of from that day to this, it is spozed that
they eat him up some years ago.

But it is thought that Submit hain't gin up hope
yet. We spoze so, but don't know, on account of
her never sayin' anything on the subject. But we
judge from the plate.

Wall, as I say (and I have episoded fearfully,
fearfully), Submit took supper with me that night.
And after Josiah had put out his horse (he had been
to Jonesville for the evenin' mail, and stopped for us
at the meetin' house on his way back), he took the

World out of his pocket, and perused it for some time, and from that learned the great news that wimmen wuz jest about to be held up agin, to see if her strength wuz sufficient to set on the Conference.

And oh! how Josiah Allen went on about it to Submit and me, all the while we wuz a eatin' supper—and for more'n a hour afterwuds.

CHAPTER XII.

UBMIT wuz very skairt to heern him go on (she felt more nervous on account of an extra hard day's work), and I myself wuz beat out, but I wuzn't afraid at all of him, though he did go on elegant, and dretful empressive and even skairful.

He stood up on the same old ground that men have always stood up on, the ground of man's great strength and capability, and wimmen's utter weakness, helplessness, and incapacity. Josiah enlarged almost wildly on the subject of how high, how inaccessibley lofty the Conference wuz, and the utter impossibility of a weak, helpless, fragaile bein' like a women ever gettin' up on it, much less settin' on it.

And then, oh how vividly he depictered it, how he and every other male Methodist in the land loved wimmen too well, worshipped 'em too deeply

to put such a wearin' job onto 'em.   Oh how Josiah
Allen soared up in eloquence.   Submit shed tears, or,
that is, I thought she did—I see her wipe her eyes
any way.   Some think that about the time the Samuel Danker anniversary comes round, she is more
nervous and deprested.   It wuz very near now, and
take that with her hard work that day, it accounts
some for her extra depression—though, without any
doubt, it wuz Josiah's talk that started the tears.

I couldn't bear to see Submit look so mournful
and deprested, and so, though I wuz that tired myself that I could hardly hold my head up, yet I did
take my bits in my teeth, as you may say, and asked
him—

What the awful hard job wuz that he and other
men wuz so anxus to ward offen wimmen.

And he sez, " Why, a settin' on the Conference."

And I sez, " I don't believe that is such a awful
hard job to tackle."

" Yes, indeed, it is," sez Josiah in his most skairful axent, " yes, it is."

And he shook his head meenin'ly and impressively,
and looked at me and Submit in as mysterius and
strange a way, es I have ever been looked at in my

life, and I have had dretful curius looks cast onto
me, from first to last. And he sez in them deep
impressive axents of hisen,

"You jest try it once, and see—I have sot on it,
and I know."

Josiah wuz sent once as a delegate to the Methodist Conference, so I spozed he did know.

But I sez, "Why you come home the second
day when you sot as happy as a king, and you told
me how you had rested off durin' the two days, and
how you had visited round at Uncle Jenkins'es, and
Cousin Henn's, and you said that you never had
had such a good time in your hull life, as you did
when you wuz a settin'. You looked as happy as a
king, and acted so."

Josiah looked dumbfounded for most a quarter
of a minute. For he knew my words wuz as true
es anything ever sot down in Matthew, Mark, or
Luke, or any of the other old patriarks. He knew
it wuz Gospel truth, that he had boasted of his good
times a settin', and as I say for nearly a quarter of a
minute he showed plain signs of mortification.

But almost imegietly he recovered himself, and
went on with the doggy obstinacy of his sect :

"Oh, wall! Men can tackle hard jobs, and get some enjoyment out of it too, when it is in the line of duty. One thing that boys em' up, and makes em' happy, is the thought that they are a keepin' trouble and care offen wimmen. That is a sweet thought to men, and always wuz. And there wuz great strains put onto our minds, us men that sot, that wimmen couldn't be expected to grapple with, and hadn't ort to try to. It wuz a great strain onto us."

"What was the nater of the strain?" sez I. "I didn't know as you did a thing only sot still there and go to sleep. You wuz fast asleep there most the hull of the time, for it come straight to me from them that know. And all that Deacon Bobbet did who went with you wuz to hold up his hand two or three times a votin'. I shouldn't think that wuz so awful wearin'."

And agin I sez, "What wuz the strain?"

But Josiah didn't answer, for that very minute he remembered a pressin' engagement he had about borrowin' a plow. He said he had got to go up to Joe Charnick's to get his plow. (*I* don't believe he wanted a plow that time of night.)

But he hurried away from the spot. And soon after Submit went home lookin' more depressed and down-casted than ever.

And Josiah Allen didn't get home till *late* at night. I dare persume to say it wuz as late as a quarter to nine when that man got back to the bosom of his family.

And I sot there all alone, and a-meditatin' on things, and a-wonderin' what under the sun he wuz a-traipsin up to Joe Charnick's for at that time of night, and a-worryin' some for fear he wuz a-keepin' Miss Charnick up, and a-spozin' in my mind what Miss Charnick would do, to get along with the meetin' house, and the Conference question, if she wuz a member. (She is a *very* sensible woman, Jenette Charnick is, *very*, and a great favorite with me, and others.)

And I got to thinkin' how prosperus and happy she is now, and how much she had went through. And I declare the hull thing come back to me, all the strange and curius circumstances connected with her courtship and marriage, and I thought it all out agin, the hull story, from beginnin' to end.

The way it begun wuz —and the way Josiah Allen

and me come to have any connectin with the story wuz as follers :

Some time ago, and previus, we had a widder come to stay with us a spell, she that wuz Tamer Shelmadine, Miss Trueman Pool that now is.

Her husband died several years ago, and left her not over and above well off. And so she goes round a-visitin', and has went ever sense his death. And finds sights of faults with things wherever she is, sights of it.

Trueman wuz Josiah's cousin, on his own side, and I always made a practice of usin' her quite well. She used to live neighbor to me before I wuz married, and she come and stayed nine weeks.

She is a tall spindlin' woman, a Second Adventist by perswasion, and weighs about ninety-nine pounds.

Wall, as I say, she means middlin' well, and would be quite agreeable if it wuzn't for a habit she has of thinkin' what she duz is a leetle better than anybody else can do, and wantin' to tell a leetle better story than anybody else can.

Now she thinks she looks better than I do. But Josiah sez she can't begin with me for looks, and

I don't spoze she can, though of course it hain't to be expected that I would want it told of that I said so. No, I wouldn't want it told of pro or con, es-

"SHE IS A TALL SPINDLIN' WOMAN."

pecially con. But I know Josiah Allen has always been called a pretty good judge of wimmen's looks.

And now she thinks she can set hens better than I can—and make better riz biscuit. She jest the same as told me so. Any way, the first time I baked bread after she got here, she looked down on my loaves real haughty, yet with a pityin' look, and sez:

" It is very good for yeast, but I always use milk emptin's."

And she kinder tosted her head, and sort o' swept out of the room, not with a broom, no, she would scorn to sweep out a room with a broom or help me in any way, but she sort o' swept it out with her mean. But I didn't care, I knew my bread wuz good.

Now if anybody is sick, she will always tell of times when she has been sicker. She boasts of layin' three nights and two days in a fit. But we don't believe it, Josiah and me don't. That is, we don't believe she lay there so long, a-runnin'.

We believe she come out of 'em occasionally.

But you couldn't get her to give off a hour or a minute of the time. Three nights and two days she lay there a-runnin', so she sez, and she has said it so long, that we spoze, Josiah and me do, that she believes it herself now.

CHAPTER XIII.

URIUS, hain't it? How folks will get to tellin' things, and finally tell 'em so much, that finally they will get to believin' of 'em themselves— boastin' of bein' rich, etc., or bad. Now I have seen folks boast over that, act real haughty because they had been bad and got over it. I've seen temperance lecturers and religious exhorters boast sights and sights over how bad they had been. But they wuzn't tellin' the truth, though they had told the same thing so much that probable they had got to thinkin' so.

But in the case of one man in petickuler, I found out for myself, for I didn't believe what he wuz a sayin' any of the time.

Why, he made out in evenin' meetin's, protracted and otherwise, that he had been a awful villain. Why no pirate wuz ever wickeder than he made himself out to be, in the old times before he turned round and become pious.

But I didn't believe it, for he had a good look

"His face wuz a good moral face."

to his face, all but the high headed look he had, and sort o' vain.

But except this one look, his face wuz a good moral face, and I knew that no man could cut up and act as he claimed that he had, without carryin' some marks on the face of the cuttin' up, and also of the actin'.

And so, as it happened, I went a visitin' (to Josiah's relations) to the very place where he had claimed to do his deeds of wild badness, and I found that he had always been a pattern man— never had done a single mean act, so fur as wuz known.

Where wuz his boastin' then? As the Bible sez, why, it wuz all vain talk. He had done it to get up a reputation. He had done it because he wuz big feelin' and vain. And he had got so haughty over it, and had told of it so much, that I spoze he believed in it himself.

Curius! hain't it? But I am a eppisodin', and to resoom. Trueman's wife would talk jest so, jest so haughty and high headed, about the world comin' to a end.

She'd dispute with everybody right up and down if they disagreed with her—and specially about that religion of hern. How sot she wuz, how ex-tremely sot.

But then, it hain't in me, nor never wuz, to fight anybody for any petickuler religion of theirn.

There is sights and sights of different religions round amongst different friends of mine, and most all on 'em quite good ones.

That is, they are agreeable to the ones who believe in 'em, and not over and above disagreeable to me.

Now it seems to me that in most all of these different doctrines and beliefs, there is a grain of truth, and if folks would only kinder hold onto that grain, and hold themselves stiddy while they held onto it, they would be better off.

But most folks when they go to follerin' off a doctrine, they foller too fur, they hain't megum enough.

Now, for instance, when you go to work and whip anybody, or hang 'em, or burn 'em up for not believin' as you do, that is goin' too fur.

It has been done though, time and agin, in the world's history, and mebby will be agin.

But it hain't reasonable. Now what good will doctrines o' any kind do to anybody after they are burnt up or choked to death?

You see such things hain't bein' megum. Because I can't believe jest as somebody else duz, it

hain't for me to pitch at 'em and burn 'em up, or
even whip 'em.

No, indeed! And most probable if I should
study faithfully out their beliefs, I would find one

" EF I FELL ON A STUN."

grain, or mebby a grain and a half of real truth
in it.

Now, for instance, take the doctrines of Christian
Healin', or Mind Cure.

Now I can't exactly believe that if I fell down and hurt my head on a stun—I cannot believe as I am a layin' there, that I hain't fell, and there hain't no stun—and while I am a groanin' and a bathin' the achin' bruise in anarky and wormwood, I can't believe that there hain't no such thing as pain, nor never wuz.

No, I can't believe this with the present light I have got on the subject.

But yet, I have seen them that this mind cure religion had fairly riz right up, and made 'em nigher to heaven every way—so nigh to it that seemin'ly a light out of some of its winders had lit up their faces with its glowin' repose, its sweet rapture.

I've seen 'em, seen 'em as the Patent Medicine Maker observes so frequently, "before and after takin'."

Folks that wuz despondent and hopeless, and wretched actin', why, this belief made 'em jest blossom right out into a state of hopefulness, and calmness, and joy—refreshin' indeed to contemplate.

Wall now, the idee of whippin' anybody for believin' anything that brings such a good change to

'em, and fills them and them round 'em with so
much peace and happiness.

Why, I wouldn't do it for a dollar bill. And as
for hangin' 'em, and brilin' 'em on gridirons, etc.,
why, that is entirely out of the question, or ort
to be.

And now, it don't seem to me that I ever could
make a tree walk off, by lookin' at it, and com-
mandin' it to—or call some posys to fall down into
my lap, right through the plasterin'—

Or send myself, or one of myselfs, off to Injy,
while the other one of me stayed to Jonesville.

Now, honestly speakin', it don't seem to me that
I ever could learn to do this, not at my age, any way,
and most dead with rheumatiz a good deal of the
time.

I most know I couldn't.

But then agin I have seen believers in Theosiphy
that could do wonders, and seemed indeed to have
got marvelous control over the forces of Natur.

And now the idee of my whippin' 'em for it.
Why you wouldn't ketch me at it.

And Spiritualism now! I spoze, and I about know
that there are lots of folks that won't ever see into

any other world than this, till the breath leaves
their body.

Yet i've seen them, pure sweet souls too, as I ever
see, whose eyes beheld blessed visions withheld
from more material gaze.

Yes, i've neighbored with about all sorts of religius believers, and never disputed that they had a
right to their own religion.

And i've seen them too that didn't make a practice of goin' to any meetin' houses much, who
lived so near to God and his angels that they felt
the touch of angel hands on their forwards every
day of their lives, and you could see the glow
of the Fairer Land in their rapt eyes.

They had outgrown the outward forms of religion
that had helped them at first, jest as children out-
grow the primers and A B C books of thier child-
hood and advance into the higher learnin'.

I've seen them folks i've neighbored with 'em.
Human faults they had, or God would have taken
them to His own land before now.   Their imper-
fections, I spoze sort o' anchored 'em here for a spell
to a imperfect world.

But you could see, if you got nigh enough to

their souls to see anything about 'em—you could
see that the anchor chains wuz slight after all, and
when they wuz broke, oh how lightly and easily
they would sail away, away to the land that their
rapt souls inhabited even now.

Yes, i've seen all sorts of religius believers and I
wuzn't goin' to be too hard on Tamer for her
belief, though I couldn't believe as she did.

CHAPTER XIV.

HE come to our house a visitin' along the first week in June, and the last day in June wuz the day they had sot for the world to come to an end. I, myself, didn't believe she knew positive about it, and Josiah didn't either. And I sez to her, "The Bible sez that it hain't agoin' to be revealed to angels even, or to the Son himself, but only to the Father when that great day shall be." And sez I to Trueman's wife, sez I, "How should *you* be expected to know it?"

Sez she, with that same collected together haughty look to her, "My name wuzn't mentioned, I believe, amongst them that *wuzn't* to know it!"

And of course I had to own up that it wuzn't. But good land! I didn't believe she knew a thing more about it than I did, but I didn't dispute with her much, because she wuz one of the relatives on

his side—you know you have to do different with
'em than you do with them on your own side—you
have to. And then agin, I felt that if it didn't
come to an end she would be convinced that she
wuz in the wrong on't, and if she did we should
both of us be pretty apt to know it, so there wuzn't
much use in disputin' back and forth.

But she wuz firm as iron in her belief. And she
had come up visitin' to our home, so's to be nigh
when Trueman riz. Trueman wuz buried in the
old Risley deestrict, not half a mile from us on a back
road. And she naterally wanted to be round at the
time.

She said plain to me that Trueman never could
seem to get along without her. And though she
didn't say it right out, she carried the idea (and
Josiah resented it because Trueman was a favorite
cousin of his'n on his own side.) She jest the
same as said right out that Trueman, if she wuzn't
by him to tend to him, would be jest as apt to come
up wrong end up as any way.

Josiah didn't like it at all.

Wall, she had lived a widowed life for a number
of years, and had said right out, time and time agin,

that she wouldn't marry agin.   But Josiah thought,
and I kinder mistrusted myself, that she wuz kinder
on the lookout, and would marry agin if she got a
chance—not fierce, you know, or anything of that

"BURIED IN THE OLD RISLEY DEESTRICT."

kind, but kinder quietly lookin' out and standin'
ready.   That wuz when she first come; but before
she went away she acted fierce.

Wall, there wuz sights of Adventists up in the

Risley deestrict, and amongst the rest wuz an old bachelder, Joe Charnick.

And Joe Charnick wuz, I s'poze, of all Advents, the most Adventy. He jest *knew* the world wuz a comin' to a end that very day, the last day of June, at four o'clock in the afternoon. And he got his robe all made to go up in. It wuz made of a white book muslin, and Jenette Finster made it. Cut it out by one of his mother's nightgowns—so she told me in confidence, and of course I tell it jest the same; I want it kep.

She was afraid Joe wouldn't like it, if he knew she took the nightgown for a guide, wantin' it, as he did, for a religious purpose.

But, good land! as I told her, religion or not, anybody couldn't cut anything to look anyhow without sumpthin' for a guide, and she bein' an old maiden felt a little delicate about measurin' him.

His mother wuz as big round as he wuz, her weight bein' 230 by the steelyards, and she allowed 2 fingers and a half extra length—Joe is tall. She gathered it in full round the neck, and the sleeves (at his request) hung down like wings, a breadth for each wing wuz what she allowed.

Jenette owned up to me (though she wouldn't
want it told of for the world, for it had been sposed
for years, that he and she had a likin' for each other,
and mebby would make a match some time, though
what they had been a-waitin' for for the last 10
years nobody knew).   But she allowed to me that
when he got his robe on, he wuz the worst lookin'
human bein' that she ever laid eyes on, and sez she,
for she likes a joke, Jenette duz: " I should think
if Joe looked in the glass after he got it on, his
religion would be a comfort to him ; I should think
he would be glad the world *wuz* comin' to a end."

But he *didn't* look at the glass, Jenette said he
didn't ; he wanted to see if it wuz the right size
round the neck.   Joe hain't handsome, but he is
kinder good-lookin', and he is a good feller and got
plenty to do with, but bein' kinder big-featured, and
tall, and hefty, he must have looked like fury in the
robe.   But he is liked by everybody, and everybody
is glad to see him so prosperous and well off.

He has got 300 acres of good land, " be it more
or less," as the deed reads; 30 head of cows, and
7 head of horses (and the hull bodies of 'em).   And
a big sugar bush, over 1100 trees, and a nice little su-

gar house way up on a pretty side hill amongst the maple trees. A good, big, handsome dwellin' house, a
sort of cream color, with green blinds; big barn, and
carriage house, etc., etc., and everything in the very
best of order. He is a pattern farmer and a pattern
son—yes, Joe couldn't be a more pattern son if he
acted every day from a pattern.

He treats his mother dretful pretty, from day to
day. She thinks that there hain't nobody like Joe;
and it wuz s'pozed that Jenette thought so too.

But Jenette is, and always wuz, runnin' over with
common sense, and she always made fun and laugh-
ed at Joe when he got to talkin' about his religion,
and about settin' a time for the world to come to a
end. And some thought that that wuz one reason
why the match didn't go off, for Joe likes her, everybody could see that, for he wuz jest such a great, honest, open-hearted feller, that he never made any secret
of it. And Jenette liked Joe *I* knew, though she
fooled a good many on the subject. But she wuz
always a great case to confide in me, and though
she didn't say so right out, which wouldn't have
been her way, for, as the poet sez, she wuzn't one
" to wear her heart on the sleeves of her bask waist,"

still, I knew as well es I wanted to, that she thought her eyes of him.   And old Miss Charnick jest about worshipped Jenette, would have her with her, sewin' for her, and takin' care of her—she wuz sick a good deal, Mother Charnick wuz.   And she would have been tickled most to death to have had Joe marry her and bring her right home there.

And Jenette wuz a smart little creeter, "smart as lightnin'," as Josiah always said.

She had got along in years, Jenette had, without marryin', for she staid to hum and took care of her old father and mother and Tom.   The other girls married off, and left her to hum, and she had chances, so it wuz said, good ones, but she wouldn't leave her father and mother, who wuz gettin' old, and kinder bed-rid, and needed her.   Her father, specially, said he couldn't live, and wouldn't try to, if Jenette left 'em, but he said, the old gentleman did, that Jenette should be richly paid for her goodness to 'em.

That wuzn't what made Jenette good, no, indeed ; she did it out of the pure tenderness and sweetness of her nature and lovin' heart.   But I used to love to hear the old gentleman talk that way, for he wuz well

off, and I felt that so far as money could pay for the
hull devotion of a life, why, Jenette would be looked
out for, and have a good home, and enough to do
with. So she staid to hum, as I say, and took care
of 'em night and day; sights of watching and wearisome care she had, poor little creeter; but she took
the best of care of 'em, and kep 'em kinder com-
forted up, and clean, and brought up Tom, the young-
est boy, by hand, and thought her eyes on him.

And he wuz a smart chap—awful smart, as it
proved in the end; for he married when he wuz 21,
and brought his wife (a disagreeable creeter) home
to the old homestead, and Jenette, before they had
been there 2 weeks, wuz made to feel that her room
wuz better than her company.

That wuz the year the old gentleman died; her
mother had died 3 months prior and beforehand.

Her brother, as I said, wur smart, and he and his
wife got round the old man in some way and sot
him against Jenette, and got everything he had.

He wuz childish, the old man wuz; used to try to
put his pantaloons on over his head, and get his feet
into his coat sleeves, etc., etc.

And he changed his will, that had gi'n Jenette

half the property, a good property, too, and gi'n it all
to Tom, every mite of it, all but one dollar, which
Jenette never took by my advice.

For I wuz burnin' indignant at old Mr. Finster
and at Tom.   Curius, to think such a girl as Jenette
had been—such a patient, good creeter, and such a
good-tempered one, and everything—to think her
pa should have forgot all she had done, and suffered,
and gi'n up for 'em, and give the property all to that
boy, who had never done anything only to spend
their money and make Jenette trouble.

But then, I s'poze it wuz old Mr. Finster's mind,
or the lack on't, and I had to stand it, likewise so
did Jenette.

But I never sot a foot into Tom Finster's house,
not a foot after that day that Jenette left it.   I
wouldn't.   But I took her right to my house, and
kep her for 9 weeks right along, and wuz glad to.

That wuz some 10 years prior and before this,
and she had gone round sewin' ever sense.   And
she wuz beloved by everybody, and had gone round
highly respected, and at seventy-five cents a day.

Her troubles, and everybody that knew her, knew
how many she had of 'em, but she kep 'em all to

herself, and met the world and her neighbors with a bright face.

If she took her skeletons out of the closet to air 'em, and I s'poze she did, everybody duz; they have to at times, to see if their bones are in good order, if for nothin' else.   But if she ever did take 'em out and dust 'em, she did it all by herself.   The closet door wuz shet up and locked when anybody wuz round.   And you would think, by her bright, laughin' face, that she never heard the word skeleton, or ever listened to the rattle of a bone.

And she kep up such a happy, cheerful look on the outside, that I s'poze it ended by her bein' cheer· ful and happy on the inside.

The stiddy, good-natured, happy spirit that she cultivated at first by hard work, so I s'poze; but at last it got to be second nater, the qualities kinder struck in and she *wuz* happy, and she *wuz* contented —that is, I s'poze so.

Though I, who knew Jenette better than anybody else, almost, knew how tuff, how fearful tuff it must have come on her, to go round from home to home—not bein' settled down at home anywhere. I knew jest what a lovin' little home body she wuz.

And how her sweet nater, like the sun, would love
to light up one bright lovin' home, and shine kinder
stiddy there, instead of glancin' and changin' about
from one place to another, like a meteor.

Some would have liked it ; some like change and
constant goin' about, and movin' constantly through
space—but I knew Jenette wuzn't made on the
meteor plan. I felt sorry for Jenette, down deep in
my heart, I did; but I didn't tell her so ; no, she
wouldn't have liked it; she kep a brave face to the
world. And as I said, her comin' wuz looked for
weeks and weeks ahead, in any home where she wuz
engaged to sew by the day.

Everybody in the house used to feel the presence
of a sunshiny, cheerful spirit. One that wuz determined to turn her back onto troubles she couldn't
help and keep her face sot towards the Sun of Happiness. One who felt good and pleasant towards
everybody, wished everybody well. One who could
look upon other folks'es good fortune without a mite
of jealousy or spite. One who loved to hear her
friends praised and admired, loved to see 'em happy.
And if they had a hundred times the good things
she had, why, she was glad for their sakes, that they

had 'em, she loved to see 'em enjoy 'em, if she couldn't.

And she wuz dretful kinder cunnin' and cute, Jenette wuz.   She would make the oddest little

"DRETFUL KINDER CUNNIN' AND CUTE, JENETTE WUZ."

speeches; keep everybody laughin' round her, when she got to goin'.

Yes, she wuz liked dretful well, Jenette wuz. Her face has a kind of a pert look on to it, her black eyes snap, a good-natured snap, though, and her nose turns up jest enough to look kinder cunnin', and her hair curls all over her head.

Smart round the house she is, and Mother Charnick likes that, for she is a master good housekeeper. Smart to answer back and joke. Joe is slow of speech, and his big blue eyes won't fairly get sot onto anything, before Jenette has looked it all through, and turned it over, and examined it on the other side, and got through with it.

Wall, she wuz to work to Mother Charnick's makin' her a black alpacka dress, and four new calico ones, and coverin' a parasol.

A good many said that Miss Charnick got dresses a purpose for Jenette to make, so's to keep her there. Jenette wouldn't stay there a minute only when she wuz to work, and as they always kep a good, strong, hired girl, she knew when she wuz needed, and when she wuzn't. But, of course, she couldn't refuse to sew for her, and at what she wuz sot at, though she must have known and felt that Miss Charnick wuz lavish in dresses. She had 42 calico dresses, and everybody knew it, new ones, besides woosted. But, anyway, there she was a sewin' when the word came that the world was a comin' to a end on the 30th day of June, at 4 o'clock in the afternoon.

Miss Charnick wuz a believer, but not to the extent that Joe was. For Jenette asked her if she should stop sewin', not sposin' that she would need the dresses, specially the four calico ones, and the parasol in case of the world's endin'.

And she told Jenette, and Jenette told me, so's I know it is true, "that she might go right on, and get the parasol cover, and the trimmins to the dresses, cambrick, and linin' and things, and hooks and eyes."

And Miss Charnick didn't prepare no robe. But Jenette mistrusted, though Miss Charnick is close-mouthed, and didn't say nothin', but Jenette mistrusted that she laid out, when she sees signs, to use a nightgown.

She had piles of the nicest ones, that Jenette had made for her from time to time, over 28, all trimmed off nice enough for day dresses, so Jenette said, trimmed with tape trimmin's, some of 'em, and belted down in front.

Wall, they had lots of meetin's at the Risley

school-house, as the time drew near. And Miss Trueman Pool went to every one on 'em.

She had been too weak to go out to the well, or to the barn. She wanted dretfully to see some new stanchils that Josiah had been a makin', jest like some that Pool had had in his barn. She wanted to see 'em dretful, but was too weak to walk. And I had had kind of a tussle in my own mind, whether or not I should offer to let Josiah carry her out; but kinder hesitated, thinkin' mebby she would get stronger.

But I hain't jealous, not a mite. It is known that I hain't all through Jonesville and Loontown. No, I'd scorn it. I thought Pool's wife would get better and she did.

One evenin' Joe Charnick came down to bring home Josiah's augur, and the conversation turned onto Adventin'. And Miss Pool see that Joe wuz congenial on that subject; he believed jest as she did, that the world would come to an end the 30th. This was along the first part of the month.

He spoke of the good meetin's they wuz a-havin' to the Risley school-house, and how he always attended to every one on 'em. And the next mornin' Miss

"JOE CHARNICK CAME DOWN TO BRING HOME JOSIAH'S AUGUR."

Trueman Pool gin out that she wuz a-goin' that evenin'. It wuz a good half a mile away, and I reminded her that Josiah had to be away with the team, for he wuz a-goin' to Loontown, heavy loaded, and wouldn't get back till along in the evenin'.

But she said " that she felt that the walk would do her good."

I then reminded her of the stanchils, but she said "stanchils and religion wuz two separate things." Which I couldn't deny, and didn't try to. And she sot off for the school-house that evenin' a-walkin' a foot. And the rest of her adventins and the adventins of Joe I will relate in another epistol; and I will also tell whether the world come to an end or not. I know folks will want to know, and I don't love to keep folks in onxiety—it hain't my way.

CHAPTER XV.

WALL, from that night, Miss Trueman Pool attended to the meetins at the Risley school-house,
stiddy and constant. And before
the week wuz out Joe Charnick
had walked home with her twice.
And the next week he carried her to Jonesville
to get the cloth for her robe, jest like his'n, white
book muslin. And twice he had come to consult
her on a Bible passage, and twice she had walked
up to his mother's to consult with her on a passage
in the Apockraphy. And once she went up to see
if her wings wuz es deep and full es his'n. She
wanted 'em jest the same size.

Miss Charnick couldn't bear her. Miss Charnick
wuz a woman who had enjoyed considerble poor
health in her life, and she had now, and had been
havin' for years, some dretful bad spells in her
stomach—a sort of a tightness acrost her chest.

And Trueman's wife argued with her that her spells had been worse, and her chest had been tighter. And the old lady didn't like that at all, of course. And the old lady took thoroughwert for 'em, and Trueman's wife insisted on't that thoroughwert wuz tightenin'.

And then there wuz some chickens in a basket out on the stoop, that the old hen had deserted, and Miss Charnick wuz a bringin' 'em up by hand. And Mother Charnick went out to feed 'em, and Trueman's wife tosted her head and said, " she didn't approve of it—she thought a chicken ought to be brung up by a hen."

But Miss Charnick said, "Why, the hen deserted 'em ; they would have perished right there in the nest."

But Trueman's wife wouldn't gin in, she stuck right to it, "that it wuz a hen's business, and nobody else's."

And of course she had some sense on her side, for of course it is a hen's business, her duty and her prevelege to bring up her chickens. But if she won't do it, why, then, somebody else has got to— they ought to be brung.

I say Mother Charnick wuz in the right on't.
But Trueman's wife had got so in the habit of
findin' fault, and naggin' at me, and the other relations on Trueman's side and hern, that she couldn't
seem to stop it when she knew it wuz for her interest to stop.

And then she ketched a sight of the alpacker
dress Jenette wuz a-makin' and she said "that basks
had gone out."

And Miss Charnick was over partial to 'em (most
too partial, some thought), and thought they wuz in
the height of the fashion.   But Trueman's wife
ground her right down on it.

" Basks *wuz out*, fer she knew it, she had all her
new ones made polenay."

And hearin' 'em argue back and forth for more'n
a quarter of an hour, Jenette put in and sez (she
thinks all the world of Mother Charnick), " Wall, I
s'pose you won't take much good of your polenays,
if you have got so little time to wear 'em."

And then Trueman's wife (she wuz meen-dispo-
sitioned, anyway) said somethin' about " hired girls
keepin' their place."

And then Mother Charnick flared right up and

took Jenette's part. And Joe's face got red ; he couldn't bear to see Jenette put upon, if she wuz makin' fun of his religeon. And Trueman's wife see that she had gone too fur, and held herself in, and talked good to Jenette, and flattered up Joe, and he went home with her and staid till ten o'clock.

They spent a good deal of their time a-huntin' up passages, to prove their doctrine, in the Bible, and the Apockraphy, and Josephus, and others.

It beat all how many Trueman's wife would find, and every one she found Joe would seem to think the more on her. And so it run along, till folks said they wuz engaged, and Josiah and me thought so, too.

And though Jenette wuzn't the one to say any-thing, she begun to look kinder pale and mauger. And when I spoke of it to her, she laid it to her liver. And I let her believe I thought so too. And I even went so fur as to recommend tansey and camomile tea, with a little catnip mixed in—I did it fur blinders. I knew it wuzn't her liver that ailed her. I knew it wuz her heart. I knew it wuz her heart that wuz a-achin'.

Wall, we had our troubles, Josiah and me did.

Trueman's wife wuz dretful disagreeable, and would argue us down, every separate thing we tried to do or say. And she seemed more high-headed and disagreeable than ever sence Joe had begun to pay attention to her. Though what earthly good his attention wuz a-goin' to do, wuz more than I could see, accordin' to her belief.

But Josiah said, " he guessed Joe wouldn't have paid her any attention, if he hadn't thought that the world wuz a-comin' to a end so soon. He guessed he wouldn't want her round if it wuz a-goin' to stand."

Sez I, " Josiah, you are a-judgin' Joe by yourself." And he owned up that he wuz.

Wall, the mornin' of the 30th, after Josiah and me had eat our breakfast, I proceeded to mix up my bread. I had set the yeast overnight, and I wuz a mouldin' it out into tins when Trueman's wife come down-stairs with her robe over her arm. She wanted to iron it out and press the seams.

I had baked one tin of my biscuit for breakfast, and I had kep 'em warm for Trueman's wife, for she had been out late the night before to a meetin' to Risley school-house, and didn't come down to breakfast.   I had also kep some good coffee warm for her, and some toast and steak.

She laid her robe down over a chair-back, and sot down to her breakfast, but begun the first thing to find fault with me for bein' to work on that day. She sez, " The idee, of the last day of the world, and you a-bein' found makin' riz biscuit, yeast ones !" sez she.

" Wall," sez I, " I don't know but I had jest as soon be found a-makin' riz biscuit, a-takin' care of my own household, as the Lord hes commanded me to, as to be found a-sailin' round in a book muslin Mother Hubbard."

" It hain't a Mother Hubbard !" sez she.

" Wall," sez I, " I said it for oritory.   But it is puckered up some like them, and you know it." Hers wuz made with a yoke.

And Josiah sot there a-fixin' his plantin' bag. He wuz a-goin' out that mornin' to plant over some corn that the crows had pulled up.   And she bitterly reproved him.   But he sez, " If the world don't come to a end, the corn will be needed."

" But it will," she sez in a cold, haughty tone.

" Wall," sez he, " if it does, I may as well be a-

"WALL," sez he, "IF IT DOES, I MAY AS WELL BE DOIN' THAT AS TO BE SETTIN' ROUND."

doin' that as to be settin' round." And he took
his plantin' bag and went out. And then she jawed
me for upholdin' him.

And sez she, as she broke open a biscuit and
spread it with butter previous to eatin' it, sez she,
" I should think *respect*, respect for the great and
fearful thought of meetin' the Lord, would scare you
out of the idea of goin' on with your work."

Sez I calmly, " Does it scare you, Trueman's
wife ?"

" Wall, not exactly scare," sez she, " but lift up,
lift up far above bread and other kitchen work."

And again she buttered a large slice, and I sez
calmly, " I don't s'poze I should be any nearer the
Lord than I am now. He sez He dwells inside of
our hearts, and I don't see how He could get any
nearer to us than that. And anyway, what I said
to you I keep a-sayin', that I think He would approve of my goin' on calm and stiddy, a-doin' my
best for the ones He put in my charge here below,
my husband, my children, and my grandchildren."
(I some expected Tirzah Ann and the babe home
that day to dinner.)

" Wall, you feel very diffrent from some wimmen

that wuz to the school-house last night, and act very
diffrent. They are good Christian females. It is
a pity you wuzn't there. P'raps your hard heart
would have melted, and you would have had
thoughts this mornin' that would soar up above riz
biscuit."

And as she sez this she begun on her third biscuit,
and poured out another cup of coffee. And I,
wantin' to use her well, sez, " What did they do
there ?"

" Do !" sez she, " why, it wuz the most glorious
meetin' we ever had. Three wimmen lay at one
time perfectly speechless with the power. And
some of em' screemed so you could hear 'em fer
half a mile."

I kep on a-mouldin' my bread out into biscuit
(good shaped ones, too, if I do say it), and sez
calmly, " Wall, I never wuz much of a screemer. I
have always believed in layin' holt of the duty next
to you, and doin' *some* things, things He has *commanded*. Everybody to their own way. I don't
condemn yourn, but I have always seemed to believe more in the solid, practical parts of religion,
than the ornimental. I have always believed more

in the power of honesty, truth, and justice, than in
the power they sometimes have at camp and other
meetins.   Howsumever," sez I, " I don't say but
what 'hat power is powerful, to the ones that have
it, only I wuz merely observin' that it never wuz
my way to lay speechless or holler much—not that
I consider hollerin' wrong, if you holler from principle, but I never seemed to have a call to."

   " You would be far better if you did," sez Trueman's wife, "far better.   But you hain't good
enough."

   " Oh !" sez I, reasonably, " I could holler if I
wanted to, but the Lord hain't deef.   He sez specilly, that He hain't, and so I never could see the *use*
in hollerin' to Him.   And I never could see the use
of tellin' Him in public so many things as some do.
Why He *knows* it.   He *knows* all these things. He
don't need to have you try to enlighten Him as if
you wuz His gardeen—as I have heard folks do
time and time agin.   He *knows* what we are, what
we need.   I am glad, Trueman's wife," sez I, " that
He can look right down into our hearts, that He is
right there in 'em a-knowin' all about us, all our
wants, our joys, our despairs, our temptations, our

resolves, our weakness, our blindness, our defects, our regrets, our remorse, our deepest hopes, our inspiration, our triumphs, our glorys. But when He *is* right there, in the midst of our soul, our life, why, *why* should we kneel down in public and holler at Him ?"

" You would be glad to if you wuz good enough," sez she ; " if you had attained unto a state of perfection, you would feel like it."

That kinder riled me up, and I sez, " Wall, I have lived in this house with them that wuz perfect, and that is bad enough for me, without bein' one of 'em myself. For more disagreeable creeters," sez I, a prickin' my biscuit with a fork, " more disagreeable creeters I never laid eyes on."

Trueman's wife thinks she is perfect, she has told me so time and agin—thinks she hain't done anything wrong in upwards of a number of years.

But she didn't say nothin' to this, only begun agin about the wickedness and immorality of my makin' riz biscuit that mornin', and the deep disgrace of Josiah Allen keepin' on with his work.

But before I could speak up and take his part, foɪ

I *will* not hear my companion found fault with by any female but myself, she had gathered up her robe, and swept upstairs with it, leavin' orders for a flat-iron to be sent up.

Wall, the believers wuz all a-goin' to meet at the Risley school-house that afternoon. They wuz about 40 of 'em, men and wimmen. And I told Josiah at noon, I believed I would go down to the school-house to the meetin'. And he a-feelin', I mistrust, that if they should happen to be in the right on't, and the world should come to a end, he wanted to be by the side of his beloved pardner, he offered to go too. But he never had no robe, no, nor never thought of havin'.

The Risley school-house stood in a clearin', and had tall stumps round it in the door-yard. And we had heard that some of the believers wuz goin' to get up on them stumps, so's to start off from there. And sure enough, we found it wuz the calculation of some on 'em.

The school-boys had made steps up the sides of some of the biggest stumps, and lots of times in political meetin's men had riz up on 'em to talk to the masses below. Why I s'poze a crowd of as many as 45 or 48, had assembled there at one time durin' the heat of the campain.

But them politicians had on their usual run of clothes, they didn't have on white book muslin robes. Good land!

CHAPTER XVI.

ALL, lots of folks had assembled to the school-house when we got there, about 3 o'clock P.M.—afternoon. Believers, and world's people, all a-settin' round on seats and stumps, for the school-house wuz small and warm, and it wuz pleasanter out-doors.

We had only been there a few minutes when Mother Charnick and Jenette walked in. Joe had been there for sometime, and he and the Widder Pool wuz a-settin' together readin' a him out of one book. Jenette looked kinder mauger, and Trueman's wife looked haughtily at her, from over the top of the him book.

Mother Charnick had a woosted work-bag on her arm. There might have been a night gown in it, and there might not. It wuz big enough to hold one, and it looked sort o' bulgy. But it wuz never known—Miss Charnick is a smart woman. It never wuz known what she had in the bag.

Wall, the believers struck up a him, and sung it through—as mournful, skairful sort of a him as I ever hearn in my hull life; and it swelled out and riz up over the pine trees in a wailin', melancholy sort of a way, and wierd—dretful wierd.

And then a sort of a lurid, wild-looking chap, a minister, got up and preached the wildest and luridest discourse I ever hearn in my hull days. It wuz enough to scare a snipe. The very strongest and toughest men there turned pale, and wimmen cried and wept on every side of me, and wept and cried.

I, myself, didn't weep. But I drawed nearer to my companion, and kinder leaned up against him, and looked off on the calm blue heavens, the serene landscape, and the shinin' blue lake fur away, and thought—jest as true as I live and breathe, I thought that I didn't care much, if God willed it to be so, that my Josiah and I should go side by side, that very day and minute, out of the certainties of this life into the mysteries of the other, out of the mysteries of this life into the certainties of the other.

For, thinks I to myself, we have got to go into that other world pretty soon, Josiah and me have. And if we went in the usual way, we had got to go alone, each on us. Terrible thought! We

"A SORT OF A LURID, WILD-LOOKING CHAP."

who had been together under shine and shade, in joy and sorrow. Our two hands that had joined at the alter, and had clung so clost together ever sence, had got to leggo of each other down there in front of the dark gateway.

Solemn gateway! So big that the hull world must pass through it—and yet so small that the hull world has got to go through it alone, one at a time.

My Josiah would have to stand outside and let me go down under the dark, mysterious arches, alone —and he knows jest how I hate to go anywhere alone, or else I would have to stop at the gate and bid him good-by. And no matter how much we knocked at the gate, or how many tears we shed onto it, we couldn't get through till our time come, we had *got* to be parted.

And now if we went on this clear June day through the crystal gateway of the bendin' heavens —we two would be together for weal or for woe. And on whatever new, strange landscape we would have to look on, or wander through, he would be right by me. Whatever strange inhabitants the celestial country held, he would face 'em with me. Close, close by my side, he would go with me through that blue, lovely gateway of the soft June skies into the City of the King. And it wuz a sweet thought to me.

Not that I really *wanted* the world to come to a

end that day. No, I kinder wanted to live along for some time, for several reasons: My pardner, the babe, the children, etc.; and then I kinder like to live for the *sake* of livin'. I enjoy it.

But I can say, and say with truth, and solemnity, that the idee didn't scare me none. And as my companion looked down in my face as the time approached, I could see the same thoughts that wuz writ in my eyes a-shinin' in his'n.

Wall, as the pinter approached the hour, the excitement grew nearly, if not quite rampant. The believers threw their white robes on over their dresses and coats, and as the pinter slowly moved round from half-past three to quarter to 4—and so on—they shouted, they sung, they prayed, they shook each other's hands—they wuz fairly crazed with excitement and fervor, which they called religion—for they wuz in earnest, nobody could dispute that.

Joe and Miss Pool kinder hung together all this time—though I ketched him givin' several wistful looks at Jenette, as much as to say, " Oh, how I hate to leave you, Jenette !"

But Miss Pool would roust him up agin, and he

would shout and sing with the frienziedest and most zealousest of 'em.

Mother Charnick stood with her bag in her hand, and the other hand on the puckerin' string. I don't say what she had in the bag, but I do say this, that she had it fixed so's she could have on-done it in a secont's time. And her eyes wuz in-tent on the heavens overhead. But they kep calm and serene and cloudless, nothin' to be seen there —no sign, no change—and Ma Charnick kep still and didn't draw the puckerin' string.

But oh, how excitement reined and grew ram-pant around that school-house! Miss Pool and Joe seemin' to outdo all the rest (she always did try to), till at last, jest as the pinter swung round to the very minute, Joe, more than half by the side of himself, with the excitement he had been in for a week, and bein' urged onto it by Miss Pool, as he sez to this day, he jumped up onto the tall stump he had been a standin' by, and stood there in his long white robe, lookin' like a spook, if any-body had been calm enough to notice it, and he sung out in a clear voice—his voice always did have a good honest ring to it:

Farewell my friends,
Farewell my foes;
Up to Heaven
Joe Charnick goes.

And jest as the clock struck, and they all shouted and screamed, he waved his arms, with their two great white wings a-flutterin', and sprung upwards, expectin' the hull world, livin' and dead, would foller him—and go right up into the heavens.

And Trueman's wife bein' right by the stump, waved her wings and jumped too—jest the same direction es he jumped. But she only stood on a camp chair, and when she fell, she didn't crack no bones, it only jarred her dretfully, and hurt her across the small of her back, to that extent that I kep bread and milk poultices on day and night for three weeks, and lobelia and catnip, half and half; she a-arguin' at me every single poultice I put on that it wuzn't her way of makin' poultices, nor her way of applyin' of 'em.

I told her I didn't know of any other way of applyin' 'em to her back, only to put 'em on it.

"FAREWELL MY FRIENDS, FAREWELL MY FOES."

But she insisted to the last that I didn't apply
'em right, and I didn't crumble the bread into the
milk right, and the lobelia wuzn't picked right, nor
the catnip.

Not one word did she ever speak about the end of
the world—not a word—but a-naggin' about everything else.

Wall, I healed her after a time, and glad enough
wuz I to see her healed, and started off.

But Joe Charnick suffered worse and longer. He
broke his limb in two places and cracked his rib.
The bones of his arm wuz a good while a-healin',
and before they wuz healed he was wounded in a
new place.

He jest fell over head and ears in love with
Jenette Finster. For bein' shet up to home with
his mother and her (his mother wouldn't hear to
Jenette leavin' her for a minute) he jest seemed to
come to a full realizin' sense of her sweet natur'
and bright, obleegin' ways; and his old affection
for her bloomed out into the deepest and most
idolatrous love—Joe never could be megum.

Jenette, and good enough for him, held him off
for quite a spell—but when he got cold and re-

lapsted, and they thought he wuz goin' to die, then she owned up to him that she worshipped him— and always had.

And from that day he gained. Mother Char- nick wuz tickled most to death at the idea of havin' Jenette for her own girl—she thinks her eyes on her, and so does Jenette of her. So it wuz agree- able as anything ever wuz all around, if not agree- abler.

Jest as quick as she got well enough to walk, and before he got out of his bed, Trueman's wife walked over to see Joe. And Joe's mother hatin' her so, wouldn't let her step her foot into the house. And Joe wuz glad on't, so they say.

Mother Charnick wuz out on the stoop in front of the house, when Trueman's wife got there, and told her that they had to keep the house still; that is, they say so, I don't know for certain, but they say that Ma Charnick offered to take Trueman's wife out to see her chickens, the ones she had brought up by hand, and Trueman's wife wantin' to please her, so's to get in, consented. And Miss Char- nick showed her the hull 14 of 'em, all fat and flourishin',—they wuz well took care of. And

Miss Charnick looked down on 'em fondly, and sez :

"I lay out to have a good chicken pie the day that Joe and Jenette are married."

"I LAY OUT TO HAVE A GOOD CHICKEN PIE THE DAY THAT JOE AND JENETTE ARE MARRIED."

"Married !" sez Trueman's wife, in faint and horrified axcents.

"Yes, they are goin' to be married jest as soon as my son gets well enough. Jenette is fixin' a new dress for me to wear to the weddin'—with a bask," sez she with emphasis. And es she said it, they say she stooped down and gathered some sprigs of thoroughwert, a-mentionin' how much store she set by it for sickness.

But if she did, Trueman's wife didn't sense it, she wuz dumbfoundered and sot back by the news. And she left my home and board the week before the weddin'.

They had been married about a year, when Jenette wuz here a-visitin'—and she asked me in confidence (and it *must* be kep, it stands to reason it must), "if I s'posed that book muslin robe would make two little dresses?"

And I told her, "Good land! yes, three on 'em," and it did.

She dresses the child beautiful, and I don't know whether she would want the neighbors to know jest what and when and where she gets the materials—

It looks some like her and some like Joe—and they both think their eyes on it—but old Miss Charnick worships it—

Wall, though es I said (and I have eppisoded to a extent that is almost onprecidented and onheard on).

Though Josiah Allen made a excuse of bor-rowin' a plow (a *plow*, that time of night) to get away from my arguments on the Conference, and Submit's kinder skairt face, and so forth, and so on—

He resumed the conversation the next mornin' with more energy than ever. (He never said nuthin' about the plow, and I never see no sign on it, and don't believe he got it, or wanted it.)

He resumed the subject, and kep on a-resumin' of it from day to day and from hour to hour.

He would nearly exhaust the subject at home, and then he would tackle the wimmen on it at the Methodist Meetin' House, while we Methodist wim-men wuz to work.

After leavin' me to the meetin' house, Josiah would go on to the post-office for his daily *World*, and then he would stop on his way back to give us female wimmen the latest news from the Con-ference, and give us his idees on't.

And sometimes he would fairly harrow us to the

"He never had time to help."

very bone, with his dretful imaginins and fears that wimmen would be allowed to overdo herself, and ruin her health, and strain her mind, by bein' permitted to set!

Why Submit Tewksbury, and some of the other weaker sisters, would look fairly wild-eyed for some time after he would go.

He never could stay long. Sometimes we would beset him to stay and do some little job for us, to help us along with our work, such as liftin' somethin' or movin' some bench, or the pulpit, or somethin'.

But he never had the time; he always had to hasten home to get to work. He wuz in a great hurry with his spring's work, and full of care about that buzz saw mill.

And that wuz how it wuz with every man in the meetin' house that wuz able to work any. They wuz all in a hurry with their spring's work, and their buzz saws, and their inventions, and their agencys, etc., etc., etc.

And that wuz the reason why we wimmen wuz havin' such a hard job on the meetin' house.

CHAPTER XVII.

OU see the way on't wuz: we had to do sumthin' to raise the minister's salary, which wuz most half a year behindhand, to say nothin' of the ensuin' year a-comin'. And as I have hinted at before but hain't gi'n petickulers, the men in the meetin' house had all gi'n out, and said they had gi'n every cent they could, and they couldn't and they wouldn't do any more, any way.

As I have said more formally, there wuz a hardness arozen amongst the male brethern.

Deacon Peedick thought he had gi'n more than his part in proportion, and come right out plain and said so.

And Deacon Bobbet said " he wuzn't the man to stand it to be told right to his face that he hadn't done his share," and he said " he wuzn't the man either, to be hinted at from the pulpit about things."

I don't believe he wuz hinted at, and Sister Bobbet don't.   And she felt like death to have him so
riz up in his mind, and act so.   I know what the
tex' wuz ; it wuz these words :

"The Lord loveth a cheerful giver."

The minister didn't mean nothin' only pure gospel, when he preached about it. But it proved to be
a tight-breasted, close-fittin' coat to several of the
male brothers, and it fitted 'em so well it fairly
pinched 'em.

But there it wuz, Deacon Bobbet wouldn't gi'n a
cent towards raisin' the money.   And there wuz
them that said, and stuck to it, that he said " he
wouldn't give a *darn* cent."

But I don't know as that is so.   I wouldn't want
to be the one that said that he had demeaned himself
to that extent.

Wall, he wouldn't give a cent, and Peedick wouldn't
give, and Deacon Henzy and Deacon Sypher
wouldn't.   They said that there wuz certain members of the meetin' house that had said to . certain
people suthin' slightin' about buzz saws.

I myself thought then, and think still, that the
subject of buzz saws had a great deal to do in makin'

'em act so riz up and excited. I believe the subject rasped 'em, and made 'em nervous. But when these various hardnesses aroze amongst some of the brethern, the rest of the men kinder joined in with 'em, some on one side, and some on the other, and they all baulked right out of the harness. (Allegory.) And there the minister wuz, good old creeter, jest a-sufferin' for the necessities of life, and most half a year's salery due.

I tell you it looked dark. The men all said they couldn't see no way out of the trouble, and some of the wimmen felt about so. And old Miss Henn, one of our most able sisters, she had gi'n out, she wuz as mad as her own sirname about how her Metilda had been used.

The meetin' house had just hauled her up for levity. And I thought then, and think now, that the meetin' house wuz too hard on Metilda Henn.

She did titter right out in protracted meetin', Sister Henn don't deny it, and she felt dretful bad about it, and so did I. But Metilda said, and stuck to it, that she couldn't have helped laughin' if it had been to save her life.

And though I realized the awfulness of it, still, when some of the brethern wuz goin' on dretful about it, I sez to 'em :

" The Bible sez there is a time to laugh, and I don t know when that is, unless it is when you can't help it."

What she wuz a-laughin' at wuz this :

There wuz a widder woman by the name of Nancy Lum that always come to evenin' meetin's.

She wuz very tall and humbly, and she had been on the look out (so it wuz s'pozed) for a 3d husband for some time.

She had always made a practice of saying one thing over and over to all the protracted and Conference meetin's, and she would always bust out a-cryin' before she got it all out.

She always said " she wanted to be found always at the foot of the Cross."

She would always begin this remark dretful kinder loud and hysterical, and then would dwindle down kinder low at the end on't, and bustin' out into tears somewhere through it from first to last.

But this evenin' suthin' had occurred to make her more hysterical and melted down than usial (some say it wuz because Deacon Henshaw wuz present for the first time after his wive's death.

But any way, she riz up lookin' awful tall and humbly—she was most a head taller than any man there—and she sez out loud and strong:

"I want to be found—"

And then she busted right out a-cryin' hard. And she sobbed for some time. And then she begun agin,

"I want to be found—"

And then she busted out agin.

And so it went on for some time—she a-tellin' out ever and anon loud and firm, "that she wanted to be found—" and then bustin' into tears.

Till finally Deacon Henshaw (some mistrust that he is on the point of gettin' after her, and he always leads the singin' any way) he struck right out onto the him—

"Oh, that will be joyful!"

And Sister Lum sot down.

Wall, that wuz what made Metilda Henn titter. And that was what made me bring forward that verse of scripter.

"I WANT TO BE FOUND."

That the Bible said "'there wuz a time to laugh,' and I didn't know when it wuz unless it wuz when you couldn't help it—"

But I didn't say it to uphold Metilda—no, indeed. I only said it because they wuz so bitter on her, and laid the rules of the meetin' house down on her so heavy.

But Josiah said, "What would become of the meetin' house if it didn't punish its unruly members?"

And I sez to Josiah, "Do you remember the case of Deacon Widrig over in Loontown. He wuz rich and influential, and when he wuz complained of, and the meetin' house sot on him, they sot light, and you know it, Josiah Allen. And he was kep in the church, the meen old creeter. And Miss Henn is a widder and poor."

"Yes," sez Josiah, calmly, "she hain't been able to help the meetin' house much, and Brother Widrig contributes largely."

Sez I, in a fearful meanin' axent, "I hearn he did at the time he wuz up—I hearn he contributed *lots* to the male brethren who was a-judgin' him—but," sez I, "do you spoze, Josiah Allen, that if wimmen wuz allowed their way in the matter, that that man

would be allowed to stay in the meetin' house, and
keep on a-makin' and a-sellin' the poisen that is
sendin' men to ruin all round him—

"Makin' his hard cider by the barell and hogset
and fixin' it some way so it will make a far worse
drunk than whiskey, and then supplyin' every low
saloon fur and near with it, and peddlin' it out to
every man and boy that wants it.

"And boys think they can drink cider without doin'
any harm—so he jest entices 'em down into the road
to ruin—doin' as much agin harm as a whiskey seller

"And mothers have to set still and see it go on.
It is men that are always appinted to deal with sinners, male or female.   Men are judged by their peers,
but wimmen never are.

"I wonder if that is just?   I wonder how Deacon
Widrig would have liked it to have had Miss Henn
set on him?   He wuz dretful excited, so I hearn, about
Metilda's case—thought it wuz highly incumbient on
the meetin' house to have her made a example of,
so's to try to abolish such wicked doin's as snickerin'
out in meetin'.

"I wonder how he would have liked it to have had
Charley Lanfear's mother set on him?   She is a Sister

"Supplyin' every low saloon fur and near."

in the meetin' house and Charley is a ruined boy—
and Deacon Widrig is jest as much the cause of his
ruin—jest as guilty of murderin' all that wuz sweet
and lovely in him es if he had fed arsenic to him
with a teaspoon."

Sez I, " In that very meetin' house to Loontown, there are mothers who have to set and take
the bread and wine tokens of the blood and body
of their crucified Redeemer from a man's hands
that they know are red with the blood of their own
sons. Fur redder than human blood and deeper-
stained with the ruin of their immortal souls.

" What thoughts does these mothers keep on a-
thinkin' as they set there and see a man guilty of
worse than murder set up as a example to other
young souls ? What thoughts do they keep on a-
thinkin' of the young hearts that wuz pure before
this man laid holt of 'em. Young eyes that wuz
true and tender till this man made 'em look on his
accursed drink. Young lips that smiled on their
mothers till he gin 'em that that changed the smiles
to curses ?

" Would a delegation of wimmen keep such a
man in the meetin' house if he paved the hull floor

with fine gold ? No, you know they wouldn't. Let
a jury of mothers set on such a man, and see if he
could get up agin very easy.

" They are the ones who have suffered by him,
who have agonized, who went down into deeper
than the Valley of Death led by his hand. They
went down into that depth where they lose their
boy. Lose him eternally.

" Death, jest death, would give 'em a chance to
meet their child again. But what hope does a
mother have when down in the darkness that has no
mornin', her boy tears his hand from her weak
grasp and plunges downward ?

" How does such a mother feel as she sets there
in a still meetin' house, and the man who has done
all this passes her the emblems of a deathless love, a
divine purity ?"

Josiah sat demute and didn't say nuthin', and I
went on, for I wuz very roze up in my mind, and
by the side of myself with emotions.

And sez I, " Take the case of Simeon Lathers.
Why wuz it that Sister Irene Filkins wuz turned out
of the meetin' house and the man who wuz the
first cause of her goin' astray kep in—the handsome,

JOSIAH LOOKED UP AND SEZ, 'HOW A STEEPLE WOULD LOOK A-PINTIN' DOWN'

smooth-faced hypocrite ?—it wuz because he wuz rich
as a Jew, and jest plastered over the consciences of
them that tried him with his fine speeches and his
money.

"Fixed over the meetin' house there in Zoar, built
a new steeple, a towerin' one.   If wimmen had had
their way, that steeple would have pinted the other
way."

Josiah looked up from Ayers' Almanac, which he
wuz calmly perusin', and sez he,

"How a steeple would look a-pintin' down !"

CHAPTER XVIII.

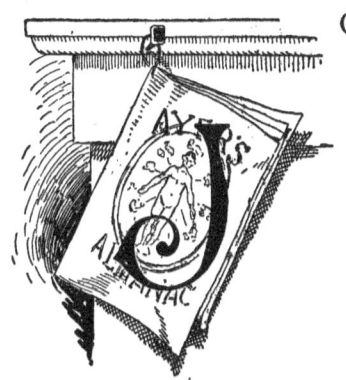

OSIAH'S face wuz smooth and placid, he hadn't took a mite of sense of what I had been a-sayin', and I knew it. Men don't. They know at the most it is only *talk*, wimmen hain't got it in their power to *do* anything. And I s'pose they reason on it in this way—a little wind storm is soon over, it relieves old Natur and don't hurt anything.

Yes, my pardner's face wuz as calm as the figger on the outside of the almanac a-holdin' the bottle, and his axent wuz mildly wonderin' and gently sarcestickle.

" How a steeple would look a-pintin' down ! That is a true woman's idee."

Sez I, " I would have it a-pintin' down towards the

depths of darkness that wuz in that man's heart
that roze it up, and the infamy of the deed that kep

SISTER FILKINS.

him in the meetin' house and turned his victim out
of it."

"Id'no as she wuz his victim," sez Josiah.

Sez I, "Every one knows that in the first place
Simeon Lathers wuz the man that led her astray."

"It wuzn't proved," sez Josiah, a-turnin' the almanac over and lookin' at the advertisement on the back side on't.

"And why wuzn't it proved?" sez I, "because he held a big piece of gold against the mouths of the witnesses."

"I didn't see any in front of my mouth," sez Josiah, lookin' 'shamed but some composed.

"And you know what the story wuz," sez he, "accordin' to that, he did it all to try her faith."

I wouldn't encourage Josiah by even smilin' at his words, though I knew well what the story wuz he referred to.

It wuz at a Conference meetin', when Simeon Lathers wuz jest a-beginnin' to take notice of how pretty Irene Filkins wuz.

She had gone forward to the anxious seat, with some other young females, their minds bein' wrought on, so it wuz spozed, by Deacon Lathers's eloquent exhortations, and urgin's to 'em to come forward and be saved.

And they had gone up onto the anxious seat a-sheddin' tears, and they all knelt down there, and Deacon Lathers he went right up and knelt down right by Sister Irene Filkins, and them that wuz there say, that right while he wuz a-prayin' loud and strong for 'em all, and her specially, he put his arm round her and acted in such a way that she resented it bitterly.

She wuz a good, virtuous girl then, any way.

And she resented his overtoors in such a indignant and decided way that it drawed the attention of a hull lot of brothers and sisters towards 'em.

And Deacon Lathers got right up from his knees and sez, "Bretheren and sisters, let us sing these lines:

"He did it all to try her faith."

I remembered this story, but I wuzn't goin' to encourage Josiah Allen by lettin' my attention be drawed off by any anectotes—nor I didn't smile— oh, no! But I went right on with a hull lot of burnin' indignatin in my axents, and sez I, "Josiah Allen, can you look me in the face and say that it wuzn't money and bad men's influence that keep such men as Deacon Widrig and Simeon Lathers in the meetin' house?" Sez I, "If they wuz poor men would they have been kep', or if it wuzn't for the influence of men that like hard drink?"

"Wall, as it were," sez Josiah, " I—that is—wall,
it is a-gettin' bed-time, Samantha."

And he wound up the clock and went to bed.

And I set there, all rousted up in my mind, for
more'n a hour—and I dropped more'n seven
stitches in Josiah's heel, and didn't care if I did.

But I have episoded fearfully, and to resoom and
go on.

Miss Henn wuz mad, and she wuz one of our
most enterprizen' sisters, and we felt that she wuz a
great loss.

Things looked dretful dark. And Sister Bobbet,
who is very tender hearted, shed tears several times
a-talkin' about the hard times that had come onto
our meetin' house, and how Zion wuz a-languishin',
etc., etc.

And I told Sister Bobbet in confidence, and also
in public, that it wuz time to talk about Zion's lan-
guishin' when we had done all we could to help her
up. And I didn't believe Zion would languish so
much if she had a little help gin her when she
needed it.

And Miss Bobbet said "she felt jest so about it,
but she couldn't help bein' cast down."

And so most all of the sisters said. Submit
Tewksbury wept, and shed tears time and agin, a-
talkin' about it, and so several of 'em did.   But I
sez to 'em—

"Good land!" sez I.   "We have seen jest as hard
times in the Methodist meetin' house before, time
and agin, and we wimmen have always laid holt
and worked, and laid plans, and worked, and worked,
and with the Lord's help have sailed the old ship
Zion through the dark waters into safety, and we
can do it agin."

Though what we wuz to do we knew not, and the
few male men who didn't jine in the hardness, said
they couldn't see no way out of it, but what the
minister would have to go, and the meetin' house
be shet up for a spell.

But we female wimmen felt that we could not
have it so any way.   And we jined together, and
met in each other's housen (not publickly, oh no!
we knew our places too well as Methodist Sisters).

We didn't make no move in public, but we kinder
met round to each other's housen, sort o' private like,
and talked, and talked, and prayed—we all knew that
wuzn't aginst the church rules, so we jest rastled

in prayer, for help to pay our honest debts, and keep
the Methodist meetin' house from disgrace, for the
men wuz that worked up and madded, that they
didn't seem to care whether the meetin' house come
to nothin' or not.

Wall, after settin' day after day (not public settin',
oh, no! we knew our places too well, and wouldn't
be ketched a-settin' public till we had a right to).

After settin' and talkin' it over back and forth, we
concluded the very best thing we could do wuz to
give a big fair and try to sell things enough to raise
some money.

It wuz a fearful tuff job we had took onto ourselves, for we had got to make all the things to sell
out of what we could get holt of, for, of course, our
husbands all kep the money purses in their own
hands, as the way of male pardners is. But we laid
out to beset 'em when they wuz cleverer than common (owin' to extra good vittles) and get enough
money out of 'em to buy the materials to work with,
bedquilts (crazy, and otherwise), embroidered
towels, shawl straps, knit socks and suspenders, rugs,
chair covers, lap robes, etc., etc., etc.

It wuz a tremendus hard undertakin' we had took

onto ourselves, with all our spring's work on hand,
and not one of us Sisters kep a hired girl at the time,
and we had to do our own house cleanin', paintin'
floors, makin' soap, spring sewin', etc., besides our
common housework.

But the very worst on't wuz the meetin' house
wuz in such a shape that we couldn't do a thing till
that wuz fixed.

The men had undertook to fix over the meetin'
house jest before the hardness commenced. The
men and wimmen both had labored side by side to
fix up the old house a little.

The men had said that in such church work as
that wimmen had a perfect right to help, to stand
side by side with the male brothers, and do half, or
more than half, or even *all* the work. They said it
wuzn't aginst the Discipline, and all the Bishops
wuz in favor of it, and always had been. They said
it wuz right accordin' to the Articles. But when it
come to the hard and arjuous duties of drawin' sal-
leries with 'em, or settin' up on Conferences with
'em, why there a line had to be drawed, wimmen
must not be permitted to strain herself in no such
ways—nor resk the tender delicacy of her nature,

by settin' in a meetin' house as a delegate by the
side of a man once a year.   It wuz too resky.   But
we could lay holt and work with 'em in public, or in
private, which we felt wuz indeed a privelege, for the
interests of the Methodist meetin' house wuz dear
to our hearts, and so wuz our pardners' approvals—
and they wuz all on 'em unanimus on this pint—
we could *work* all we wanted to.

So we had laid holt and worked right along with
the men from day to day, with their full and free
consents, and a little help from 'em, till we had got
the work partly done.   We had got the little Sabbath-
school room painted and papered, and the cushions
of the main room new covered, and we had engaged to have it frescoed, but the frescoer had
turned out to be a perfect fraud, and, of all the lookin' things, that meetin' house wuz about the worst.
The plaster, or whatever it wuz he had put on, had
to be all scraped off before it could be papered, the
paper wuz bought, and the scrapin' had begun.

The young male and female church members had
give a public concert together, and raised enough
money to get the paper—it wuz very nice, and fifty
cents a roll (double roll).

"Appearin' in public."

These young females appearin' in public for this purpose wuz very agreeable to the hull meetin' house, and wuz right accordin' to the rules of the Methodist Meetin' House, for I remember I asked about it when the question first come up about sendin' female delegates to the Conference, and all the male members of our meetin' house wuz so horrified at the idee.

I sez, " I'll bet there wouldn't one of the delegates yell half so loud es she that wuz Mahala Gowdey at the concert. Her voice is a sulferino of the very keenest edge and highest tone, and she puts in sights and sights of quavers."

But they all said that wuz a *very* different thing.

And sez I, " How different ? She wuz a yellin' in public for the good of the Methodist Meetin' House (it wuz her voice that drawed the big congregatin, we all know). And them wimmen delegates would only have to 'yea' and 'nay' in a still small voice for the good of the same. I can't see why it would be so much more indelicate and unbecomin' in them"—and sez I, " they would have bonnets and shawls on, and she that wuz Mahala had on a low neck and short sleeves."

But they wouldn't yield, and I wouldn't nuther.

But I am a eppisodin fearful, and to resoom. Wall, as I said, the scrapin' had begun. One side of the room wuz partly cleaned so the paper could go on, and then the fuss come up, and there it wuz, as you may say, neither hay nor grass, neither frescoed nor papered nor nuthin'. And of all the lookin' sights it wuz.

Wall, of course, if we had a fair in that meetin' house, we couldn't have it in such a lookin' place to disgrace us in the eyes of Baptists and 'Piscopals.

No, that meetin' house had got to be scraped, and we wimmen had got to do the scrapin' with case knives.

It wuz a hard job. I couldn't help thinkin' quite a number of thoughts as I stood on a barell with a board acrost it, afraid as death of fallin' and a workin' for dear life, and the other female sisters a standin' round on similar barells, all a-workin' fur beyond their strengths, and all afraid of fallin', and we all a-knowin' what we had got ahead on us a paperin' and a gettin' up the fair.

CHAPTER XIX.

 COULDN'T help a-me-thinkin' to myself several times. It duz seem to me that there hain't a question a-comin' up before that Conference that is harder to tackle than this plasterin' and the conundrum that is up before us Jonesville wimmen how to raise 300 dollars out of nuthin', and to make peace in a meetin' house where anarky is now rainin' down.

But I only thought these thoughts to myself, fur I knew every women there wuz peacible and law abidin' and there wuzn't one of 'em but what would ruther fall offen her barell then go agin the rules of the Methodist Meetin' House.

Yes, I tried to curb down my rebellous thoughts, and did, pretty much all the time.

And good land! we worked so hard that we hadn't time to tackle very curius and peculier thoughts, them that wuz dretful strainin' and wear-

"EVERY NIGHT JOSIAH WOULD TACKLE ME ON IT."

in' on the mind. Not of our own accord we didn't, fur we had to jest nip in and work the hull durin' time.

And then we all knew how deathly opposed our

pardners wuz to our takin' any public part in meetin' house matters or mountin' rostrums, and that thought quelled us down a sight.

Of course when these subjects wuz brung up before us, and turned round and round in front of our eyes, why we had to look at 'em and be rousted up by 'em more or less. It was Nater.

And Josiah not havin' anything to do evenin's only to set and look at the ceilin'. Every single night when I would go home from the meetin' house, Josiah would tackle me on it, on the danger of allowin' wimmen to ventur out of her spear in Meetin' House matters, and specially the Conference.

It begin to set in New York the very day we tackled the meetin' in Jonesville with a extra grip.

So's I can truly say, the Meetin' House wuz on me day and night. For workin' on it es I did, all day long, and Josiah a-talkin' abut it till bed time, and I a-dreamin' abut it a sight, that, and the Conference.

Truly, if I couldn't set on the Conference, the Conference sot on me, from mornin' till night, and from night till mornin'.

I spoze it wuz Josiah's skairful talk that brung it

onto me, it wuz brung on nite mairs mostly, in the nite time.

He would talk *very* skairful, and what he called deep, and repeat pages of Casper Keeler's arguments, and they would appear to me (drawed also by nite mairs) every page on 'em lookin' fairly lurid.

I suffered.

Josiah would set with the *World* and other papers in his hand, a-perusin' of 'em, while I would be a-washin' up my dishes, and the very minute I would get 'em done and my sleeves rolled down, he would tackle me, and often he wouldn't wait for me to get my work done up, or even supper got, but would begin on me as I filled up my tea kettle, and keep up a stiddy drizzle of argument till bed time, and as I say, when he left off, the nite mairs would begin.

I suffered beyond tellin' almost.

The secont night of my arjuous labors on the meetin' house, he began wild and eloquent about wimmen bein' on Conferences, and mountin' rostrums. And sez he, "That is suthin' that we Methodist men can't stand."

And I, havin' stood up on a barell all day a-

"Is rostrums much higher than them barells to stand on?"

scrapin' the ceilin', and not bein' recuperated yet from the skairtness and dizziness of my day's work, I sez to him :

" Is rostrums much higher than them barells we have to stand on to the meetin' house ?"

And Josiah said, "it wuz suthin' altogether dif· ferent." And he assured me agin,

" That in any modest, unpretendin' way the Meth· odist Church wuz willin' to accept wimmen's work. It wuzn't aginst the Discipline. And that is why," sez he, "that wimmen have all through the ages been allowed to do most all the hard work in the church—such as raisin' money for church work— earnin' money in all sorts of ways to carry on the different kinds of charity work connected with it— teachin' the children, nursin' the sick, carryin' on hospital work, etc., etc. But," sez he, " this is fur, fur different from gettin' up on a rostrum, or tryin' to set on a Conference. Why," sez he, in a haughty tone, " I should think they'd know without havin' to be told that laymen don't mean women."

Sez I, " Them very laymen that are tryin' to keep wimmen out of the Conference wouldn't have got in themselves if it hadn't been for wimmen's votes. If they can legally vote for men to get in why can't men vote for them?"

"That is the pint," sez Josiah, " that is the very pint I have been tryin' to explain to you. Wimmen can help men to office, but men can't help wimmen ; that is law, that is statesmanship. I have been a-tryin' to explain it to you that the word laymen *always* means woman when she can help men in any way, but *not* when he can help her, or in any other sense."

Sez I, " It seemed to mean wimmen when Metilda Henn wuz turned out of the meetin' house."

" Oh, yes," sez Josiah in a reasonin' tone, "the word laymen always means wimmen when it is used in a punishin' and condemnatory sense, or in the case of work and so fourth, but when it comes to settin' up in high places, or drawin' sallerys, or anything else difficult, it alweys means men."

Sez I, in a very dry axent, " Then the word man, when it is used in church matters, always means wimmen, so fur as scrubbin' is concerned, and drowdgin' round ?"

" Yes," sez Josiah haughtily. " And it always

means men in the higher and more difficult matters of decidin' questions, drawin' sallerys, settin' on
Conferences, etc. It has long been settled to be so,"
sez he.

"Who settled it ?" sez I.

"Why the men, of course," sez he. "The men
have always made the rules of the churches, and
translated the Bibles, and everything else that is
difficult," sez he. Sez I, in fearful dry axents, almost
husky ones, "It seems to take quite a knack to
know jest when the word laymen means men and
when it means wimmen."

"That is so," sez Josiah. "It takes a man's mind
to grapple with it; wimmen's minds are too weak to
tackle it   It is jest as it is with that word 'men' in
the Declaration of Independence. Now that word
'men', in that Declaration, means men some of the
time, and some of the time men and wimmen both.
It means both sexes when it relates to punishment,
taxin' property, obeyin' the laws strictly, etc., etc.,
and then it goes right on the very next minute and
means men only, as to wit, namely, votin', takin'
charge of public matters, makin' laws, etc.

"I tell you it takes deep minds to foller on and

see jest to a hair where the division is made. It takes statesmanship.

" Now take that claws, ' All men are born free and equal.'

" Now half of that means men, and the other half men and wimmen. Now to understand them words perfect you have got to divide the tex. ' Men are born.' That means men and wimmen both—men and wimmen are both born, nobody can dispute that. Then comes the next claws, ' Free and equal.' Now that means men only—anybody with one eye can see that.

" Then the claws, ' True government consists.' That means men and wimmen both—consists—of course the government consists of men and wimmen, 'twould be a fool who would dispute that. ' In the consent of the governed.' That means men alone. Do you see, Samantha?" sez he.

I kep' my eye fixed on the tea kettle, fer I stood with my tea-pot in hand waitin' for it to bile—" I see a great deal, Josiah Allen."

" Wall," sez he, " I am glad on't. Now to sum it up," sez he, with some the mean of a preacher—or, ruther, a exhauster—" to sum the matter all up, the

CHURCH WORK.

words 'bretheren,' 'laymen,' etc., always means
wimmen so fur as this: punishment for all offenses,
strict obedience to the rules of the church, work of
any kind and all kinds, raisin' money, givin' money
all that is possible, teachin' in the Sabbath school,
gettin' up missionary and charitable societies, carryin' on the same with no help from the male sect
leavin' that sect free to look after their half of the
meanin' of the word—sallerys, office, makin' the
laws that bind both of the sexes, rulin' things generally, translatin' Bibles to suit their own idees,
preachin' at 'em, etc., etc. Do you see, Samantha?"
sez he, proudly and loftily.

"Yes," sez I, as I filled up my tea-pot, for the
water had at last biled. "Yes, I see."

And I spoze he thought he had convinced me,
for he acted high headeder and haughtier for as much
as an hour and a half. And I didn't say anything
to break it up, for I see he had stated it jest as he
and all his sect looked at it, and good land! I
couldn't convince the hull male sect if I tried—
clergymen, statesmen and all—so I didn't try,
and I wuz truly beat out with my day's work,
and I didn't drop more than one idee more,

I simply dropped this remark es I poured out his tea and put some good cream into it—I merely sez:

"There is three times es many wimmen in the meetin' house es there is men."

"Yes," sez he, "that is one of the pints I have been explainin' to you," and then he went on agin real high headed, and skairt, about the old ground, of the willingness of the meetin' house to shelter wimmen in its folds, and how much they needed gaurdin' and guidin', and about their delicacy of frame, and how unfitted they wuz to tackle anything hard, and what a grief it wuz to the male sect to see 'em a-tryin' to set on Conferences or mount rostrums, etc., etc.

And I didn't try to break up his argument, but simply repeated the question I had put to him—for es I said before, I wuz tired, and skairt, and giddy yet from my hard labor and my great and hazardus elevatin'; I had not, es you may say, recovered yet from my recuperation, and so I sez agin them words—

"Is rostrums much higher than them barells to stand on?"

And Josiah said agin, "it wuz suthin' entirely different;" he said barells and rostrums wuz so fur apart that you couldn't look at both on 'em in one day hardly, let alone a minute. And he went on once more with a long argument full of Bible quotations and everything.

And I wuz too tuckered out to say much more. But I did contend for it to the last, that I didn't believe a rostrum would be any more tottlin' and skairful a place than the barell I had been a-standin' on all day, nor the work I'd do on it any harder than the scrapin' of the ceilin' of that meetin house.

And I don't believe it would, I stand jest as firm on it to-day as I did then.

CHAPTER XX.

WALL, we got the scrapin' done after three hard and arjous days' works, and then we preceeded to clean the house. The day we set to clean the meetin' house prior and before paperin', we all met in good season, for we knew the hardships of the job in front of us, and we all felt that we wanted to tackle it with our full strengths.

Sister Henzy, wife of Deacon Henzy, got there jest as I did. She wuz in middlin' good spirits and a old yeller belzerine dress.

Sister Gowdy had the ganders and newraligy and wore a flannel for 'em round her head, but she wuz in workin' spirits, her will wuz up in arms, and nerved up her body.

Sister Meechim wuz a-makin' soap, and so wuz Sister Sypher, and Sister Mead, and me. But we

all felt that soap come after religion, not before.
" Cleanliness *next* to godliness."

So we wuz all willin' to act accordin', and tackle
the old meetin' house with a willin' mind.

Wall, we wuz all engaged in the very heat of
the warfare, as you may say, a-scrubbin' the floors,
and a-scourin' the benches by the door, and a-
blackin' the 2 stoves that stood jest inside of the
door. We wuz workin' jest as hard as wimmen
ever worked—and all of the wimmen who wuzn't
engaged in scourin' and moppin' wuz a-settin'
round in the pews a-workin' hard on articles for the
fair—when all of a suddin the outside door opened
and in come Josiah Allen with 3 of the other men
bretheren.

They had jest got the great news of wimmen
bein' apinted for Deaconesses, and had come down
on the first minute to tell us. She that wuz Celestine Bobbet wuz the only female present that had
heard of it.

Josiah had heard it to the post-office, and he
couldn't wait till noon to tell me about it, and
Deacon Gowdy wuz anxius Miss Gowdy should
hear it as soon es possible.

Deacon Sypher wanted his wife to know at once that if she wuzn't married she could have become a deaconess under his derectin'.

And Josiah wanted me to know immegietly that I, too, could have had the privilege if I had been a more single woman, of becomin' a deaconess, and have had the chance of workin' all my hull life for the meetin' house, with a man to direct my movements and take charge on me, and tell me what to do, from day to day and from hour to hour.

And Deacon Henzy was anxious Miss Henzy should get the news as quick as she could. So they all hastened down to the meetin' house to tell us.

And we left off our work for a minute to hear 'em. It wuzn't nowhere near time for us to go home.

Josiah had lots of further business to do in Jonesville and so had the other men. But the news had excited 'em, and exhilerated 'em so, that they had dropped everything, and hastened right down to tell us, and then they wuz a-goin' back agin immegietly.

I, myself, took the news coolly, or as cool as I could, with my temperature up to five or five and a half, owin' to the hard work and the heat.

THE LAST NEWS FROM THE CONFERENCE.

Miss Gowdy also took it pretty calm.   She leaned on her mop handle, partly for rest (for she was
tuckered out) and partly out of good manners, and
didn't say much.

But Miss Sypher is such a admirin' woman, she
looked fairly radiant at the news, and she spoke up
to her husband in her enthusiastik warm-hearted
way—

" Why, Deacon Sypher, is it possible that I, too,
could become a deacon, jest like you ?"

" No," sez Deacon Sypher solemnly, "no, Drusilly, not like me.   But you wimmen have got the
privelege now, if you are single, of workin' all your
days at church work under the direction of us men."

" Then I could work at the Deacon trade under
you," sez she admirin'ly, " I could work jest like you
—pass round the bread and wine and the contribu-
tion box Sundays ?"

" Oh, no, Drusilly," sez he condesendinly, " these
hard and arjuous dutys belong to the male deacon-
ship.   That is their own one pertickiler work, that
wimmen can't infringe upon.   Their hull strength
is spent in these duties, wimmen deacons have other
fields of labor, such as relievin' the wants of the sick

and sufferin', sittin' up nights with small-pox pa-
tients, takin' care of the sufferin' poor, etc., etc."

"But," sez Miss Sypher (she is so good-hearted, and
so awful fond of the deacon), "wouldn't it be
real sweet, Deacon, if you and I could work together as deacons, and tend the sick, relieve the suf-
ferers—work for the good of the church together—
go about doin' good?"

"No, Drusilly," sez he, "that is wimmen's work. I
would not wish for a moment to curtail the holy
rights of wimmen. I wouldn't want to stand in her
way, and keep her from doin' all this modest, unpretendin' work, for which her **weaker frame and**
less hefty brain has fitted her.

"We will let it go on in the same old way. Let
wimmen have the privelege of workin' hard, jest as
she always has. Let her work all the time, day and
night, and let men go on in the same sure old way
of superentendin' her movements, guardin' her
weaker footsteps, and bossin' her round generally."

Deacon Sypher is never happy in his choice of
language, and his method of argiment is such that
when he is up on the affirmative of a question, **the**
negative is delighted, for they know he will bring

victery to their side of the question. Now, he didn't
mean to speak right out about men's usual way of
bossin' wimmen round. It was only his unfortunate
and transparent manner of speakin'.

And Deacon Bobbet hastened to cover up the
remark by the statement that "he wuz so highly tickled that wimmen wuzn't goin' to be admitted to the
Conference, because it would *weaken* the Conference."

"Yes," sez my Josiah, a-leanin' up aginst the
meetin' house door, and talkin' pretty loud, for Sister Peedick and me had gone to liftin' round the
big bench by the door, and it wuz fearful heavy,
and our minds wuz excersised as to the best place to
put it while we wuz a-cleanin' the floor.

"You see," sez he, "we feel, we men do, we feel
that it would be weakenin' to the Conference to
have wimmen admitted, both on account of her own
lack of strength and also from the fact that every
woman you would admit would keep out a man.
And that," sez he (a-leanin' back in a still easier
attitude, almust a luxurious one), "that, you see,
would tend naterally to weakenin' the strength of
a church."

"Wall," sez I, a-pantin' hard for breath under my burden, "move round a little, won't you, for we want to set the bench here while we scrub under it. And,"

"WALL," SEZ I, "MOVE ROUND A LITTLE, WON'T YOU, FOR WE WANT
TO SET THE BENCH."

sez I, a-stoppin' a minute and rubbin' the perspiratin and sweat offen my face,

"Seein' you men are all here, can't you lay holt and help us move out the benches, so we can clean the floor under 'em ? Some of 'em are very hefty," sez I, "and all of us Sisters almost are a-makin' soap, and we all want to get done here, so we can go home and bile down ; we would dearly love a little help," sez I.

" I would help," sez Josiah in a willin' tone, " I would help in a minute, if I hadn't got so much work to do at home."

And all the other male bretheren said the same thing—they had got to git to get home to get to work. (Some on 'em wanted to play checkers, and I knew it.)

But some on 'em did have lots of work on their hands, I couldn't dispute it.

CHAPTER XXI.

WHY, Deacon Henzy, besides all his cares about the buzz saw mill, and his farm work, had bought a steam threshin' machine that made him sights of work. It was a good machine. But it wuz fairly skairful to see it a-steamin' and a-blowin' right along the streets of Jonesville without the sign of a horse or ox or anything nigh it to draw it. A-puffin' out the steam, and a-tearin' right along, that awful lookin' that it skairt she that wuz Celestine Bobbet most into fits.

She lived in a back place where such machines wuz unknown, and she had come home to her father's on a visit, and wuz goin' over to visit some of his folks that day, over to Loontown.

And she wuz a-travellin' along peacible, with her father's old mair, and a-leanin' back in the buggy a

readin' a article her father had sent over by her to
Deacon Widrig, a witherin' article about female
Deaconesses, and the stern necessity of settin' 'em
apart and sanctifyen' 'em to this one work—deacon
work—and how they mustn't marry, or tackle any
other hard jobs whatsumever, or break off into any
other enterprize, only jest plain deacon work.

It wuz a very flowery article. And she wuz en-
joyin' of it first rate, and a-thinkin', for she is a little
timid and easily skairt, and the piece had convinced
her—

She wuz jest a-thinkin' how dretful it would be
if sum female deaconess should ever venter into some
other branch of business, and what would be apt to
become of her if she did. She hated to think of
what her doom would most likely be, bein' tender
hearted.

When lo, and behold! jest as she wuz a-thinkin'
these thoughts, she see this wild and skairful machine approachin', and Deacon Henzy a-standin'
up on top of it a-drivin'. He looked wild and excited, bein' very tickled to think that he had thresh-
ed more with his machine, by twenty bushels, than
Deacon Petengill had with his.

"She see this wild and skairful machine approachin'."

There was a bet upon these two deacons, so it wuz spozed, and he wuz a-hastenin' to the next place where he wuz to be set up, so's to lose no time, and he was kinder hollerin'.

And the wind took his gray hair back, and his long side whiskers, and kinder stood 'em out, and the skirts of his frock the same.

His mean wuz wild.

And it wuz more than Celestine's old mair and she herself could bear; she cramped right round in the road (the mair did) and set sail back to old Bobbet'ses, and that great concern a-puffin' and a-steamin' along after 'em.

And by the time that she that wuz Celestine got there she wuz almost in a fit, and the mair in a perfect lather.

Wall, Celestine didn't get over it for weeks and weeks, nor the mair nuther.

And besides this enterprize of Deacon Henzy's, he had got up a great invention, a new rat trap, that wuz peculier and uneek in the extreme.

It wuz the result of arjous study on his part, by night and day, for a long, long time, and it wuz what he called "A Travellin' Rat Trap." It wuz designed to sort o' chase the rats round and skair 'em.

DEACON HENZY'S RAT TRAP (LIKE A CIRCUS FOR THE RATS).

It was spozed he got the idee in the first place from his threshin' machine. It had to be wound up, and then it would take after 'em—rats or mice, or anything—and they do say that it wuz quite a success.

Only it had to move on a smooth floor. It would travel round pretty much all night; and they say that when it wuz set up in a suller, it would chase the rats back into their holes, and they would set there and look out on it, for the biggest heft of the night. It would take up their minds, and kep 'em out of vittles and other mischief.

It wuz somethin' like providin' a circus for 'em.

But howsumever, the Deacon wuz a-workin' at this; he wuzn't quite satisfied with its runnin' gear, and he wuz a-perfectin' this rat trap every leisure minute he had outside of his buzz saw and threshin' machine business, and so he wuz fearful busy.

Deacon Sypher had took the agency for "The Wild West, or The Leaping Cow Boy of the Plain," and wuz doin' well by it.

And Deacon Bobbet had took in a lot of mustangs to keep through the winter. And he wuz a ridin' 'em a good deal, accordin' to contract, and tryin' to tame 'em some before spring. And this work, with the buzz saw, took up every minute of his time.

For the mustangs throwed him a good deal, and he had to lay bound up in linements a good deal of the time, and arneky.

"HE HAD TO LAY BOUND UP IN LINEMENTS A GOOD DEAL OF THE TIME."

So, as I say, it didn't surprise me a mite to have 'em say they couldn't help us, for I knew jest how these jobs of theirn devoured their time.

And when my Josiah had made his excuse, it

wuzn't any more than I had looked out for, to hear
Deacon Henzy say he had got to git home to
ile his threshin' machine. One of the cogs wuz out
of gear in some way.

He wanted to help us, so it didn't seem as if he
could tear himself away, but that steam threshin' machine stood in the way. And then on his way down
to Jonesville that very mornin' a new idee had come
to him about that travellin' rat trap, and he wanted
to get home jest as quick as he could, to try it.

And Deacon Bobbet said that three of them mustangs he had took in to break had got to be rid that
day, they wuz a gettin' so wild he didn't hardly dast
to go nigh 'em.

And Deacon Sypher said that he must hasten
back, for a man wuz a-comin' to see him from way
up on the State road, to try to get a agency under
him for "The Leaping Cow Boy of the Plain." And
he wanted to show the "Leaping Cow Boy" to
some agents to the tavern in Jonesville on his way
home, and to some wimmen on the old Plank
road. Two or three of the wimmen had gin hopes
that they would take the "Leaping Cow Boy."

And then they said—the hull three of the deacons

did—that any minute them other deacons who wuz
goin' into partnership with 'em in the buzz saw
business wuz liable to drive down to see 'em about
it.

And some of the other men brethren said their
farms and their live stock demanded the hull of their
time—every minute of it.

So we see jest how it wuz, we see these male deacons couldn't devote any of their time to the meetin'
house, nor those other brethren nuther.

We see that their time wuz too valuable, and
their own business devoured the hull on it.   And
we married Sisters, who wuz acestemed to the
strange and mysterius ways of male men, we ac-
ce ted the situation jest es we would any other
mysterius dispensation, and didn't say nothin'.

Good land ! We wuz used to curius sayin's
and doin's, every one on us. Curius as a dog, and
curiuser.

But Sister Meechim (onmarried), she is dretful
questinin' and inquirin' (men don't like her, they
say she prys into subjects she's no business to meddle with). She sez to Josiah :

" Why is it, Deacon Allen, that men deacons can

carry on all sorts of business and still be deacons, while wimmen deacons are obleeged to give up all other business and devote themselves wholly to their work ?"

"It is on account of their minds," sez Josiah. "Men have got stronger minds than wimmen, that is the reason."

And Sister Meechim sez agin—

" Why is it that wimmen deacons have to remain onmarried, while men deacons can marry one wife after another through a long life, that is, if they are took from 'em by death or a divorce lawyer ?"

"Wall," sez Josiah, "that, too, is on account of their brains. Their brains hain't so hefty es men's."

But I jest waded into the argument then. I jest interfered, and sez in a loud, clear tone,

"Oh, shaw !"

And then I sez further, in the same calm, clear tones, but dry as ever a dry oven wuz in its dryest times. Sez I,

" If you men can't help us any about the meetin' house, you'd better get out of our way, for we wimmen have got to go to scrubbin' right where you are a-standin'."

" Certainly," sez Josiah, in a polite axent,
" certainly."

And so the rest of the men said.

And Josiah added to his remarks, as he went
down the steps,

" You'd better get home, Samantha, in time to
cook a hen, and make some puddin', and so forth."

And I sez, with quite a lot of dignity, " Have I
ever failed, Josiah Allen, to have good dinners for
you, and on time too ?"

" No," sez he, " but I thought I would jest stop
to remind you of it, and also to tell you the last
news from the Conference, about the deaconesses."

And so they trailed down one after another,
and left us to our work in the meetin' house ; but
as they disapered round the corner, Sister Arvilly
Lanfear, who hain't married, and who has got a
sharp tongue (some think that is why, but I don't ;
I believe Arvilly has had chances).

But any way, she sez, as they went down the
steps,

" I'll bet them men wuz a-practisen' their new
parts of men superentendents, and look on us as
a lot of deaconesses."

"JOSIAH ADDED TO HIS REMARKS."

"Wall," sez Sister Gowdy—she loves to put on Arvilly—"wall, you have got one 'qualificatin', Arvilly!"

"Yes, thank the Lord," sez she.

And I never asked what she meant, but knew well enough that she spoke of her single state. But Arvilly has had chances, *I* think.

CHAPTER XXII.

GOT home in time to get a good supper, though mebbe I ortn't to say it.

Sure enough, Josiah Allen had killed a hen, and dressed it ready for me to brile, but it wuz young and tender, and I knew it wouldn't take long, so I didn't care.

Good land! I love to humor him, and he knows it.

Casper Keeler come in jest as I wuz a-gettin' supper and I thought like as not he would stay to supper; I laid out to ask him. But I didn't take no more pains on his account. No, I do jest as well by Josiah Allen from day to day, as if he wuz company, or lay out to.

Casper came over on a errent about that buzz saw mill. He wuz in dretful good spirits, though he looked kinder peaked.

He had jest got home from the city.

It happened dretful curius, but jest at this time Casper Keeler had had to go to New York on

CASPER KEELER.

business. He had to sign some papers that nobody else couldn't sign.

His mother had hearn of a investment there that promised to pay dretful well, so she had took a lot of

stock in it, and it had riz right up powerful.
Why the money had increased fourfold, and more
too, and Casper bein' jest come of age, had to go
and sign suthin' or other.

Wall, he went round and see lots of sights in
New York. His ma's money that she had left him
made him fairly luxurius as to comfort, and he had
plenty of money to go sight seein' as much as he
wanted to.

He went to all the theatres, and operas, and shows
of all kinds, and museums, and the Brooklyn Bridge,
and circuses, and receptions, and et cetery, et cetery.

He wuz a-tellin' me how much money he spent
while he wuz there, kinder boastin' on it; he had
went to one of the biggest, highest taverns in the
hull village of New York, where the price wuz
higher than the very highest pinakle on the top of it,
fur higher.

And I sez, "Did you go to the Wimmen's Ex-
change and the Workin' Wimmen's Association,
that wuz held there while you wuz there?"

And he acted real scorfin'.

"Wimmen's work!" sez he. "No, indeed! I had
too much on my hands, and too much comfort to

take in higher circles, than to take in any such little trifles as wimmen's work."

Sez I, "Young man, it is a precious little you would take in in life if it hadn't been for wimmen's work. Who earned and left you the money you are a-usin'?" sez I, "who educated you and made your life easy before you?"

And then bein' fairly drove into a corner, he owned up that his mother wuz a good woman.

But his nose wuz kinder lifted up the hull of the time he wuz a-sayin' it, as if he hated to own it up, hated to like a dog.

But he got real happified up and excited after-wards, in talkin' over with Josiah what he see to the Conference. He stayed to supper; I wuz a sea-sonin' my chicken and mashed potatoes, and garnishin' 'em for the table. I wuz out to one side a little, but I listened with one side of my brain while the other wuz fixed on pepper, ketchup, parsley, etc., etc.

Sez Casper, "It wuz the proudest, greatest hour of my life," sez he, "when I see a nigger delegate git up and give his views on wimmen keepin' down in their place. When I see a black nigger stand up

"HE SEEMED TO HAVE A HORROW OF WOMAN A-RAISIN' OUT OF HER SPEAR."

there in that Conference and state so clearly, so logically and so powerfully the reasons why poor weak wimmen should *not* be admitted into that sacred enclosure—

" When I see even a nigger a-standin' there and a-knowin' so well what wimmen's place wuz, my heart beat with about the proudest emotions I have ever experienced. Why, he said," sez Casper, "that if wimmen wuz allowed to stand up in the Conference, they wouldn't be satisfied. The next thing they would want to do would be to preach. It wuz a masterly argument," sez Casper.

" It must have been," sez my Josiah.

" He seemed to have such a horrow of a weak-minded, helpless woman a-raisin' herself up out of her lower spear."

" Well he might," sez Josiah, "well he might."

Truly, there are times when women can't, seeminly, stand no more. This wuz one on 'em, and I jest waded right into the argiment. I sez, real solemn like, a-holdin' the sprig of parsley some like a septer, only more sort o' riz up like and mysteriouser. Yes, I held that green sprig some as the dove did when it couldn't find no rest for

the soles of its feet—no foundation under it and it
sailed about seekin' some mount of truth it could
settle down on.   Oh how wobblin' and onsub-
stantial and curius I felt hearin' their talk.

"And," sez I, "nobody is tickleder than I be to
think a colored man has had the right gin him to
stand up in a Conference or anywhere else.   I
have probable experienced more emotions in his behalf," sez I, "deep and earnest, than any other female,
ancient or modern.   I have bore his burdens for
him, trembled under his lashes, agonized with him
in his unexampled griefs and wrongs and indigni-
ties, and I have rejoiced at the very depths of my
soul at his freedom.

" But," sez I, "when he uses that freedom to en-
chain another and as deservin' a race, my feelin's
are hurt and my indignations are riz up.

" Yes," sez I, a-wavin' that sprig some like a warlike banner, as my emotions swelled up under my
bask waste,

" When that negro stands there a-advocatin' the
slavery of another race, and a-sayin' that women
ortn't to say her soul is her own, and wimmen are
too weak and foolish to lift up their right hands,

much less preach, I'd love to ask him where he
and his race wuz twenty-five years ago, and where
they would be to-day if it wuzn't for a woman
usin' her right hand and her big heart and brain in
his behalf, and preachin' for him all over the world
and in almost every language under the sun.   Everybody says that 'Uncle Tom's Cabin' wuz the
searchin' harrow that loosened the old, hard ground
of slavery so the rich seed of justice could be
planted and bring forth freedom.

" If it hadn't been for that woman's preachin',
that negro exhauster would to-day most likely be a
hoin' cotton with a overseer a-lashin' him up to his
duties, and his wife and children and himself a-
bein' bought and sold, and borrowed and lent and
mortgaged and drove like so many animals.   And
I'd like to have riz right up in that Conference and
told him so."

" Oh, no," sez Josiah, lookin' some meachin', " no,
you wouldn't."

" Yes, I would," sez I. " And I'd 've enjoyed it
richly," sez I, es I turned and put my sprig round
the edge of the platter.

Casper wuz demute for as much as half a minute,

SAMANTHA EXPRESSES HER VIEWS.

and Josiah Allen looked meachin' for about the same length of time.

But, good land! how soon they got over it. They wuz as chipper as ever, a-runnin' down the idee of women settin', before they got half through dinner.

After hard and arjuous work we got the scrapin' done, and the scrubbin' done, and then we proceeded to make a move towards puttin' on the paper.

But the very day before we wuz to put on our first breadth, Sister Bobbet, our dependence and best paperer, fell down on a apple parin' and hurt her ankle jint, so's she couldn't stand on a barell for more'n several days.

And we felt dretful cast down about it, for we all felt as if the work must stop till Sister Bobbet could be present and attend to it.

But, as it turned out, it wuz perfectly providential, so fur as I wuz concerned, for on goin' home that night fearfully deprested on account of Sister Sylvester Bobbet, lo and behold! I found a letter there on my own mantletry piece that completely turned round my own plans.

It come entirely onexpected to me, and contained the startlin' intelligence that my own cousin, on my mother's own side, had come home to Loontown to his sister's, and wuz very sick with nervous prostra

TO NIGHT
CIRCUS

GROUND
LOFTY
TUMBLING

A

"SISTER BOBBET, OUR DEPENDENCE, FELL DOWN ON A APPLE PARIN'."

tion, neuralgia, rheumatism, etc., and expected par·alasys every minute, and heart failure, and such.

And his sister, Miss Timson, who wrote the letter, beset me to come over and see him. She said, Jane

Ann did (Miss Timson'ses name is Jane Ann), and
sez she in Post scriptum remark to me, sez
she—

"Samantha, I know well your knowledge of sickness and your powers of takin' care of the sick. Do
come and help me take care of Ralph, for it seems
as if I can't let him go. Poor boy, he has worked
so hard, and now I wuz in hopes that he wuz goin'
to take some comfort in life, unbeknown to him.
Do come and help him for my sake, and for Rosy's
sake." Rosy wuz Ralph's only child, a pretty girl,
but one ruther wild, and needin' jest now a father's
strong hand.

Rosy's mother died when she wuz a babe, and
Ralph, who had always been dretful religius, felt it
to be his duty to go and preach to the savages. So
Miss Timson took the baby and Ralph left all his
property with Miss Timson to use for her, and then
he girded up his lions, took his Bible and him book
and went out West and tackled the savages.

Tackled 'em in a perfectly religius way, and
done sights of good, sights and sights.. For all he
wuz so mild and gentle and religius, he got the
upper hand of them savages in some way, and he

brung 'em into the church by droves, and they jest worshipped him.

Wall, he worked so hard a-tryin' to do good and

RALPH SMITH ROBINSON.

save souls that wuz lost—a-tryin' single-handed to overthrow barberus beliefs and habits, and set up the pure and peaceful doctrines of the Master he loved and followed, that his health gin out after a time—he felt weak and mauger.

And jest about this time his sister wrote to him that Rosy havin' got in with gay companions, wuz a gettin' beyond her influence, and she *needed* a father's control and firm hand to guide her right, or else she would be liable to go to the wrong, and draw lots of others with her, for she wuz a born leader amongst her mates, jest as her father wuz—so wouldn't Ralph come home.

Wall, Ralph come. His sister and girl jest worshipped him, and looked and longed for his comin', as only tender-hearted wimmen can love and worship a hero. For if there wuz ever a hero it wuz Ralph Smith Robinson.

Wall, Ralph had been in the unbroken silences of nature so long, that the clack, and crash, and clamor of what we call civilized life almost crazed him.

He had been where his Maker almost seemed to come down and walk with him through the sweet, unbroken stillnesses of mornin' and evenin'. The world seemed so fur off to him, and the Eternal Verities of life so near, that truly, it sometimes seemed to him as if, like one of old, " he walked with God."

Of course the savages war-whooped some, but they wuz still a good deal of the time, which is more than you can say for Yankees.

And Loontown when he got home was rent to its very twain with a Presidential election.

Ralph suffered.

But above all his other sufferin's, he suffered from church bells.

Miss Timson lived, as it wuz her wish, and often her boast, right under the droppin's of the sanctuary.

She lotted on it when she bought the place. The Baptist steeple towered up right by the side of her house. Her spare bed wuz immegietly under the steeple.

Wall, comin' as he did from a place where he wuz called to worship by the voice of his soul and his good silver watch—this volume of clamor, this rushin' Niagara of sound a-pourin' down into his ears, wuz perfectly intolerable and onbeerable. He would lay awake till mornin' dreadin' the sound, and then colapse under it, till it run along and he come down with nervous fever.

He wuz worn out no doubt by his labors before

he come, and any way he wuz took bed-sick, and couldn't be moved so's the doctor said, and he bein' outside of his own head, delerius, couldn't of course advance no idees of his own, so he lay and suffered.

CHAPTER XXIII.

MISS TIMSON'S letter wuz writ to me on the 6th day of his sickness, and Josiah and me set sail for Loontown on the follerin' day after we got it.

I laid the case before the female Sisters of the meetin' house, and they all counselled me to go. For, as they all said, on account of Sister Bobbet's fallin' on the apple parin' we could not go on with the work of paperin' the meetin' house, and so the interests of Zion wouldn't languish on account of my absence for a day or two any way. And, as the female Sisters all said, it seemed as if the work I wuz called to in Loontown wuz a fair and square case of Duty, so they all counselled me to go, every one on 'em. Though, as wuz nateral, there wuz severel divisions of opinions as to the road I should take a-goin' there, what day I should come back, what remiedies wuz best for me to recommend when I got there, what dress I should wear, and whether I should wear a hankerchif pin or not—or a bib apron, or a plain banded one, etc., etc., etc., etc.

But, as I sez, as to my goin' they wuz every one on 'em unanimus. They meen well, those sisters in the meetin' house do, every one on 'em.

Josiah acted real offish at first about goin'. And he laid the case before the male brothers of the meetin' house, for Josiah wuz fearful that the interests of the buzz saw mill would languish in his absence. One or two of the weaker brethren joined in with him, and talked kinder deprestin' about it.

But Deacon Sypher and Deacon Henzy said they would guard his interests with eagle visions, or somethin' to that effect, and they counselled Josiah warmly that it wuz his duty to go.

We hearn afterwards that Deacon Sypher and Deacon Henzy wanted to go into the North Woods a-fishin' and a-huntin' for 2 or 3 days, and it has always been spozed by me that that accounted for their religeus advice to Josiah Allen.

Howsumever, I don't *know* that. But I do know

that they started off a-fishin' the very day we left for Loontown, and that they come back home about the time we did, with two long strings of trout.

THE RETURN OF THE HUNTERS.

And there wuz them that said that they ketched the trout, and them that said they bought 'em.

And they brung back the antlers of a deer in their game bags, and some bones of a elk.

And there are them that sez that they dassent, either one of 'em, shoot off a gun, not hardly a pop gun.   But I don't know the truth of this.   I know what they *said*, they *said* the huntin' wuz excitin' to the last degree, and the fishin' superb.

And there wuz them that said that they should think the huntin' would be excitin', a-rummagin' round on the ground for some old bones, and they should think the fishin' would be superb, a-dippin' 'em out of a barell and stringin' 'em onto their own strings.

But their stories are very large, that I know. And each one on 'em, accordin' to their tell, ketched more trouts than the other one, and fur bigger ones, and shot more deers.

Wall, Deacon Sypher'ses advice and Deacon Henzy's influenced Josiah a good deal, and I said quite a few words to him on the subject, and, suffice it to say, that the next day, about 10 A.M., we set out on our journey to Loontown.

Miss Timson and Rosy seemed dretful glad to see me, but they wuz pale and wan, wanner fur than I expected to see 'em ; but after I had been there a spell I see how it wuz.   I see that Ralph

"Miss Timson and Rosy seemed dretful glad to see me."

wuz their hero as well as their love, and they worshipped him in every way, with their hearts and their
souls and their idealized fancies.

Wall, he wuz a noble lookin' man as I ever see,
fur or near, and as good a one as they make, he wuz
strong and tender, so I couldn't blame 'em.

And though I wouldn't want Josiah to hear me
say too much about it, or mebby it would be best
that he shouldn't, before I had been there 24 hours
I begun to feel some as they did.

But my feelin's wuz strictly in a meetin' house
sense, strictly.

But I begun to feel with them that the middle of
the world wuz there in that bedroom, and the still,
white figure a-layin' there wuz the centre, and the
rest of the world wuz a-revolvin' round him.

His face wuz worn and marked by the hand of
Time and Endeaver. But every mark wuz a good
one. The Soul, which is the best sculptor after all,
had chiselled into his features the marks of a deathless endeavor and struggle toward goodness, which
is God. Had marked it with the divine sweetness
and passion of livin' and toilin' for the good of
others.

He had gi'n his life jest as truly to seek and save
them that wuz lost as ever any old prophet and
martyr ever had sense the world began. But under
all these heavenly expressions that a keen eye could
trace in his good lookin' face, could be seen a deathly
weakness, the consumin' fire that wuz a-consumin'
of him.

Miss Timson wept when she see me, and Rosy
threw herself into my arms and sobbed. But I
gently ondid her arms from round my neck and give
Miss Timson to understand that I wuz there to
help 'em if I could.

"For," sez I softly, "the hull future time is left for
us to weep in, but the present wuz the time to
try to help Ralph S. Robinson."

Wall, I laid to, Josiah a-helpin' me nobly, a-pick-
in' burdock leaves or beet leaves, as the case might
be, and a-standin' by me nobly all through the follerin' night (that is, when he wuz awake).

Josiah and I took care on him all that night,
Miss Timson refusin' to give him into the charge
of underlin's, and we a-offerin' and not to be refused.

Wall, Josiah slept some, or that is, I s'poze he did

I didn't hear much from him from 10 P.M. to 5 A.M., only once I heard him murmur in his sleep, "buzz saw mill."

"DIDN'T SEE HOW FOLKS NEEDED SO MUCH SLEEP."

But every time I would come out into the settin' room where he sot and roust him up to get sunthin' for me, he would say, almost warmly—

"Samantha, that last remark of your'n wuz very powerful."

And I wouldn't waste my time nor hisen by tel·
lin' him that I hadn't made no remark, nor thought
on't.   I see it would hurt his feelin's, specilly as
he would add in haste—

"That he didn't see how folks needed so much
sleep; as for him, it wuz a real treat to keep awake
all night, now and then."

No, I would let it go, and ask him for burdock
or beet, as the case might be.   Truly I had enugh
on my mind and heart that night without disputin''
with my Josiah.

Ralph S. Robinson would lay lookin' like a
dead man some of the time, still and demute, and
then he would speak out in a strange language,
stranger than any I ever heard.   He would preach
sermons in that language, I a-knowin' it wuz a ser-
men by his gestures, and also by my feelin's.   And
then he would shet up his eyes and pray in that
strange, strange tongue, and anon breakin' out into
our own language.   And once he said :

"And now may the peace of God be with you all.
Amen.   The peace of God ! the peace ! the peace !"

His voice lingered sort o' lovin'ly over that word,
and I felt that he wuz a-thinkin' then of the real

peace, the onbroken stillness, outside and inside, that
he invoked.

Rosy would steal in now and then like a sweet
little shadow, and bend down and kiss her Pa, and
cry a little over his thin, white hands which wuz a-
lyin' on the coverlet, or else lifted in that strange
speech that sounded so curius to us, a-risin' up
out of the stillness of a Loontown spare bedroom
on a calm moonlit evenin'.

Wall, Friday and Saturday he wuz crazier'n a
loon, more'n half the time he wuz, but along Saturday afternoon the Doctor told us that the fever
would turn sometime the latter part of the night,
and if he could sleep then, and not be disturbed,
there would be a chance for his life.

Wall, Miss Timson and Rosy both told me how
the ringin' of the bells seemed to roust him up
and skair him (as it were) and git him all excited
and crazy. And they both wuz dretful anxius about
the mornin' bells which would ring when Ralph
would mebby be sleepin'. So thinkin' it wuz a case
of life and death, and findin' out who wuz the one
to tackle in the matter, I calmly tied on my bonnet and walked over and tackled him.

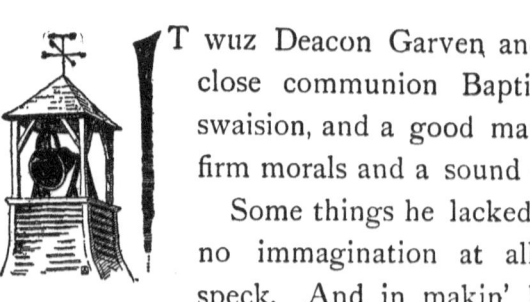IT wuz Deacon Garven and he wuz a close communion Baptist by perswaision, and a good man, so fur as firm morals and a sound creed goes.

Some things he lacked : he hadn't no immagination at all, not one speck. And in makin' him up, it seems as if he had a leetle more justice added to him to make up a lack of charity and pity. And he had a good deal of sternness and resolve gin him, to make up, I spoze, for a lack of tenderness and sweetness of nater.

A good sound man Deacon Garven wuz, a man who would cheat himself before he would cheat a neighber. He wuz jest full of qualities that would hender him from ever takin' a front part in a scandel and a tragedy. Yes, if more men wuz like Deacon Garven the pages of the daily papers would fairly suffer for rapiners, embezzlers, wife whippers, etc.

Wall, he wuz in his office when I tackled him. The hired girl asked me if I come for visitin' purposes or business, and I told her firmly, " business !"

So she walked me into a little office one side of the hall, where I spoze the Deacon transacted the business that come up on his farm, and then he wuz Justice of the Peace, and trustee of varius concerns (every one of 'em good ones).

He is a tall, bony man, with eyes a sort of a steel gray, and thin lips ruther wide, and settin' close together. And without lookin' like one, or, that is, without havin' the same features at all, the Deacon did make me think of a steel trap. I spoze it wuz because he wuz so sound, and sort o' firm. A steel trap is real firm when it lays hold and tries to be.

Wall, I begun the subject carefully, but straight to the pint, as my way is, by tellin' him that Ralph S. Robinson wuz a-layin' at death's door, and his life depended on his gettin' sleep, and we wuz afraid the bells in the mornin' would roust him up,

"THE DEACON DID MAKE ME THINK OF A STEEL TRAP."

and I had come to see if he would omit the ringin'
of 'em in the mornin'.

"Not ring the bells!" sez he, in wild amaze.
"Not ring the church bells on the Sabbath day?"

His look wuz skairful in the extreme, but I
sez—

"Yes, that is what I said, we beg of you as a
Christian to not ring the bells in the mornin'."

"A Christian! A Christian! Advise me as a
Christian to not ring the Sabbath bells!"

I see the idee skairt him. He wuz fairly pale
with surprise and horrow. And I told him agin',
puttin' in all the perticilers it needed to make the
story straight and good, how Ralph S. Robinson
had labored for the good of others, and how his
strength had gin out, and he wuz now a-layin' at
the very pint of death, and how his girl and his
sister wuz a-breakin' their hearts over him, and
how we had some hopes of savin' his life if he
could get some sleep, that the doctors said his life
depended on it, and agin I begged him to do what
we asked.

But the Deacon had begin to get over bein'
skairt, and he looked firm as anybody ever could,

as he sez : " The bells never hurt anybody, I know, for here I have lived right by the side of 'em for 20 years. Do I look broke down and weak ?" sez he.

" No," sez I, honestly. " No more than a grannit monument, or a steel trap."

"Wall," sez he, "what don't hurt me won't hurt nobody else."

" But," sez I, " folks are made up different." Sez I, " The Bible sez so, and what might not hurt you, might be the ruin of somebody else. Wuz you ever nervous ?" sez I.

" Never," sez he. And he added firmly, " I don't believe in nerves. I never did. There hain't no use in 'em."

" It wuz a wonder they wuz made, then," sez I. " As a generel thing the Lord don't make things there hain't no use on. Howsumever," sez I, " there hain't no use in disputin' back and forth on a nerve. But any way, sickness is so fur apart from health, that the conditions of one state can't be compared to the other; as Ralph S. Robinson is now, the sound of the bells, or any other loud noise means torture and agony to him, and, I am

afraid, death.   And I wish you would give orders
to not have 'em rung in the mornin'."

"Are you a professor?" sez he.

"Yes," sez I.

"What perswaision?"   sez he.

"Methodist Episcopal," sez I.

"And do you, a member of a sister church, which,
although it has many errors, is still a-gropin' after
the light! Do you counsel me to set aside the
sacred and time honored rules of our church, and
allow the Sabbath to go by unregarded, have the
sanctuary desecrated, the cause of religion languish—I cannot believe it.   Think of the wide-
spread desolation it would cause if, as the late
lamented Mr. Selkirk sung:

> "'The sound of the church-going bells,
> These valleys and hills never heard.'"

"No church, no sanctuary, no religius observ-
ances."

"Why," sez I, "that wouldn't hinder folks from
goin' to church.   Folks seem to get to theatres,
lectures, and disolvin' views on time, and better
time than they do to meetin'," sez I.   "In your
opinin' it hain't necessary to beat a drum and sound

on a bugle as the Salvation Army duz, to call folks to meetin'; you are dretful hard on them, so I hear."

"Yes, they make a senseless, vulgar, onnecessary racket, disturbin' and agrivatin' to saint and sinner."

"But," sez I, "they say they do it for the sake of religion."

"Religion hain't to be found in drum-sticks," sez he bitterly.

"No," sez I, "nor in a bell clapper."

"Oh," sez he, "that is a different thing entirely, that is to call worshippers together, that is necessary."

Sez I, "One hain't no more necessary than the other in my opinion."

Sez he, "Look how fur back in the past the sweet bells have sounded out."

"Yes," sez I candidly, "and in the sweet past they wuz necessary," sez I. "In the sweet past, there wuzn't a clock nor a watch, the houses wuz fur apart, and they needed bells. But now there hain't a house but what is runnin' over with clocks —everybody knows the time; they know it so much

that time is fairly a drug to 'em. Why, they time
themselves right along through the day, from breakfast to midnight. Time their meals, their business,
their pleasures, their music, their lessons, their visits,
their visitors, their pulse beats, and their dead beats.
They time their joys and their sorrows, and everything and everybody, all through the week, and
why should they stop short off Sundays? Why not
time themselves on goin' to meetin'? They do,
and you know it. There hain't no earthly need of
the bells to tell the time to go to meetin', no more
than there is to tell the time to put on the tea-kettle
to get supper. If folks want to go to meetin' they
will get there, bells or no bells, and if they don't
want to go, bells hain't a-goin' to get 'em started.

"Take a man with the Sunday *World* jest brung
in, a-layin' on a lounge, with his feet up in a chair,
and kinder lazy in the first place, bells hain't a-goin'
to start him.

"And take a woman with her curl papers not took
down, and a new religeus novel in her hand, and a
miliner that disapinted her the night before, and
bells hain't a-goin' to start her. No, the great bell
of Moscow won't start 'em.

"And take a good Christian woman, a widow, for instance, who loves church work, and has a good handsome Christian pasture, who is in trouble, lost

"Bells hain't a-goin' to start him."

his wife, mebby, or sunthin' else bad, and the lack of bells hain't a-goin' to keep that women back, no, not if there wuzn't a bell on earth."

"Oh, wall, wavin' off that side of the subject," sez

he (I had convinced him, I know, but he wouldn't
own it, for he knew well that if folks wanted to go
they always got there, bells or no bells). " But," sez
he wavin' off that side of the subject, " the ob-
servance is so time honored, so hallowed by tender
memories and associations all through the past."

" Don't you 'spoze, Deacon Garven," sez I, " that
I know every single emotion them bells can bring
to anybody, and felt all those memorys and associations. I'll bet, or I wouldn't be afraid to bet, if I believed in bettin', that there hain't a single emotion
in the hull line of emotions that the sound of them
bells can wake up, but what I have felt, and felt
'em deep too, jest as deep as anybody ever did, and
jest es many of 'em.   But it is better for me to do
without a upliftin', soarin' sort of a feelin' ruther than
have other people suffer agony."

" Agony !" sez he, " talk about their causin' agony,
when there hain't a more heavenly sound on earth."

" So it has been to me," sez I candidly. " To me
they have always sounded beautiful, heavenly.
Why," sez I, a-lookin' kinder fur off, beyond
Deacon Garven, and all other troubles, as thoughts
of beauty and insperation come to me borne out of

"A-LEANIN' OVER THE FRONT GATE ON A STILL SPRING MORNIN'."

the past into my very soul, by the tender memories of the bells—thoughts of the great host of believers who had gathered together at the sound of
the bells—the great army of the Redeemed—

'Some of the host have crossed the flood, and some
    are crossin' now,'

thinks I a-lookin' way off in a almost rapped way.
And then I sez to Deacon Garven in a low soft voice,
lower and more softer fur, than I had used to him,

   " Don't I know what it is to stand a-leanin' over
the front gate on a still spring mornin', the smell of
the lilacs in the air, and the brier roses.   A dew
sparklin' on the grass under the maples, and the
sunshine a-fleckin' the ground between 'em, and the
robins a-singin' and the hummin' birds a-hoverin'
round the honeysuckles at the door.   And over all
and through all, and above all clear and sweet, comin' from fur off a-floatin' through the Sabbath stillness, the sound of the bells, a-bringin' to us sweet
Sabbath   messages of love and joy.   Bringin'
memories too, of other mornin's as fair and sweet,
when other ears listened with us to the sound,
other eyes looked out on the summer beauty, and
smiled at the sound of the bells.

"Heavenly emotions, sweet emotions come to me on the melody of the bells, peaceful thoughts, inspirin' thoughts of the countless multitude that has flocked together at the sound of the bells. The aged feet, the eager youthful feet, the children's feet, all, all walkin' to the sound of the bells. Thoughts of the happy youthful feet that set out to walk side by side, at their ringin' sounds. Thoughts of the aged ones grown tired, and goin' to their long dreamless sleep to their solemn sound. Thoughts of the brave hero's who set out to protect us with their lives while the bells wuz ringin' out their approval of such deeds. Thoughts of how they pealed out joyfully on their return bearin' the form of Peace. Thoughts of how the bells filled the mornin' and evenin' air, havin' throbbed and beat with every joy and every pain of our life, till they seem a part of us (as it were) and the old world would truly seem lonesome without 'em.

"As I told you, and told you truly, I don't believe there is a single emotion in the hull line of emotions, fur or near, but what them bells have rung into my very soul.

"But such emotions, beautiful and inspirin' though

they are, can be dispensed with better than justice
and mercy can. Sweet and tender sentiment is
dear to me, truly, near and dear, but mercy and
pity and common sense, have also a powerful grip
onto my right arm, and have to lead me round a
good deal of the time.

" Beautiful emotion, when it stands opposed to
eternal justice, ort to step gently aside and let justice have a free road. Sentiment is truly sweet, but
any one can get along without it, take it right along
through the year, better than they can without sleep.

" You see if you can't sleep you must die, while a
person can worry along a good many years without
sentiment. Or, that is, I have been told they could
I don't know by experience, for I have always had
a real lot of it. You see my experience has been
such that I could keep sentiment and comfort too.
But my mind is such, that I have to think of
them that hain't so fortunate as I am.

" I have looked at the subject from my own standpoint, and have tried also to look at it through
others' eyes, which is the only way we can get a
clear, straight light on any subject. As for me, as
I have said, I would love to hear the sweet, far off

sound of the bells a-tremblin' gently over the hills
to me from Jonesville; it sounds sweeter to me
than the voices of the robins and swallers, a-comin'
home from the South in the spring of the year.
And I would deerly love to have it go on and on as
fur as my own feelins are concerned. But I have
got to look at the subject through the tired eyes,
and feel it through the worn-out nerves of others,
who are sot down right under the wild clamor of
the bells.

" What comes to me as a heavenly melody freighted
full of beautiful sentiment and holy rapture comes
to them as an intolerable agony, a-maddenin' discord, that threatens their sanity, that rouses 'em
up from their fitful sleep, that murders sleep—the
bells to them seem murderus, strikin' noisily with
brazen hands, at their hearts.

" To them tossin' on beds of nervous sufferin', who
lay for hours fillin' the stillness with horror, with
dread of the bells, where fear and dread of 'em
exceed the agony of the clangor of the sound when
it comes at last. Long nights full of a wakeful
horror and expectency, fur worse than the realiza-
tion of their imaginin's. To them the bells are a

"'Tossin' on beds of nervous sufferin'.'"

instrument of torture jest as tuff to bear as any of
the other old thumb screws and racks that wrung
and racked our old 4 fathers in the name of Religion.

"I have to think of the great crowd of humanity
huddled together right under the loud clangor of
the bells whose time of rest begins when the sun
comes up, who have toiled all night for our comfort and luxury. So we can have our mornin'
papers brought to us with our coffee. So we can
have the telegraphic messages, bringing us good
news with our toast. So's we can have some of
our dear ones come to us from distant lands in the
morning. I must think of them who protect us
through the night so we can sleep in peace.

"Hundreds and hundreds and hundreds of these,
our helpers and benafacters, work all night for our
sakes, work and toil. The least we can do for
these is to help 'em to the great Restorer, sleep,
all we can.

"Some things we can't do; we can't stop the
creakin' sounds of the world's work; the big roar
of the wheel of business that rolls through the
week days, can't be oiled into stillness; but Sundays

they might get a little rest.   Sunday is the only day
of rest for thousands of men and wimmen, nervous,
pale, worn by their week's hard toil.

" The creakin' of the wheels of traffic are stopped
on this day. They could get a little of the rest
they need to carry on the fight of life to help
support wife, child, father, husband ; but religeon is
too much for 'em—the religeon that the Bible
declares is mild, peacible, tender.   It clangs and
bangs and whangs at 'em till the day of rest is a
torment.

" Now the Lord wouldn't approve of this. I know
He wouldn't, for He was always tender and pitiful
full of compassion.   I called it religeon for oritory,
but it hain't religeon, it is a relict of old Bar-
berism who, under the cloak of Religeon, whipped
quakers and hung prophetic souls, that the secrets
of Heaven had been revealed to, secrets hidden
from the coarser, more sensual vision."

Sez Deacon Garven : " I consider the bells as
missionarys.   They help spread the Gospel."

"And," sez I, for I wuz full of my subject, and kep
him down to it all I could, " Ralph S. Robinson
has spread the Gospel over acres and acres of land,

and brung in droves and droves of sinners into the fold without the help of church or steeple, let alone bells, and it seems es if he ortn't to be tortured to death now by 'em."

" Wall," he said, " he viewed 'em as Gospel means, a..d he couldn't, with his present views of his duty to the Lord, omit 'em."

Sez I, " The Lord didn't use 'em. He got along without 'em."

" Wall," he said, " it wuz different times now."

Sez I, " The Lord, if He wuz here to-day, Deacon Garven, if He had bent over that form racked with pain and sufferin' and that noise of any kind is murderous to, He would help him, I know He would, for He wuz good to the sick, and tender hearted always."

" Wall, *I* will help him," sez Deacon Garven, " I will watch, and I will pray, and I will work for him."

Sez I, " Will you promise me not to ring the bells to-morrow mornin'; if he gets into any sleep at all durin' the 24 hours, it is along in the mornin', and I think if we could keep him asleep, say all the forenoon, there would be a chance for him. Will **you** promise me ?"

"Wall," sez he kinder meltin' down a little, " I will talk with the bretheren."

Sez I, " Promise me, Deacon Eben Garven, before you see 'em."

Sez he, " I would, but I am so afraid of bringin' the Cause of Religeon into contempt. And I dread meddlin' with the old established rules of the church."

Sez I, " Mercy and justice and pity wuz set up on earth before bells wuz, and I believe it is safe to foller 'em."

But he wouldn't promise me no further than to talk with the bretheren, and I had to leave him with that promise. As things turned out afterwuds, I wuz sorry, sorry es a dog that I didn't shet up Deacon Garven in his own smoke house, or cause him to be shet, and mount a guard over him, armed nearly to the teeth with clubs.

But I didn't, and I relied some on the bretheren.

Ralph wuz dretful wild all the forepart of the night. He'd lay still for a few minutes, and then he would get all rousted up, and he would set up in bed and call out some words in that strange tongue.

And he would lift up his poor weak right arm, strong then in his fever, and preach long sermons in that same strange curius language. He would preach his sermon right through, earnest and fervent as any sermon ever wuz. I would know it by the looks of his face. And then he would sometimes sing a little in that same singular language, and then he would lay down for a spell.

But along towards mornin' I see a change, his fever seemed to abate and go down some—very gradual, till just about the break of day, he fell into a troubled sleep—or it wuz a troubled sleep at first—but growin' deeper and more peaceful every minute. And along about eight o'clock he wuz a-sleepin' sweet for the first time durin' his sickness; it wuz a quiet restful sleep, and some drops of presperation and sweat could be seen on his softened features.

We all wuz as still, almost, as if we wuz automatoes, we wuz so afraid of makin' a speck of noise to disturb him. We kep almost breathless, in our anxiety to keep every mite of noise out of his room. But I did whisper to Rosy in a low still voice—

"THE LORD BE PRAISED, WE SHALL PULL HIM THROUGH."

"Your father is saved, the Lord be praised, we shall pull him through."

She jest dropped onto her knees, and laid her head in my lap and cried and wept, but soft and quiet so's it wouldn't disturb a mice.

Miss Timson wuz a-prayin', I could see that. She wuz a-returnin' thanks to the Lord for his mercy.

As for me, I sot demute, in that hushed and darkened room, a-watchin' every shadow of a change that might come to his features, with a teaspoon ready to my hand, to give him nourishment at the right time if he needed it, or medicine.

When all of a sudden—slam! bang! rush! roar! slam! slam! ding! dong! bang!!! come right over our heads the wild, deafening clamor of the bells.

Ralph started up wilder than ever because of his momentary repose. He never knew us, nor anything, from that time on, and after sufferin' for another 24 hours, sufferin' that made us all willin' to have it stop, he died.

And so he who had devoted his hull life to religeon wuz killed by it. He who had gin his hull life for the true, wuz murdered by the false.

"AND I THOUGHT HE WUZ PRONOUNCIN' A BENEDICTION ON THE SAVAGES."

His last move wuz to spread out his hands, and utter a few of them strange words, as if in benediction over a kneelin' multitude. And I thought then, and I think still, that he wuz pronouncin' a benediction on the savages. And I have always hoped that the mercy he besought from on High at that last hour brought down God's pity and forgiveness on all benighted savages, and bigoted ones, Deacon Garven, and the hull on 'em.

CHAPTER XXV.

HE very next day after I got home from Miss Timson'ses, we wimmen all met to the meetin' house agin as usial, for we knew very well that the very hardest and most arjuous part of our work lay before us.

For if it had been hard and tuckerin' to what it seemed the utmost limit of tucker, to stand up on a lofty barell, and lift up one arm, and scrape the ceilin', what would it be, so we wildly questioned our souls, and each other, to stand up on the same fearful hites, and iift *both* arms over our heads, and get on them fearful lengths of paper smooth.

I declare, when the hull magnitude of the task we had tackled riz before us, it skairt the hull on us, and nuthin' but our deathless devotion to the Methodist meetin' house, kep us from startin' off to our different homes on the run.

But lovin' it as we did, as the very apples in our

eyes, and havin' in our constant breasts a deter-
minate to paper that meetin' house, or die in the attempt, we made ready to tackle it.

"WE HAD TO WAIT FOR THE PASTE TO BILE."

Yet such wuz the magnitude of the task, and
our fearful apprehensions, that after we had looked
the ceilin' all over, and examined the paper—we all
sot down, as it were, instinctivly, and had a sort of
a conference meetin' (we had to wait for the paste
to bile anyway, it wuz bein' made over the stove in
the front entry).

The subject of our conference wuz, our great
work already accomplished, and to be undertook.
The big fair that wuz a-loomin' up ahead on us,
and what each one on us wuz a-goin' to do for this
same fair.

And jest how he would get holt of the money to
buy the materials that we had to have, to make up
the articles to carry to the fair.

We all knew and realized only too well, what
fearful hard work it wuz for a woman to get holt of
a cent of money to give away in charity; it is all she
can do, more'n a good deal of the time, to get money to
buy necessaries with—so we all set and confided in
each other and conferred, and laid on our plans,
and cut the edges offen the paper at the same time,
for we all felt that we couldn't set idle in such a
time es this.

Wall, cuttin' the edges offen the paper we found
wuz a long and petickuler job, and by the time
we got ready to paste the first breath—the paste
havin' been sot out to cool on the ground in a ten
quart pan—the very first move we made with the
brush, the handle come out.

Another delay and reverse for us, but we took

"WE ALL SET AND LAID ON OUR PLANS, AND CUT THE EDGES OFFEN THE
PAPER."

it middlin calm, and Miss Gowdy offered to be the
one to carry it back to Jonesville, and change it
that very afternoon—for we could not afford to buy
a new one, and we had the testimony of as many
as twenty-one or two pairs of eyes, that the handle
didn't come out by our own carelessness, but by its
own inherient weakness—so we spozed he would
swap it, we spozed so.   But it wuz arrainged before we disbanded (the result of our conference),
that the next mornin' we would each one on us
bring our offerin's to the fair, and hand 'em in to
the treasurer, so's she would know in time what to
depend on, and what she had to do with.

And we agreed (also the result of our conference) that we would, each one on us, tell jest how we
got the money and things to give to the fair.

And then we disbanded and started off home,
but I'll bet that each one on us, in a sort of secret
unbeknown way, gin a look on that lofty
ceilin', them dangerus barells, and that pile of
paper, and groaned a low melancholy groan all to
herself.

I know I did, and I know Submit Tewksbury did,
for I stood close to her and heard her.   But then to be

exactly jest, and not a mite underhanded, I ort mebby
to say, that her groan may be caused partly by the
fact that that aniversery of hern wuz a-drawin' so

"THE HANDLE COME OUT."

near. Yes, the very next day wuz the day jest 20
years ago that Samuel Danker went away from Submit Tewksbury to heathen lands. Yes, the next

day wuz the one that she always set the plate on for
him—the gilt edged chiny with pink sprigs.

But I'll bet that half or three quarters of that low
melancholy groan of her'n wuz caused by the hardness of the job that loomed up in front of us, and
the hull of mine wuz.

Wall, that night Josiah Allen wuz a-feelin' dretful neat, fer he had sold our sorell colt for a awful
big price.

It wuz a good colt; its mother wuz took sick when
it wuz a few days old, and we had brung it up as a
corset, or ruther I did, fer Josiah Allen at that time
had the rheumatiz to that extent that he couldn't
step his foot on the floor for months, so the care of
the corset come on me, most the hull on it, till it got
big enough to run out in the lot and git its own
livin'.

Night after night I used to get up and warm milk
for it, when it wuz very small, for it wuz weakly, and
we didn't know as we could winter it.

We kep it in a little warm shed offen the wood
house for quite a spell, but still I used to find it considerable cold when I would meander out there in a
icy night to feed it.

"I WOULD MEANDER OUT THERE IN A ICY NIGHT TO FEED IT."

But jest as it is always the way with wimmen, the more care I took on it, the more it needed me and depended on me, the better I liked it.

Till I got to likin' it so well that it wuzn't half so hard a job for me to go out to feed it in the night as it would have been to laid still in my warm bed and think mebby it wuz cold and hungry.

So I would pike out and feed it two or three times a night.

That is the nater of wimmen, the weaker it wuz and the humblier it wuz, and the more it needed me, the more I thought on it.

And as is the nater of man, Josiah Allen didn't seem to care so much about it while it wuz weak and humbly and spindlin'.

He told me time and agin, that I couldn't save it, and it never would amount to anythin', and wuzn't nothin' but legs any way, and lots of other slightin' remarks. And he'd call it "horse corset" in a kind of a light, triflin' way, that wuz apt to gaul a woman when she come back with icy night-gown and frosty toes and fingers, way along in the night.

He'd wake up, a-layin' there warm and comfortable on his soft goose feather piller and say to me:

"BEEN OUT TO TEND TO YOUR 'HORSE CORSET,' HAVE YOU?"

" Been out to tend to your ' horse corset,' have
you ?"

" *Horse corset /* Wall, what if it wuz ?"

Such language way along in the night, from a
warm comfortable pardner to a cold one, is apt to
make some words back and forth.

And then he'd speak of its legs agin, in the most
slightin' terms—and he'd ask me if didn't want its
picter took—etc., etc., etc.

(I believe one thing that ailed Josiah Allen wuz
he didn't want me to get up and get my feet so cold).

But, as I wuz a-sayin', though I couldn't deny some
of his words, for truly its legs did seem to be at the
least calculation a yard and a half long, specilly in
the night, why they'd look fairly pokerish.

And though I knew it wuz humbly still I perse-
vered, and at last it got to thrivin' and growin' fast.
And the likelier it grew, and the stronger, and the
handsomer, so Josiah Allen's likin' for it grew and
increased, till he got to settin' a sight of store by it.

And now it wuz a two-year-old, and he had sold
it for two hundred and fifteen dollars. It wuz spozed
it wuz goin' to make a good trotter.

Wall, seein' he had got such a big price for the

colt, and knowin' well that I wuz the sole cause of its bein' alive at this day, I felt that it wuz the best time in the hull three hundred and sixty-five days of the year to tackle him for sunthin' to give to the fair. I felt that the least he could do would be to give me ten or fifteen dollars for it. So consequently after supper wuz out of the way, and the work done up, I tackled him.

CHAPTER XXVI.

E wuz jest a-countin' out his money prior to puttin' it away in his tin box, and I laid the subject before him strong and eloquent, jest the wants and needs of the meetin' house, and jest how hard we female sisters wuz a-workin', and jest how much we needed some money to buy our ingregiencies with for the fair.

He set still, a-countin' out his money, but I know he heard me. There wuz four fifty dollar bills, a ten, and a five, and I felt that at the very least calculation he would hand me out the ten or the five, and mebby both on 'em.

But he laid 'em careful in the box, and then pulled out his old pocket-book out of his pocket, and handed me a ten cent piece.

I wuz mad. And I hain't a-goin' to deny that we had some words. Or at least I said some words

"HANDED ME A TEN CENT PIECE."

to him, and gin him a middlin' clear idee of how I felt on the subject.

Why, the colt wuz more mine than his in the first place, and I didn't want a cent of money for myself, but only wanted it for the good of the Methodist meetin' house, which he ort to be full as interested in as I wuz.

Yes, I gin him a pretty lucid idee of what my feelin's wuz on the subject—and spozed mebby I had convinced him. I wuz a-standin' with my back to him, a-ironin' a shirt for him, when I finished up my piece of mind. And thought more'n as likely as not he'd break down and be repentent, and hand me out a ten dollar bill.

But no, he spoke out as pert and cheerful as any-thing and sez he:

" Samantha, I don't think it is necessary for Chris-tians to give such a awful sight. Jest look at the widder's mit."

I turned right round and looked at him, holdin' my flat-iron in my right hand, and sez I:

"What do you mean, Josiah Allen? What are you talkin' about?"

" Why the widder's mit that is mentioned in Scrip-

"WHAT DO YOU MEAN, JOSIAH ALLEN? WHAT ARE YOU TALKIN' ABOUT?"

ter, and is talked about so much by Christians to this day. Most probable it wuz a odd one, I dare persume to say she had lost the mate to it. It specilly mentions that there wuzn't but one on 'em. And jest see how much that is talked over, and praised up clear down the ages, to this day. It couldn't have been worth more'n five cents, if it wuz worth that."

"How do you spell mit, Josiah Allen?" sez I.

"Why m-i-t-e, mit."

"I should think," sez I, "that that spells mite."

"Oh well, when you are a-readin' the Bible, all the best commentaters agree that you must use your own judgment. Mite! What sense is there in that? Widder's mite! There hain't any sense in it, not a mite."

And Josiah kinder snickered here, as if he had made a dretful cute remark, bringin' the "mite" in in that way. But I didn't snicker, no, there wuzn't a shadow, or trace of anything to be heard in my lineament, but solemn and bitter earnest. And I set the flat-iron down on the stove, solemn, and took up another, solemn, and went to ironin' on his shirt collar agin with solemnety and deep earnest.

"No," Josiah Allen continued, "there hain't no sense in that—but mit! there you have sense. All wimmen wear mits; they love 'em. She most probable had a good pair, and lost one on 'em, and then give the other to the church. I tell you it takes men to translate the Bible, they have such a realizin' sense of the weaknesses of wimmen, and how necessary it is to translate it in such a way as to show up them weaknesses, and quell her down, and make her know her place, make her know that man is her superior in every way, and it is her duty as well as privilege to look up to him."

And Josiah Allen crossed his left leg over his right one, as haughty and over bearin' a-crossin' as I ever see in my life, and looked up haughtily at the stove-pipe hole in the ceilin', and resoomed,

"But, as I wuz sayin' about her mit, the widder's, you know. That is jest my idee of givin', equinomical, savin', jest as it should be."

"Yes," sez I, in a very dry axent, most as dry as my flat-iron, and that wuz fairly hissin' hot. "She most probable had some man to advise her, and to tell her what use the mit would be to support a big meetin' house."

Oh, how dry my axent wuz. It wuz the very dryest, and most irony one I keep by me—and I keep dretful ironikle ones to use in cases of necessity.

" Most probable," sez Josiah, " most probable she did." He thought I wuz praisin' men up, and he acted tickled most to death.

" Yes, some man without any doubt, advised her, told her that some other widder would lose one of hern, and give hers to the meetin' house, jest the mate to hern. That is the way I look at it," sez he " and I mean to mention that view of mine on this subject the very next time they take up a subscription in the meetin' house and call on me."

But I turned and faced him then with the hot flat-iron in my hand, and burnin' indignation in my eys, and sez I:

" If you mention that, Josiah Allen, in the meetin' house, or to any livin' soul on earth, I'll part with you." And I would, if it wuz the last move I ever made.

But I gin up from that minute the idea of gettin' anything out of Josiah Allen for the fair. But I had some money of my own that I had got by sell-in' three pounds of geese feathers and a bushel of dried apples, every feather picked by me, and every quarter of apple pared and peeled and strung and dried by me. It all come to upwerds of seven dollars, and I took every cent of it the **next day out**

"HER CHILDREN ARE VERY HARD ON THEIR TROUSES."

of my under bureau draw and carried it to the meetin' house and gin it to the treasurer, and told 'em, at the request of the hull on 'em, jest how I got the money.

And so the hull of the female sisters did, as they handed in their money, told jest how they come by it.

Sister Moss had seated three pairs of children's trouses for young Miss Gowdy, her children are very hard on their trouses (slidin' down the banesters and such). And young Miss Gowdy is onexperienced yet in mendin', so the patches won't show And Sister Moss had got forty-seven cents for the job, and brung it all, every cent of it. with the exception of three cents she kep out to buy peppermint drops with. She has the colic fearful, and peppermint sometimes quells it.

Young Miss Gowdy wuz kep at home by some new, important business (twins). But she sent thirty-two cents, every cent of money she could rake and scrape, and that she had scrimped out of the money her husband had gin her for a woosted dress. She had sot her heart on havin' a ruffle round the bottom (he didn't give her enough for a overshirt), but she concluded to make it plain, and sent the ruffle money.

And young Sister Serena Nott had picked geese for her sister, who married a farmer up in Zoar. She

had picked ten geese at two cents apiece, and Serena that tender-hearted that it wuz like pickin' the
feathers offen her own back.

And then she is very timid, and skairt easy, and

"SHE HAD PICKED TEN GEESE AT TWO CENTS APIECE."

she owned up that while the pickin' of the geese almost broke her heart, the pickin' of the ganders
almost skairt her to death. They wuz very high
headed and warlike, and though she put a stockin'

over their heads, they would lift 'em right up, stockin' and all, and hiss, and act, and she said she picked 'em at what seemed to her to be at the resk of her life.

But she loved the meetin' house, so she grin and bore it, as the sayin' is, and she brung the hull of her hard earned money, and handed it over to the treasurer, and everybody that is at all educated knows that twice ten is twenty. She brung twenty cents.

Sister Grimshaw had, and she owned it right out and out, got four dollars and fifty-three cents by sellin' butter on the sly. She had took it out of the butter tub when Brother Grimshaw's back wuz turned, and sold it to the neighbors for money at odd times through the year, and besides gettin' her a dress cap (for which she wuz fairly sufferin'), she gin the hull to the meetin' house.

There wuz quite dubersome looks all round the room when she handed in the money and went right out, for she had a errent to the store.

And Sister Gowdy spoke up and said she didn't exactly like to use money got in that way.

But Sister Lanfear sprunted up, and brung Jacob

right into the argument, and the Isrealites who borrowed jewelry of the Egyptians, and then she
brung up other old Bible characters, and held 'em
up before us.

But still we some on us felt dubersome. And
then another sister spoke up and said the hull
property belonged to Sister Grimshaw, every mite of
it, for he wuzn't worth a cent when he married her—
she wuz the widder Bettenger, and had a fine property. And Grimshaw hadn't begun to earn what he
had spent sense (he drinks). So, sez she, it all be-
longs to Sister Grimshaw, by right.

Then the sisters all begin to look less dubersome.
But I sez:

" Why don't she come out openly and take the
money she wants for her own use, and for church
work, and charity ?"

" Because he is so hard with her," sez Sister Lanfear, " and tears round so, and cusses, and commits
so much wickedness. He is willin' she should dress
well—wants her to—and live well. But he don't want
her to spend a cent on the meetin' house. He is a
atheist, and he hain't willin' she should help on the
Cause of religeon. And if he knows of her givin' any

to the Cause, he makes the awfulest fuss, scolds, ana swears, and threatens her, so's she has been made sick by it, time and agin."

" Wall," sez I, " what business is it to him what she does with her own money and her own property ?"

I said this out full and square. But I confess that I did feel a little dubersome in my own mind. I felt that she ort to have took it more openly.

And Sister Grimshaw's sister Amelia, who lives with her (onmarried and older than Sister Grimshaw, though it hain't spozed to be the case, for she has hopes yet, and her age is kep). She had been and contoggled three days and a half for Miss Elder Minkley, and got fifty cents a day for contogglin'.

She had fixed over the waists of two old dresses, and contoggled a old dress skirt so's it looked most as well as new. Amelia is a good contoggler and a good Christian. And I shouldn't be surprised any day to see her snatched away by some widower or bachelder of proper age. She would be willin', so it is spozed.

Wall, Sister Henn kinder relented at the last, and brung two pairs of fowls, all picked, and tied up by their legs. And we thought it wuz kinder funny and

providential that one Henn should bring four more
of 'em.

But we wuz tickled, for we knew we could sell

" SUBMIT TEWKSBURY DID BRING THAT PLATE."

'em to the grocer man at Jonesville for upwerds of
a dollar bill.

And Submit Tewksbury, what should that good
little creeter bring, and we couldn't any of us hardly

believe our eyes at first, and think she could part
with it, but she did bring *that plate*. That pink
edged, chiny plate, with gilt sprigs, that she had
used as a memorial of Samuel Danker for so many
years. Sot it up on the supper table and wept in
front of it.

Wall, she knew old china like that would bring
a fancy price, and she hadn't a cent of money she
could bring, and she wanted to do her full part towerds helpin' the meetin' house along—so she tore
up her memorial, a-weepin' on it for hours, so we
spozed, and offered it up, a burnt chiny offerin' to the
Lord.

Wall, I am safe to say, that nothin' that had took
place that day had begun to affect us like that.

To see that good little creeter lookin' pale and
considerble wan, hand in that plate and never groan
over it, nor nothin', not out loud she didn't, but we
spozed she kep up a silent groanin' inside of her,
for we all knew the feelin' she felt for the plate.

It affected all on us fearfully.

But the treasurer took it, and thanked her almost
warmly, and Submit merely sez, when she wuz
thanked :

"Oh, you are entirely welcome to it, and I hope it will fetch a good price, so's to help the cause along."

And then she tried to smile a little mite. But I declare that smile wuz more pitiful than tears would have been.

Everybody has seen smiles that seemed made up, more than half, of unshed tears, and withered hopes, and disappointed dreams, etc., etc.

Submit's smile wuz of that variety, one of the very curiusest of 'em, too. Wall, she gin, I guess, about two of 'em, and then she went and sot down.

CHAPTER XXVII.

ND now I am goin' to relate the very singulerist thing that ever happened in Jonesville, or the world—although it is eppisodin' to tell on it now, and also a-gettin' ahead of my story, and hitchin', as you may say, my cart in front of my horse. But it has got to be told and I don't know but I may as well tell it now as any time.

Mebby you won't believe it. I don't know as I should myself, if it wuz told to me, that is, if it come through two or three   But any way it is the livin' truth.

That very night as Submit Tewksbury sat alone at her supper table, a-lookin' at that vacent spot on the table-cloth opposite to her, where the plate laid for Samuel Danher had set for over twenty years, she heard a knock at the door, and she got up hasty and wiped away her tears and opened the door.

A man stood there in the cold a-lookin' into the warm cosy little room. He didn't say nothin', he acted strange. He gin Submit a look that pierced clear to her heart (so they say). A look that had in it the crystallized love and longin' of twenty years of faithfulness and heart hunger and homesickness. It wuz a strange look.

Submit's heart begun to flutter, and her face grew red and then white, and she sez in a little fine tremblin' voice,

" Who be you ?"

And he sez,

" I am Samuel Danker."

And then they say she fainted dead away, and fell over the rockin' chair, he not bein' near enough to ketch her.

And he brung her to on a burnt feather that fell out of the chair cushion when she fell. There wuz a small hole in it, so they say, and the feather oozed out.

I don't tell this for truth, I only say that *they say* thus and so.

But as to Samuel's return, that I can swear to, and so can Josiah. And that they wuz married that

"I AM SAMUEL DANKER."

very night of his return, that too can be swore to.
A old minister who lived next door to Submit—
superanuated, but life enough in him to marry 'em
safe and sound, a-performin' the ceremony.

It made a great stir in Jonesville, almost enormus.

But they wuz married safe enough, and happy as
two gambolin' lambs, so they say. Any way Submit looks ten years younger than she did, and I
don't know but more. I don't know but she looks
eleven or twelve years younger, and Samuel, why
they say it is a perfect sight to see how happy he
looks, and how he has renewed his age.

The hull affair wuz very pleasin' to the Jonesvillians. Why there wuzn't more'n one or two villians
but what wuz fairly delighted by it, and they wuz
spozed to be envius.

And I drew severel morals from it, and drew 'em
quite a good ways too, over both religous and seckuler grounds.

One of the seckuler ones wuz drawed from her
not settin' the table for him that night, for the first
time for twenty years, givin' away the plate, and settin' on (with tears) only a stun chiny one for herself.

How true it is that if a female woman keeps dressed up slick, piles of extra good cookin' on hand,

"THEY DON'T COME!"

and her house oncommon clean, and she sets down
in a rockin' chair, lookin' down the road for company.

They don't come!

But let her on a cold mornin' leave her dishes on-washed, and her floors onswept, and put on her hus-band's old coat over her meanest dress, and go out (at his urgent request) to help him pick up apples before the frost spiles 'em. She a-layin' out to cook up some vittles to put on to her empty shelves when she goes into the house, she not a-dreamin' of com-pany at that time of day.

They come!

Another moral and a more religeus one. When folks set alone sheddin' tears on their empty hands, that seem to 'em to be emptied of all hope and hap-piness forever. Like es not some Divine Compen-sation is a-standin' right on the door steps, ready to enter in and dwell with 'em.

Also that when Submit Tewksbury thought she had gin away for conscience' sake, her dearest treas-ure, she had a dearer one gin to her—Samuel Dan-ker by name.

Also I drew other ones of various sizes, needless to recapitulate, for time is hastenin', and I have eppisoded too fur, and to resoom, and take up agin on my finger the thread of my discourse, that

"THEY COME."

I dropped in the Methodist meetin' house at Jones-ville, in front of the treasurer.

Wall, Submit brought the plate.

Sister Nash brought twenty-three cents all in pennys, tied up in the corner of a old handkercif. She is dretful poor, but she had picked up these here and there doin' little jobs for folks.

And we hadn't hardly the heart to take 'em, nor the heart to refuse takin' 'em, she wuz so set on givin' 'em. And it wuz jest so with Mahala Crane, Joe Cranes'es widder.

She, too, is poor, but a Christian, if there ever wuz one. She had made five pair of overhawls for the clothin' store in Loontown, for which she had received the princely revenue of fifty cents.

She handed the money over to the treasurer, and we wuz all on us extremely worked upon and wrought up to see her do it, for she did it with such a cheerful air. And her poor old calico dress she had on wuz so thin and wore out, and her dingy alpaca shawl wuz thin to mendin', and all darned in spots. We all felt that Mahala had ort to took the money to get her a new dress.

But we dasted none on us to say so to her. I

"SISTER ARVILLY LANFEAR, CANVASSIN' FOR A BOOK."

wouldn't have been the one to tell her that for a dollar bill, she seemed to be so happy a-givin' her part towerds the fair, and for the good of the meetin' house she loved.

Wall, Sister Meachim had earned two dollars above her wages—she is a millinner by perswasion, and works at a millinner's shop in Jonesville. She had earned the two dollars by stayin' and workin' nights after the day's work wuz done.

And Sister Arvilly Lanfear had earned three dollars and twenty-eight cents by canvassin' for a book. The name of the book wuz:

" The Wild, Wicked, and Warlike Deeds of Man."

And Arvilly said she had took solid comfort a-sellin' it, though she had to wade through snow and slush half way up to her knees some of the time, a-trailin' round from house to house a-takin' orders fer it. She said she loved to sell a book that wuz full of truth from the front page to the back bindin'.

As for me I wouldn't gin a cent for the book, and I remember we had some words when she come to our house with it. I told her plain that I wouldn't buy no book that belittled my companion, or tried to—sez I, "Arvilly, men are *jest* as good as wimmen and no better, not a mite better."

And Arvilly didn't like it, but I made it up to her

"OLD MISS ·BALCH."

in other ways.   I gin her some lamb's wool yarn for a pair of stockin's most immegietly afterwerds, and a half bushel of but'nuts.   She is dretful fond of but'nuts.

Wall, Sister Shelmadine had sold ten pounds of maple sugar, and brought the worth on it.

And Sister Henzy brung four dollars and a half, her husband had gin her for another purpose, but she took it for this, and thought there wuzn't no harm in it, as she laid out to go without the four dollars and a half's worth. It was fine shoes he had gin the money for, and she calculated to make the old ones do.

And Sister Henzy's mother, old Miss Balch, she is eighty-three years old, and has inflamatery rheumatiz in her hands, which makes 'em all swelled up and painful. But Sister Henzy said her mother had knit three pairs of fringed mittens (the hardest work for her hands she could have laid holt of, and which must have hurt her fearful). But Miss Henzy said a neighbor had offered her five dollars fer the three pairs, and so she felt it wuz her duty to knit 'em, to help the fair along. She is a very strong Methodist, and loved to forwerd the interests of Zion.

She wuz goin' to give every cent of the money to the meetin' house, so Sister Henzy said, all but ten cents, that she *had* to have to get Pond's Extract with, to bathe her hands. They wuz in a fearful state.

We all felt bad for old Miss Balch, and I don't believe there wuz a woman there but what gin her some different receipt fer helpin' her hands, besides sympathy, lots and lots of it, and pity.

Wall, Sister Sypher'ses husband is clost, very clost with her. She don't have anythin' to give, only her labor, as well off as they be. And now he wuz so wrapped up in that buzz saw mill business that she wouldn't have dasted to approach him any way, that is, to ask him for a cent.

Wall, what should that good little creeter do but gin all the money she had earned and saved durin' the past year or two, and had laid by for emergincies or bunnets.

She had got over two dollars and seventy-five cents, which she handed right over to the treasurer of the fair to get materials for fancy work. When they wuz got she proposed to knit three pairs of men's socks out of zephyr woosted, and she said she was goin' to try to pick enough strawberrys to buy a pair of the socks for Deacon Sypher. She said it would be a comfort for her to do it, for they would be so soft for the Deacon's feet.

Wall, Sister Gowdy wuz the last one to gin in

dress gin to her by her uncle out to the Ohio. It
wuz gin her to mourn for her mother-in-law in.

And what should that good, willin' creeter do but
bring that dress and gin it to the fair to sell.

We hated to take it, we hated to like dogs, for
we knew Sister Gowdy needed it.

But she would make us take it; she said "if her
Mother Gowdy wuz alive, she would say to
her,

" Sarah Ann, I'd ruther not be mourned for in
bombazeen than to have the dear old meetin' house in
Jonesville go to destruction. Sell the dress and
mourn fer me in a black calico."

That Sister Gowdy said would be, she knew,
what Mother Gowdy would say to her if she wuz
alive.

And we couldn't dispute Sarah Ann, for we all knew
that old Miss Gowdy worked for the meetin' house
as long as she could work for anything. She loved
the Methodist meetin' house better than she loved
husband or children, though she wuz a good' wife
and mother. She died with cramps, and her last
request wuz to have this hymn sung to her funeral:

"I LOVE THY KINGDOM, LORD."

> " I love thy kingdom, Lord,
>   The house of thine abode,
>   The church our dear Redeemer bought
>   With His most precious blood."

The quire all loved Mother Gowdy, and sung it accordin' to her wishes, and broke down, I well remember, at the third verse—

> " For her my tears shall fall,
>   For her my prayers ascend,
>   For her my toil and life be given,
>   Till life and toil shall end."

The quire broke down, and the minister himself shed tears to think how she had carried out her belief all her life, and died with the thought of the church she loved on her heart and its name on her lips.

Wall, the dress would sell at the least calculation for eight dollars; the storekeeper had offered that, but Sarah Ann hoped it would bring ten to the fair.

It wuz a cross to Sarah Ann, so we could see, for she had loved Mother Gowdy dretful well, and loved the uncle who had gin it to her, and she hadn't a nice black dress to her back.

But she said she hadn't lived with Mother Gowdy twenty years for nothin', and see how she would always sacrifice anything and everything but principle for the good of the meetin' house.

Sister Gowdy is a good-hearted woman, and we all on us honored her for this act of hern, though we felt it wuz almost too much for her to do it.

Wall, Sister Gowdy wuz the last one to gin in her testimony, and havin' got through relatin' our experiences we proceeded to business and paperin'.

CHAPTER XXVIII.

ISTER Sylvester Bobbet and I had been voted on es the ones best qualified to lead off in the arjeous and hazerdous enterprize.

And though we deeply felt the honor they wuz a-heapin' on to us, yet es it hes been, time and agin, in other high places in the land, if it hadn't been fer duty that wuz a-grippin' holt of us, we would gladly have shirked out of it and gin the honor to some humble but worthy constituent.

Fer the lengths of paper wuz extremely long, the ceilin' fearfully high, and oh! how lofty and tottlin' the barells looked to us. And we both on us, Sister Sylvester Bobbet and I, had giddy and dizzy spells right on the ground, let alone bein' perched up on barells, a-liftin' our arms up fur, fur beyond the strength of their sockets.

But duty wuz a-callin' us, and the other wimmen

"WE FELT NERVED UP TO DO OUR BEST."

also, and it wuzn't for me, nor Sister Sylvester Bobbet to wave her nor them off, or shirk out of haz-
erdous and dangerous jobs when the good of the
Methodist Meetin' House wuz at the Bay.

No, with as lofty looks as I ever see in my life
(I couldn't see my own, but I felt 'em), and with as
resolute and martyrous feelin's as ever animated two
wimmen's breasts, Sister Sylvester Bobbet and I
grasped holt of the length of paper, one on each end
on it, Sister Arvilly Lanfear and Miss Henzy a-
holdin' it up in the middle like Aaron and Hur
a-holdin' up Moses'ses arms. We advanced and
boldly mounted up onto our two barells, Miss Gowdy and Sister Sypher a-holdin' two chairs stiddy
for us to mount up on.

Every eye in the meetin' house wuz on us. We
felt nerved up to do our best, even if we perished
in so doin', and I didn't know some of the time but
we would fall at our two posts. The job wuz so
much more wearin' and awful than we had foreboded,
and we had foreboded about it day and night for
weeks and weeks, every one on us.

The extreme hite of the ceilin'; the slipperyness
and fragility of the lengths of paper; the fearful
hite and tottlin'ness of the barells; the dizzeness

that swept over us at times, in spite of our marble efforts to be calm. The dretful achin' and strainin' of our armpits, that bid fair to loosen 'em from their four sockets. The tremenjous responsibility that laid onto us to get the paper on smooth and on-wrinkled.

It wuz, takin' it altogether, the most fearful and wearisome hour of my hull life.

Every female in the room held her breath in deathless anxiety (about thirty breaths). And every eye in the room wuz on us (about fifty-nine eyes—Miss Shelmadine hain't got but one workin' eye, the other is glass, though it hain't known, and must be kep).

Wall, it wuz a-goin' on smooth and onwrinkled —smiles broke out on every face, about thirty smiles —a half a minute more and it would be done, and done well. When at that tryin' and decisive mo-ment when the fate of our meetin' house wuz, as you may say, at the stake, we heard the sound of hur-ryin' feet, and the door suddenly opened, and in walked Josiah Allen, Deacon Sypher, and Deacon Henzy followed by what seemed to me at the time to be the hull male part of the meetin' house.

But we found out afterwerds that there wuz a few

men in the meetin' house that thought wimmen ort
to set; they argued that when wimmen had been
standin' so long they out to set down; they wuz
good dispositioned. But as I sez at the time, it
looked to us as if every male Methodist in the land
wuz there and present.

They wuz in great spirits, and their means wuz triumphant and satisfied.

They had jest got the last news from the Conference in New York village, and had come down in a
body to disseminate it to us.

They said the Methodist Conference had decided
that the seven wimmen that had been stood up there
in New York for the last week, couldn't set, that
they wuz too weak and fraguile to set on the Conference.

And then the hull crowd of men, with smiles and
haughty linements, beset Josiah to read it out to us.

So Josiah Allen, with his face nearly wreathed
with a smile, a blissful smile, but as high headed a
one as I ever see, read it all out to us. But he
should have to hurry, he said, for he had got to carry
the great and triumphant news all round, up as fur
as Zoar, if he had time.

And so he read it out to us, and as we see that

"THE METHODIST CONFERENCE HAD DECIDED THAT WIMMEN WUZ TOO
WEAK TO SET."

that breadth wuz spilte, we stopped our work for a minute and heard it.

And after he had finished it, they all said it wuz a masterly dockument, the decision wuz a noble one, and it wuz jest what they had always said. They said they had always known that wimmen wuz too weak, her frame wuz too tender, she was onfitted by Nater, in mind and in body to contend with such hardship. And they all agreed that it would be puttin' the men in a bad place, and takin' a good deal offen their dignity, if the fair sex had been allowed by them to take such hardships onto 'em. And they sez, some on 'em, " Why! what are men in the Methodist meetin' house for, if it hain't to guard the more weaker sect, and keep cares offen 'em ?"

And one or two on 'em mentioned the words, " cooin' doves " and " sweet tender flowerets," as is the way of men at such times. But they wuz in too big a hurry to spread themselves (as you may say) in this direction. They had to hurry off to tell the great news to other places in Jonesville and up as fer as Loontown and Zoar.

But Sister Arvilly Lanfear, who happened to be a-standin' in the door as they went off, she said she heard 'em out as fer as the gate a-congratilatin' themselves and the Methodist Meetin' House and the nation on the decesion, for, sez they,

" Them angels hain't strong enough to set, and I've known it all the time."

And Sister Sylvester Gowdy sez to me, a-rubbin' her achin' armpits—

" If they are as beet out as we be they'd be glad to set down on anything—a Conference or anything else."

And I sez, a-wipin' the presperatin of hard labor from my forwerd,

" For the land's sake! Yes! I should think so."

And then with giddy heads and strainin' armpits we tackled the meetin' house agin.

The End

PUBLISHERS' APPENDIX.

In view of the frequent reference, in this work, to the discussion in and preceding the General Conference of the Methodist Episcopal Church of 1888, in regard to the admission of women delegates, the publishers have deemed it desirable to append the six following addresses delivered on the floor of the Conference during the progress of that discussion.

The General Conference of the Methodist Episcopal Church is the highest legislative body of that denomination. It is composed of delegates, both ministerial and lay, the former being elected by the Annual Conferences, and the latter by Lay Electoral Conferences. The sessions of the General Conference are held quadrennially.

Prior to the session held in May, 1888, in New York City, women delegates were elected, one each, by the four following Lay Electoral Conferences—namely, The Kansas Conference, The Minnesota Conference, The Pittsburgh Conference, and The Rock River Conference. Protest was made against the admission of these delegates on the ground that the admission of women delegates was not in accord with the constitutional provisions of the Church, embodied in what are termed the Restrictive Rules. A special Committee on the Eligibility of Women to Member-

ship in the General Conference was appointed, consisting
of seventeen members, to whom the protest was referred.
On May 3d the Committee reported adversely to the admission of the four women delegates, the report alleging
"that under the Constitution and laws of the Church as
they now are, women are not eligible as lay delegates in
the General Conference." From the discussion following
this report, and lasting several days, the following six addresses, three in favor of and three against the admission
of the women delegates, are selected and presented, with
a few verbal corrections, as published in the official
journal of the Conference.

ADDRESS OF REV. DR. THEODORE L. FLOOD.

I AM in accord, in the main, with Dr. Potts and Dr. Brush in what they have said on this question, unless it may be where my friend who last spoke said that these ladies, these elected delegates to this body, ought to be admitted. My judgment and my conscience before the Discipline of the Methodist Episcopal Church and the Restrictive Rules is that these women elected by these Electoral Conferences are in this General Conference.

Their names may not have been called when the roll was called, and yet it was distinctly stated by the Bishop presiding that morning that they would be called, and the challenges presented with their names; and afterward demanded it, the names of these delegates who were not enrolled with the others were called, and the protests were read. Their names have been called as members of this body, and they are simply here as " challenged" members. From that standpoint this question must be discussed, and any disposition of this case under the circumstances must be in this direction. These women delegates must be put out of this General Conference if they are not granted the rights and privileges of members here. It is not a question of "admitting" them. Before this report, before the bar of history, we stand, and will be called upon to vote and act, and millions of people will hold us responsible, and I dare say that our votes will be recorded as to whether they shall be "put out" or "stay in."

Why, sir, the government of the Methodist Episcopal Church exists for the ministry and membership of the Church. The ministry and the membership of the Church do not exist for the government. The world was made for man, and not man for the world. That is the fundamental idea in the government of God, as He treats us as human beings. That is the fundamental idea in the government of the Methodist Episcopal Church, as we are enlisted in the support of that government as ministers and members of the Church. Now under this system of ecclesiastical government a time came in our history when we submitted a grave question to the membership of the Church. It was not a question simply of petition, asking the membership to send petitions up to the General Conference. On the contrary, it was submitting a constitutional question not simply to the male members of the Church, for that grand and noble man of the Methodist Church, Dr. David Sherman of the New England Conference, moved himself to strike out the word "male" from the report of the Committee on Lay Delegation. It came to a vote, and it was stricken out, two to one in the vote. When that was done, then the General Conference of our Church submitted to the membership of the Church the question of lay delegation. But back of the question of lay delegation was as grave a question, and that was granting the right of suffrage to the women of the Church. The General Conference assumed the responsibility of giving to the women the right to vote. It may be questioned this way; it may be explained that way; but the facts abide that the General Conference granted to the women of the Church the right to vote on a great and important question in ecclesiastical law. Now if you run a parallel along the line of our government—and it has often been said that there are parallels in the government of the United States corresponding to lines of legislation and legislative action in the government of the Church—you will find that the right of suffrage in the country at the ballot-box has been a gradual growth. One of the most sacred rights that a man, an American citizen, enjoys is the right to cast a ballot for the man or men he would have legislate for him; and for no trivial reason can that right, when once granted to the American citizen, be taken away from him. Go to the State of Massachusetts, and trace the history of citizen suffrage, and you find it commenced in this way: First, a man could vote under the government there who was a member of the Church. Next, he could vote if he were a freeholder. A little later on he could vote if he paid a poll-tax. In the government, and under the legislation of our Church, first the women were granted the right to vote on the principle of lay delegation, not on the "plan" of lay delegation, but on the "principle" of lay delegation. That was decided by Bishop Simpson in the New Hampshire Conference, and by Bishop Janes afterward in one of the New York Conferences. On the principle of lay delegation, the women of the Church were granted the right of suffrage; presently they appeared in the Quarterly Conference, to vote as class-leaders, stewards, and Sunday-school superintendents; and it created a little excitement.

a feverish state of feeling in the Church, and the General Conference simply passed a resolution or a rule interpreting that action on the part of women claiming this privilege in the Quarterly Conference as being a " right," and it was continued. Presently, as the right of suffrage of women passed on and grew, they voted in the Electoral Conferences, and there was no outcry made against it. I have yet to hear of any Bishop in the Church, or any presiding elder, or any minister challenging the right of women to vote in Electoral Conferences or Quarterly Conferences; and yet for sixteen years they have been voting in these bodies; voting to send laymen here to legislate; to send laymen to the General Conference to elect Bishops and Editors and Book Agents and Secretaries. They come to where votes count in making up this body; they have been voting sixteen years, and only now, when the logical result of the right of suffrage that the General Conference gave to women appears and confronts us by women coming here to vote as delegates, do we rise up and protest. I believe that it is at the wrong time that the protest comes. It should have come when the right to vote was granted to women in the Church. It is sixteen years too late, and as was very wisely said by Dr. Potts, the objection comes not so much from the Constitution of the Church as from the " constitution of the men," who challenge these women.

Now, sir, another parallel. You take the United States Government just after the war, when the colored people of the South, the freedmen of our land, unable to take care of themselves, their friends, that had fought the battles of the war, in Congress determined that they should be protected, if no longer by bayonets and cannon, that they should be protected by placing the ballot in their hands, and the ballot was placed in the hands of the freedman of the South by the action of the National Congress, Congress submitting a constitutional amendment to the legislatures of the States; and when enough of them had voted in favor of it, and the President had signed the bill, it became an amendment to the Constitution of the United States, granting to the people of the South, who had been disfranchised, the right of suffrage.

Now, what does the right of suffrage do? It carries with it the right to hold office. Where women have the privileges of voting on the school question, they are granted the privilege of being school directors, holding the office of superintendents, and the restriction on them stops at that point under statute law. If you go a little further you will find that when the freedmen were enfranchised, and they sent men of their own color to the House of Representatives, did that body say "stop!" "we protest, you cannot come in because of illegality"? No. They were admitted on the face of their credentials because they had first been granted the right of suffrage. When men of their color went to the United States Senate and submitted their credentials, they were not protested against, but they were admitted as members of the United States Senate on the face of their credentials. And why? Because the right of suffrage granted to the freedmen of the South under a constitutional amendment of the nation, carried with it the right of the men whom we fought to free, and did free, in an awful war, to hold office in the nation. Now, sir, you must interpret the law somewhat by the spirit of the times in which you live. That is a mistaken notion to say that you must always go to the men that made the law to get the interpretation of it. If that were true, would it not always be wise for legislators to give their affidavits and place on file their interpretation of the law they had confirmed, and placed on the statute books? There are legal gentlemen in this body who will tell you that it goes for very little when you come to interpret law. And yet you will find this to be true, that a law must be interpreted somewhat by the spirit of the time in which you live. Why, twenty years ago, when the General Conference handed the question of lay delegation down to the Annual Conferences, and the members of our Church, there was not a woman practising law in the Supreme Court of the United States. Go back through the history of jurisprudence of this country and in England, and you will find that it had never been known that a woman practised law in the Supreme Court of this country or England. But to-day women have been admitted to practise law in the Supreme Court of the United States. No amendment to the Constitution of the United States had to be adopted in order to secure this privilege for them. But this is true, that the judges of the Supreme Court, by a more liberal interpretation of the Constitution of the United States, said, "Women may be officers of the Supreme Court, and may practise law there." The same kind of a spirit, in interpreting the Discipline and the Restrictive Rules of the Discipline of the Church, will place these women delegates in this body where they have been sent. The same thing is true of the Supreme Court of Pennsylvania and in the Courts of Philadelphia. There is no way out, as my judgment sees, and as my conscience tells me, since before the government of God man and woman are equally responsible. There is no way out of this dilemma for this General Conference, but to say that these women delegates shall sit in this body, where they have been sent, and where their names have been called.

Why, take the missionary operations. The Woman's Missionary Society is to-day raising more money and doing more missionary work than the Parent Missionary Society did fifty years ago. And yet men legislate concerning the missionary operations of women, and give them no voice directly in this body.

We bring up the temperance question here against license and in favor of Prohibition, and we pass our resolutions after we have given our discussions, and yet the Methodist Church has the honor of having in the ranks of her membership— (Time called.)

ADDRESS OF REV. DR. JAMES M. BUCKLEY.

MR. PRESIDENT, while the last speaker was on the floor, a modification of a passage of Scripture occurred to me, " The enemy cometh in like a flood, but I will lift up a standard against him." It is somewhat peculiar that he should begin by making a statement about one of the most honored names in American Methodism, a statement that has been published in the papers, and that nine tenths of this body knew as well as he did. It must have been intended as a part of his argument, and I regard it as of as much force as anything he said after it. But in point of fact the question does not turn upon the person, but upon the principle. I have received an anonymous letter containing the following among other things, " Beware how you attack the holy cause of woman. Do you not know that obstacles to progress are rem-o-o-v-e-d out of the way?" The signature of that letter is ingenious. I cannot tell whether it was a man or a woman, for it reads as follows, "A Lover of your Soul and of Woman." Now, Mr. President, the only candlestick that ought to be removed out of its place is the candlestick that contains a candle that does not burn the pure oil of truth. And I believe, sir, that with the best of intentions the three speakers who have appeared have given us three chapters in different styles of a work of fiction, and it is my duty to undertake to show where they have slipped. The Apocrypha says, " An eloquent man is known far and near; but a man of understanding discerneth where he slippeth." I have no claim to eloquence ; never pretended to have any ; but I have a claim to some knowledge of Methodist history, to some ability to state my sentiments, and to be without any fear of the results, either present or prospective.

Now, Mr. President, you notice from my friends that if they cannot command the judgment of the Conference they propose to say the women are in, and defy us to put them out. I am sorry that my friend did not take in the full significance of that. And they say that everybody who has a certificate in form is in until he is put out. Why, they do not discriminate between ordinary contested cases and a case where the constitutional point is involved. If these women have a right here, they have had it from the beginning by the Constitution. It is not a contested case as to whether John Smith was voted for by the people who ought to vote for him, or in the right place. Now, they talk of bringing up documents here. I wrote to the Hon. George F. Edmunds, the most distinguished member of the United States Senate, and simply put this question, If a certificate of election in the Senate shows anything that would prove the person unworthy of a seat, would he be seated pending an investigation or not ? He did not know what it referred to, and I read it *verbatim*. I never mentioned the name of Methodist, and I read *verbatim* from his letter :

" No officer of the Senate has any right to decide any such question, and, therefore, every person admitted to a seat is admitted by, in fact, a vote of the Senate. The ordinary course in the Senate is, when the cre-

dentials appear to be perfectly regular, and there is no notorious and un-
disputed fact or circumstance against the qualifications and election of a
senator, to admit him at once and settle the question of his right afterward.   But there have been cases in which the Senate declined to admit
a claimant holding a regular certificate upon the ground that enough was
known to the Senate to justify its declining to receive him until an inquiry should be had.   Very truly yours,

"GEORGE F. EDMUNDS."

Now, Mr. President, all this twaddle about the women
being in is based upon the pretence that one woman is
there now.   The certificate shows that they were women,
though as yet no action has been taken in regard to them
at all.   If they were in, they were in with a constitutional challenge.   I champion the holy cause of women.   I
stand here to champion their cause against their being introduced into this body without their own sex having had
the opportunity of expressing their opinion upon the subject.   I stand here to protect them against being connected with movements without law or contrary to law, and
those who wish to bring them in and those who say
it is the constitution of the man and prejudice (my friend,
Dr. Potts, said prejudice), they are persons, indeed, to
stand up here as *par excellence* the champions of women!
Is it the constitution of the men?   Have you read the
letter of Mrs. Caroline Wright in the *Christian Advocate*,
one of our most distinguished American Methodist wom-
en?   She does not wish to see them here.   It is the
constitution of the woman in that case, and I am opposed
to their being admitted until the general sentiment of the
women and the men of our Church have an opportunity
of being heard upon it.

Now, Mr. President, note these facts. . . . This is not

a fact, but my opinion. 'I solemnly believe that there was never an hour in the Methodist Episcopal Church when it was in so great danger as it is to-day, not on account of the admission of these women, two of whom I believe to be as competent to sit in judgment on this question as any man on this floor. That is not the question, as I propose to show. I assert freely, here and now, if the women are in under the Restrictive Rules, no power ought to put them out. If they are not in under the Restrictive Rules, nothing has been done since, in my judgment, bearing upon it. I am astounded that these brethren fancy that this question has no bearing at all on the mean· ing of that rule. That is a wonderful thing. But we affirm that when the Church voted to introduce lay dele- gation, it not only did not intend to introduce women, but it did intend to fill up the whole body with men. That is what we affirm. If we can prove it, it is a tower of help to us. If we cannot prove it, we cannot make out our case. But our contention is, that the Church did not undertake to put women in, and it did undertake to fill up the capacities and relations of the body with men. Now, look at it. No man goes to the dictionary to find the meaning of the word "layman." There is not a man that can find out the meaning of our Restrictive Rules from the dictionary. No living man can make out the meaning of a word in the Restrictive Rules from Web- ster's dictionary. You must get it from the history of the Church. Who is the "General Superintendent" by Web- ster or Worcester? The Methodist Episcopacy is the thing that is protected by the Restrictive Rules. The dictionary does not tell how the Chartered Fund shall be

taken care of. Now they talk about laymen. They do
not seem, I think, to understand the history of the thing.
Some of them do not appear to understand the history of
the English language. Why was the word " layman" ever
introduced? Because there was a separate class of clergymen in the world, but there was not a class of clergywom-
en in the world. If there had been, there would have been
a term for laywomen and for clergywomen. And the
word was invented to distinguish the laymen from the
*clergy*men. Had there been clergywomen, there would
have been laywomen. The " laity" means all the people,
men, women, and children. A woman is one of the laity,
and so is every child in the country or in the Church one
of the laity. But when you speak of man acting as a
unit he is a layman, but you never say a laywoman. You
say: a woman. Abraham Lincoln said, " All these
things are done and suffered, that government of the people, for the people, and by the people should not perish
from the earth." Now, people, the dictionary says, are
men, women, and children. Did Abraham Lincoln mean
that any women or children can take any part in the
government of the nation? No, no, no! He meant this.
When he stood up and delivered his inaugural speech,
he said this, " The intent of the lawmaker is the law."

I give them something from one of the greatest lawyers
that ever lived to think of awhile—John Selden: " The
only honest meaning of any word is the intent of the
man that wrote it." At the time that the plan of lay
delegation was adopted, there was not a single Conference
of the Church on this wide globe, not one that distinguished between the ministry and the laity that allowed

women to take any part in its law-making body. Some one will talk about the Quakers. But they deny the existence of the Church, the sacraments of the Church, and make no distinction between the ministry and the laity. Let them get up and show that there was ever one Church in the world worthy of the name that allowed women to make its laws. There is not one to-day. Let them name a Church, let them name one that has allowed women in its law-making body; and yet such is the blinding power of gush that men will say that our fathers all understood it and proposed to put women in. The fact is, that they only proposed to allow them to put us in. As soon as the General Conference adjourned the women made an appeal in a public statement. They were asked to vote for lay delegation, and were told that then they could set the Church right. The opponents appealed to them to vote against it on the ground that it would not make any difference to them. James Porter, Daniel Curry, Dr. Hodgson (Professor Little thinks he was the greatest of them all) wrote a series of articles in the *Advocate*, and it never occurred to them that the women could come into the General Conference. Lay delegation was only admitted by 33 votes. Had there been a change of 33 votes they would not have come in. Every member of the New York East Conference knows that Dr. Curry's influence was so powerful that he could almost get a majority against it. And they know if any one had set up an opposition to it on this ground, the whole Conference would have voted against the movement, and that if it had not been for Bishop Ames and Bishop Janes, who went to the Wyoming Conference where the majority

was opposed to lay delegation, and by their influence
there converted my friend Olin and others, he knows
that if this matter of the women had been in or understood, the whole Conference would have been against it.
It would not have been possible. Dr. Potts says that it
is prejudice. Nothing of the kind. Do you know there
are 12,000 Methodist ministers that are ciphers all the
time except when they vote for delegates? Are you going to presume that when the Church has a multitude of
members, that it is going to sit here and change, by an
interpretation, a Restrictive Rule, or put in what was never
in, and never understood to be in ? The Restrictive Rule
fills up the ministerial delegates. Every time you put a
woman in, you put a man out. This subject has never
come up here before. The question is this, Do those
Restrictive Rules mean anything ? If they do, you cannot put in anything that the fathers did not put in. And
if you put in women as lawmakers; if you can read those
Rules and put them in there, you can change any one of
the Restrictive Rules by a majority of one. And I want
to say to you, that if you do it, you will prove to the
Methodist Episcopal Church that the sole protection we
have against the caprice of a majority of the General Conference is not worth the paper it is written on. All you
have to do is to get a majority of the Conference against
the Episcopacy, and then put any interpretation, and
then you get a few women admitted, and this you call the
progress of the age. Mr. Chairman, I believe in progress,
and when the Church progresses far enough, it can change
this law in a constitutional way. But it has not yet gone
far enough. These men believe that the Church has

never done it, or that it is best. Dr. Flood said that they must be brought in in the light of progress. I affirm that Dr. Flood's arguments all point in that direction—they must be interpreted in the light of progress. When you do that you have got a despotism. I want to go back to my constituents and say this: I exercise all the power that our Charter gives me. But at the moment that anything is proposed, and we put in what the fathers did not have before their eyes, at that moment I stop and say, Thus far, but no farther. A despotism is a despotism, whether it is a despotism without restraint, the Czar with his wife, the Czar without his wife. You will turn this house into a despotism, and you will find it difficult to defend Methodism by its peculiar Constitution before the American people.

If you want women in, there is another way to bring them in. Send the question around as you did for lay delegation. There was only a doubt in the General Conference of 1868, and yet they had a sense of candor. John M'Clintock fought in favor of taking them in. But he said, " I think it best to send the question around." True progress is not gained in any other way. Some prefer a shorter cut. Let me say to you, " He that cometh in by the door," the same hath a right to come in ; but he that cometh in another way, is not as respectable as in the other case.

ADDRESS OF REV. DR. A. B. LEONARD.

MR. CHAIRMAN, unfortunately for me, I have received no anonymous letters. And so I have nothing either sensational or startling with which to introduce my speech. I shall not speak this morning under any fear of being removed as an obstruction, or of having my future prospects blasted. It is my privilege, therefore, to speak to you this morning upon this subject calmly and dispassionately, having no motive to either suppress or exaggerate the truth. The party who wrote Dr. Buckley, threatening to remove him as an obstruction, must be highly gratified to know that that obstruction has already been removed. Brother Hughey removed the obstruction, extinguished the candle, and destroyed the candlestick.

We are to approach this question this morning, to discuss it purely upon its merits. The ground of constitutional law was traversed thoroughly yesterday morning in the opening speech by Dr. Potts, a speech that, though he did not hear it himself, was heard by this body, and will be heard through the length and breadth of the Church everywhere. It remains for us who follow him simply to turn on a few side-lights here and there, or to give an opportunity of viewing this question from a new point of view. And, first, there is a line of argument that may be helpful to some that has already been presented in part touching the administration of our law and the interpretation of terms that is worthy, I think, of still further consideration.

Dr. Buckley said in the New York *Christian Advocate* of March 15th, 1888:

" The question of eligibility turns, first, upon whether the persons claiming seats are laymen ; secondly, whether they have been members of the Church for five years consecutively, and are at least twenty-five years of age ; and, thirdly, upon whether they have been duly elected. If women are found to be eligible under the law, they would stand upon the same plane with men, in this particular, that they must be twenty-five years, etc."

Now, then, is a woman legally qualified to sit in the General Conference as a lay delegate? Is she a layman in the sense of that word in the Discipline? If she be not in, she cannot be introduced contrary to law by a mere majority vote of the General Conference. The Doctor sometimes writes more clearly than he speaks, and it was so in the occasion of writing this article. Over against this we have one of (as Dr. Hamilton would say) the " subtle insinuations" of the Episcopal Address, which declares that no definition of " layman" settles the question of eligibility as to any class of persons. For many are classed as laymen for the purposes of lay representation, and have to do with it officially as laymen, yet themselves are ineligible as delegates. Well, in this case, we have the Episcopal Board over against the editor. Both are right and both are wrong. The editor is right when he said of a woman, if she be a lay member her right is clear as that of any duly elected man. But he is wrong when he denies to her a right to a seat in this body as a layman. The Episcopal Address is wrong when it says that " no defini-

tion of the word 'layman' settles the question of eligibil
ity." But it is right when it says, "Many are classed as
laymen for purposes of lay representation, and have to do
with it officially as lay members who are not themselves
eligible as delegates."

In the practical work of the Church, and in the administration of its laws, women have been regarded as laymen
from the beginning until now. They pay quarterage. If
they did not pay quarterage some of our salaries would be
very short. They contribute to our benevolent collections,
and if it were not for their contributions, we would not
to-day be shouting over the "Million dollars for Missions."
They pray and testify in our class-meetings and prayer-
meetings, and but for their presence among us, many of
those meetings would be as silent as the grave. They are
amenable to law, and must be tried by the very same process by which men are tried. They are subject to the
same penalty. They may be suspended; they may be
expelled. In all these respects they have been regarded
as laymen from the beginning. Indeed, we have never
recognized more than two orders in our Church. We have
laymen and ministers. Up to 1872 but one of these orders
was represented in this General Conference. This General Conference was strictly a clerical organization. But
in 1872 we marked a new epoch in Methodist history, and
a new element came into this body, and has been in all
our sessions since that date. The first step, as has been
mentioned here before, was taken in 1868, when the question of lay delegation was sent down to the members of
the Church over twenty-one years of age, and to the Annual Conferences. Dr. Queal, if I understood him, made

what is, in my judgment, a fatal concession on this question. He distinctly stated, if I understood him correctly, and I have not had time to refer to the report of his speech (if I misinterpret him he will correct me), that when the motion to strike out the word "male" was made, it was done for the purpose of putting a "rider" on the motion and cause its defeat, and when that fact was made known to those in favor of lay delegation, they said they would accept it then with that interpretation, and the interpretation was that the amendment would let women into the General Conference.

Now, that being true, all this talk about the idea of the "women coming in" being never entertained until very recently falls to the ground. It was present on that occasion. It was understood by those that opposed lay delegation, and that favored it, that if they passed this amendment and the laymen were allowed to come in, it would open the door to allow women to come in also.

L. C. Queal said:

I think I am entitled now to correct this putting of the case.

Bishop Foss:

Are you misrepresented?

L. C. Queal:

I am misrepresented in this, that while I stated that Dr. Sherman put that on as a "rider," with a view to defeating the bill, that immediately after thinking so I thought it might be the occasion of securing the approval of the principle in the laity of the Church. That is all I stated. All the rest of Dr. Leonard's statement is his own inference—a misconstruction of the fact.

A. B. Leonard:

I understood Dr. Queal as I stated. I have not had time to refer to the speech he made. I leave his statement with you, and you have the privilege of consulting his speech as it is printed this morning, in reference to this matter. It came to my thought very distinctly that the idea of the possibility of women coming in was then lodged in the minds that were both in favor of and opposed to lay delegation.

Now, then, this vote that was taken, in accordance with the order of 1868, laid the foundation stone for the introduction of women into this body. That sent the question of lay delegation down to be voted on by the laity of the Church. If the women were not to be recognized as laity here, why allow them to vote on the question of the laity at all? And, having allowed them to vote on the question of the laity, settling the very foundation principle itself, with what consistency can we disallow them a place in this General Conference, when by their votes they opened the way for the laymen coming into this General Conference? Do you not remember that we had a vote previously, and the men only voted, and that the lay delegation scheme was defeated, and the *Methodist*, that was published in this city, being the organ of the lay delegationists, said that "votes ought to be weighed, not counted"? And then the question was sent back to be voted upon by both the men and the women? And let the laymen of this General Conference remember that they are in this body to-day by reason of the votes of the women of the Methodist Episcopal Church. In 1880 we went still further. We went into the work of construing

pronouns. There had been women in the Quarterly Conferences previously to that date ; but there was a mist in
the air with regard to their legality there. The General
Conference by its action did not propose to admit women
to the Quarterly Conferences. It simply proposed to
clear away the mist and recognize their legal right to sit
in the Quarterly Conference. Being in the Quarterly
Conference, and in the District Conference, they have the
right to vote on every question that comes before such
bodies. They vote to license ministers, to recommend
ministers to Annual Conferences, to recommend local
preachers for deacons' and elders' orders. They vote on
sending delegates to our Lay Electoral Conferences, and
they vote in elections for delegates to Lay Electoral Conferences, and they vote in elections for delegates from
Lay Electoral Conferences to this General Conference.
And there are men on this floor to-day that would not be
in this at all if they had not received the support of
women in Lay Electoral Conferences. Now, brethren,
let it be remembered that the votes of the women to send
delegates to the Lay Electoral Conferences were never
challenged until they came here asking for seats. They
were good enough to elect laymen to this body, but not
good enough to take seats with laymen in this body
With what consistency can laymen accept seats by the
votes of the women and then deprive women of their seats ?
I am surprised at some of the " subtle insinuations" of the
Episcopacy concerning constitutional law. Allow me to
say at this point that, having introduced into the Quarterly Conference these women, and having given them a
right to vote there, and in the District Conferences, and

in the Lay Electoral Conferences, in all honesty we must do one of two things, if we would be consistent, we must go back and take up that old foundation of lay delegation that we laid in 1868, or we must go forward and allow these women to have their seats. In a word, we must either lay again the " foundation of repentance from dead work, or go forward to perfection." And I am not in favor of going back.

If it is true that the body of the Constitution is outside of the Restrictive Rules, and cannot be changed except in the way prescribed for altering the Restrictive Rules, then I say that this General Conference has again and again been both lawless and revolutionary. Every paragraph of the chapter, known as the Constitution, beginning with § 63, and closing with § 69, was put into that Constitution without any voice from an Annual Conference of this foot-stool. Not one single one of them was ever submitted to an Annual Conference; § 20, ¶ 183, stood for many years in the Constitution of the Church, but was transferred bodily from that Constitution by the General Conference to the position it now occupies. You come and tell us to-day that we cannot change the Constitution outside of the Restrictive Rules without going down to the Annual Conferences; it is too late in the day to say that. We have made too much history on that point. The present plan of lay delegation was not submitted to the Annual Conferences. Bishop Simpson definitely stated when he reported to the General Conference the result of the vote ordered in 1868 that the question simply of the introduction of the laity into the General Conference was presented to be voted upon by the laity and by

the Annual Conferences, but the "plan" was not submitted to either to be voted upon, and the "plan" for lay
delegation by which these lay brethren occupy their seats
here this morning was made in every jot and tittle by the
General Conference without any reference to the Annual
Conferences at all.

I want to know, then, by what propriety we come
here in this General Conference to say that there can be
no change of Part I. of the Constitution outside of the
Restrictive Rules. The General Conference cannot alter
our articles of faith, it cannot abolish our Episcopacy; it
cannot deprive our members of a right to trial and appeal.
These come under the Restrictive Rules, and cannot be
touched by this body without the consent of the Annual
Conferences; but all else has been from beginning, and
is now in the hands of the General Conference. Let it be
remembered that this General Conference is a unique
body. It is at once a legislative and a judicial body; in
the former capacity it makes law; in the latter capacity it
has the power to construe law.

It is at once a Congress, if you please, to enact law,
and a supreme court to interpret law. Now, then, in admitting women to our General Conference, we are simply
construing the Constitution, and not changing the Constitution. The Supreme Court of the United States gives
decisions on the construing of the Constitution, and who
ever heard of a decision of the Supreme Court being sent
down to be ratified by the State Legislatures? The Supreme Court of the United States construes the Constitution, without any reference to the State Legislatures, and
so we construe law without any reference to the Annual

Conferences.   If we touch the law inside of the Restrictive Rules, we must go down to the Annual Conferences. Outside we are free to legislate as we may.

What is the Constitution for?   The Constitution is designed simply to limit the powers of the Legislature.   In my own State of Ohio, for illustration, we have an article in our Constitution that forbids our Legislature to license the liquor traffic, but our legislators give a license under the guise of taxing, but they cannot give us a license law in form.   The Constitution prevents it.   There are States that have Constitutions that have no word to say about the liquor traffic at all, while they may either tax, license, or prohibit.

This is a fact that is well settled, that the Constitution is a limitation of legislative power, and where there is no such limitation there is no restriction.

ADDRESS OF REV. DR. ALFRED WHEELER.

MR. PRESIDENT, it will be well for us, so far as we have progressed in this discussion, to see how near and how far we agree. It is admitted by the friends of the report, or by the committee, that this is a question of law, and to be decided exclusively upon principles of law. So far as those who are opposed to the report have spoken, they conceive, as I understand it, that the position taken by the committee is taken by those who are advocating its adoption. Then we are agreed that it is not a matter of sentiment, it is not a matter of chivalry. There is no place for knighthood, or any of its laws, or any other of the principles that dominated the contests of the knights of old. If it were a matter of knighthood there is not a man on this floor that would deem it necessary to bring a lance into this body. All would be peace and quiet.

There are none that would hail with more joy and gladness the women of the Church to a seat in this body than those of us who now, under the circumstances, oppose their coming in.

It is not either a matter of progressive legislation regarding the franchise of colored men, or of anybody else in the country. It is a question of law, Methodist law, and Methodist law alone.

Now, so far as the intention is concerned of those who made the law, I do not see how those who have kept themselves conversant with the history of lay delegation can for a moment claim that it was even the most remote intention of those who introduced lay delegation into the General Conference to bring in the women, and for us to transfer the field now toward women, in view of their magnificent work in the last ten or fifteen years, back to twenty years, is to commit an anachronism that would be fatal to all just interpretation of law.

I myself was in the very first meeting that was ever called to initiate the movement that at last brought in lay delegation. I voted for it; I wrote for it; I spoke for it in the General Conference and in the Annual Conferences. I was a member of the first lay committee, or Committee on Lay Delegation, that was appointed here by the General Conference in 1868. And during all these various processes of discussion, so far as I know, the thought was never suggested that under it women would come in to represent the laity, nor was it ever suggested that it was desirable that they should; so that the intention of the law-maker could never have embraced this design—the design of bringing women into the General Conference. I leave that.

Now, I claim that the General Conference has no legal authority to admit them here. We are not an omnipotent body. I know that the Supreme Court of the United States, in that contest between the Northern Church, or the Methodist Episcopal Church, and the Church South, decided that the General Conference was the Methodist Episcopal Church. I used that argument myself upon the Conference floor in 1868, that the General Conference could, without any other process, by mere legislation, introduce the laity into this body. I claimed there and then that, according to that decision, the Methodist Episcopal Church was in the General Conference. The General Conference refused to accept that indorsement of that Court, or that proposition concerning the prerogatives of this body. And through all the processes that have been ordered concerning the introduction of lay delegation that interpretation of the constitution of the Church has been repudiated. The Church herself rejected the interpretation that the Supreme Court placed upon her constitution, and as a loyal son of the Church I accepted her interpretation of her own constitution, so that now I claim that the General Conference has no authority whatever to change the *personnel* of the General Conference without the vote of the Annual Conferences. Before it can be done constitutionally, you must obtain the consent of the brethren of the Annual Conferences, and I am in favor of that, and of receiving an affirmative vote on their part. But until this is done I do not see how they can come in only as we trample the organic law of our Church under our feet. And to do this, there is nothing but peril ahead of us.

A simple body may disregard law with comparative impunity, but an organic body that is complicated, complex in its nature, will find its own security in adhering earnestly, strictly, and everlastingly, to the law that that body passes for the government of its own conduct.

Let us see, now, with regard to this Restrictive Rule. As I have said, it has been admitted all along that the action of the Annual Conferences must be secured. Here comes in the decision of the General Conference of 1872

I do not need to recite it. But let us bear in mind two facts. One is, that this General Conference is a legislative body, and that it is also a judicial body. As a judicial body, it interprets law; as a legislative body, it makes law. The General Conference of 1872 interpreted law, and the General Conference may reverse itself with just as much propriety as a court can reverse itself. And if it be the judgment of this General Conference that that interpretation was incorrect, it is perfectly competent for this Conference to say so, and have its action correspond with its own decision.

There is another point. The case that was before the General Conference of 1876 was a specific case. It was the case of the relation that local preachers sustain to the Church, a particular case. This is the principle of all decisions in law, that when a particular case is decided in general terms, the scope and comprehension of the decision must be limited to the particular case itself. And if a court in its decision embraces more than was involved in the particular case, it has no force whatever. And as this was a particular case submitted to the General Conference, and the decision was in general terms, it comprehends simply the case that was before it, and cannot be advanced to comprehend more. And the reason of this is very obvious; for if it was not the case, then cases might be brought before the court for its decision that had never occurred.

There is another point I wish to notice. The General Conference of 1880 did not see the effect that legislation would have by admitting women to certain offices. Certain affirmative legislation is also negative legislation.

When saloons are permitted to sell in quantities of one
gallon, it forbids to sell in quantities of less than one
gallon ; when it says you can sell in quantities of one
barrel, it forbids them to sell in quantities of two. When
the General Conference of 1880 decided that women
should be eligible in the Quarterly Conferences as superintendents of Sunday-schools, class-leaders, and as stewards,
by that very affirmative conclusion, the subject was passed
upon about their taking any other position. That, I
think, must be regarded as sound, and a just interpretation of the law.

But suppose it is not; the General Conference of 1880
certainly did not understand the matter as the General
Conference of 1872 did. For if it had, there would have
been no necessity for legislation at all, there would have
been no need for putting in the law as it now stands, that
the pronoun " he," wherever employed, shall not be considered as prohibiting women from holding the offices of
Sunday-school Superintendent, Class Leader, and Steward.

Now, for this reason,.and for the further reason that it
is a matter of immense importance that we guard against
despotism, I oppose changing the *personnel* of the General Conference without my Annual Conference has a right
to vote upon it, and it is voted upon. Despotism is a
suitable term. A General Conference may become a
despot, and just as soon as it goes outside of its legitimate province, then it usurps, and so far as it usurps, it
becomes despotic, and is a despot ; and you and I, so
far as our Annual Conferences are concerned, do well to

regard with a deep jealousy an infringement upon our organic rights. The only safety of the Church is the equipoise that is constituted by the relation the Annual Conferences sustain to the General Conference, and far safer is it for us to bring these women of the Church, elect, honorable women, into the General Conference of the Church by the same way that their husbands and brothers are here.

There is another thought that I wish to suggest. What are the possibilities with regard to lay delegation, supposing the design of those who wish to bring women in without further action is successful? You make lay delegation a farce in this body. The presiding elders and pastors of the Church may act in co-operation, and they can elect their own wives as delegates to this General Conference, and thus lay delegation comes to be a farce. Some of you may laugh at this suggestion, but it is an *in posse*, and it may easily be made an *in esse*. It is important to us that the laity should hold the place they have by the regulations we have, and they should be changed only to make them more perfect.

No body is safe without adherence to law. We may set lightly by law ; we may regard it as a thing to be laid aside at the command of excitement or passion, but the nation that does that is a doomed nation, and the Church that does that has its history already written. The only safe course for us to pursue is to pursue the wise, careful, judicious, and conservative—I mean every word—and conservative course we have heretofore pursued through all our history. When we boast of what Methodism has

done, or what she is going to do, let us remember it is because of her firm adherence to law.

It is with her as it is with the German nation and the
Anglo-Saxon race—everywhere our glory is in our adherence to wise laws, and if we pass unwise laws, in repealing
them in the same wise.

ADDRESS OF GENERAL CLINTON .B. FISK.

MR. PRESIDENT and Brethren, to an onlooker of this remarkable scene, this great debate now in the third day of its progress must be suggestive of some of the marvellous plays, woven into song, which have made the hearts of the thronging multitudes who have crowded this place of meeting in the past throb alternately with emotions of hope and fear as to the outcome of the parties involved in plot and counterplot. The visitors to this General Conference, seated in their boxes and in the family circle, will say surely these honored men of God who have been called as Superintendents of the affairs of our great conquering Church, these chosen ministers of reconciliation and peace, these *male* laymen called by their brethren to their high places in this General Conference, whose names at home are the synonym of chivalrous goodness—surely all these of rank and talent and authority, whose able and eloquent words have been ringing through the arches and dome of this temple of music on the wrong side of the question, are but simply acting the parts assigned them. In the final scene they will join hands around the eligible women elect, who, in obedience to the call of the laity in their several Conferences, are in their seats with us, and say, "Whom God hath joined, let not *male* put asunder." My brothers, let us briefly restate the case. Five noble women of the laymen of the Methodist Episcopal Church have been chosen as delegates to this General Conference under the Constitution and by the forms prescribed by the laws of the Church. As they enter, or attempt to enter, the portals of this great assemblage they hear a voice from the platform, in words not to be misunderstood, " Thou shalt not," and voices from all parts of the house take up the prohibitory words, and supplement the voices of the Bishops, "Thou shalt not." And one would think, from the vehement oratory of the resisting delegates of this General Conference, that the foundations of the Church were in imminent peril by the presence of these " elect ladies" among us.

Let us turn back a moment, and review the history of the rise, progress, and triumph of the cause of lay representation. I claim to know a little something about it, as I was on the skirmish line in the conflict, and in all its battles fought until the day of victory.

In 1861, to the male members of the Church, was submitted the question of lay representation. It failed of securing a majority vote. Had it carried, there would have been plausibility in the argument this day made against the eligibility of women to seats in this General Conference. The evolution of the succeeding eight years lifted woman to a higher appreciation of her position in the Methodist Church, and her rights and privileges became the theme of discussion throughout the bounds of the Church. Among the champions for woman was that magnificent man, that grand old man, Dr. Daniel D. Whedon, who, in discussing this question, said :

" If it is *rights* they talk of, every competent member of the Church of Christ, of either sex and of every shade of complexion, has equal original rights. Those rights, they may be assured, when that question comes fairly up, will be firmly asserted and maintained."

And in answer to the expected fling, " But you are a woman's rights man," he replied :

" We are a human rights man. And our mother was a human being. And our wives, sisters, and daughters are all human, beings. And that these human beings are liable as any other human beings to be oppressed by the stronger sex, and as truly need in self-defence a check upon oppression, the history of all past governments and legislation does most terribly demonstrate. What is best in the State is not indeed with us the question ; but never, with our consent, shall the Church of the living God disfranchise her who gave to the world its divine Redeemer. When that disfranchisement comes to the debate, may the God of eternal righteousness give us strength equal to our will to cleave it to the ground !"

The General Conference of 1868, after full discussion, submitted the question of Lay Representation to a vote of all the members of the Church, male and female, thus recognizing the women as laymen, as belonging to the great body of the laity, and as vitally interested in the government of the Church, and having rights under that government. During the debate on the report of the Committee on the plan for submitting the question as in 1861, to the male members, Dr. Sherman moved to strike out the word " male." While that motion was under consideration, Dr. Slicer, of Baltimore, said, " If it were the last moment I should spend, and the last articulate sound I should utter, I should speak for the wives, mothers, and daughters of the Methodist Episcopal Church. . . . I am for women's rights, sir, *wherever church privileges are concerned.*"

Dr. Sherman's motion was carried by a vote of 142 to 70, and the question of lay representation was submitted to all the members of the Church over twenty-one years of age. The General Conference did not ask women to vote on a proposition that only male members of the Church should be represented in the General Conference, and it did not then enter the thought of any clear-headed man that women were to be deprived of their rights to a seat in the General Conference. There were a few noisy, disorderly brethren who cried out from their seats, " No, no," but they were silenced by the presiding Bishop and the indignation of the right thinking, orderly delegates.

What does the Rev. Dr. David Sherman, the mover of the motion to strike out the word " male," now say of the prevailing sentiment on that day of great debate? I have his freshly written words in response to an inquiry made a few weeks ago. On March 21st he made this statement :

" Some of us believed that women were laymen, that the term 'men' in the Discipline, as elsewhere, often designated not sex, but genus ; and that those who constituted a main part of many of our churches should have a voice in determining under what government they would live. We believed in the rightful equality òf the sexes before the law, and hence that women should have the same right as men to vote and hold office. The Conference of 1868 was a reform body, and it seemed possible to take these views on a stage ; hence the amendment was offered, and carried with a rush and heartiness even beyond my expectations. . . . The latter interpretation of the Conference making all not members of Conferences laymen, fully carried out these views, as they were understood at the moment by the majority party. Some, to be sure, cried out against it, but their voices were not heard amid the roar of victory. Who can go back of the interpretation of the supreme court of the Church ?"

It is amazing that brethren will stand here to-day and utterly ignore the decision of our Supreme Court in defining who are laymen. Could the utterances of any Court be more definite and clear than those of the General Conference when it said, " The General Conference holds that in all matters connected with the election of lay delegates the word 'laymen' must be understood to include all the members of the Church who are not members of the Annual Conferences "? This decision must include women among the laity of the Church. I know it is said that this means the classification of local preachers. We respond that that only appears from the debate. The General Conference was settling a great principle in which the personal rights and privileges of two thirds of the membership of our Church were involved. Surely, our Supreme Court would have made a strange decision had they, in defining laymen, excepted women. Let us see how it would look in cold type had they said, " The General Conference holds that in all matters connected with the election of lay delegates the word laymen must be understood to include all the members of the Annual Conferences, *and who are not women.*" We would have become the laughing-stock of Christendom had we made such an utterance. The Church universal in all ages has always divided its membership into two great classes, and two only, the clergy and the laymen, using the terms laity and laymen synonomously and interchangeably. See Bingham's "Antiquities," Blackstone's "Commentaries," Schaff's "History," and kindred authorities. It is sheer trifling for sensible males to talk about a distinction between lay*men* and lay*women.*

Women were made class-leaders, stewards, and Sunday-school superintendents, and employed in these several capacities long before the specific interpretations of the pronouns were made. They were so appointed and employed in Saint Paul's Church in this city during the pastorate of that sainted man, John M'Clintock, in 1860, and could the voice of that great leader and lover of the Church reach us to day from the skies it would be in protest against the views presented in this debate by the supporters of the committee's report and its amendment.

It is a well-established and incontrovertible principle of law that any elector is eligible to the office for which said elector votes, unless there be a *specific enactment discriminating against the elector*. Our law says that a lay delegate shall be twenty-five years of age, and five years a member of the Methodist Episcopal Church. It does not say that a delegate must not be a woman, or must be a man.

Women are eligible to membership in this General Conference. Women have been chosen delegates as provided by law. They are here in their seats ready for any duty on committees, or otherwise, as they may be invited. We cannot turn them out and slam the door on their exit. It would be revolutionary so to do by a simple vote of this body. It would be a violation of the guarantees of personal liberty, a holding of the just rights of the laity of the Church. We cannot exclude them from membership in the General Conference, except by directing the Annual Conferences to vote on the question of their exclusion. Are we ready to send that question in that form down to the Annual Conferences for their action? I trust that a large majority of this General Conference will say with emphasis we are not ready for any such action.

The women of our Methodism have a place in the heart of the Church from which they cannot be dislodged. They are our chief working members. They are at the very front of every great movement of the Church at home or abroad. In the spirit of rejoicing consecration our matrons and maids uphold the banner of our Lord in every conflict with the enemy of virtue and righteousness. Looking down upon us from these galleries, tier upon tier, are the magnificent leaders of the Woman's Foreign and the Woman's Home Missionary Societies. Our women are at the front of the battle now waging against the liquor traffic in our fair land, and they will not cease their warfare until this nation shall be redeemed from the curse of the saloon. God bless all these women of our great conquering Church of the Redeemer.

Twenty years ago Bishop Hurst accompanied me on a leisurely tour of continental Europe. In the old city of Nuremberg we wandered among the old churches and market-places, where may be seen the marvellous productions of that evangel of art, Albert Dürer. In an old schloss in that city may be found the diary of Albert Dürer, almost four centuries old. In it you may read as follows: "Master Gebhart, of Antwerp, has a daughter seventeen years old, and she has illuminated the head of a Saviour for which I gave a florin. It is a marvel that a woman could do so much." Three and a half centuries later Rosa Bonheur hangs her master-piece in the chief places of the galleries of the world, and Harriet Hosmer's studio contributes many of the best marbles that adorn the parlors of Europe and America, and no one wonders that a woman can do so much. From that day when

Martin Luther, the protesting monk, and Catherine Von Bora, the ex-nun, stood together at the altar and the twain became one, woman has by her own heroism, by her faith in her sex and in God, who made her, fought a good fight against the organized selfishness of those who would with-hold from her any right or privilege to which she is en-titled, and has lifted herself from slavery and barbarism to a place by the side of man, where God placed her in para-dise, his equal in tact and talent, moving upon the world with her unseen influences, and making our Christian civ-ilization what it is to-day. Let not our Methodism in this her chiefest council say or do ought that shall lead the world to conclude that we are retreating from our advanced position of justice to the laity of the Church. Let us rather strengthen our guarantee of loving protection of every right and privilege of every member of our Church, without distinction of race, color, or sex. Amen and Amen.

ADDRESS OF JUDGE Z. P. TAYLOR.

MR. PRESIDENT and Gentlemen, when elected a delegate I had no opinion on the constitutional question here
involved. But I had then, and I have now, a sympathy
for the women, and a profound admiration of their work.
No man on this floor stands more ready and more willing
to assist them by all lawful and constitutional means to
every right and and to every privilege enjoyed by men.

But, sir, notwithstanding this admiration and sympathy, I cannot lose sight of the vital question before the
General Conference now and here.

That question is this: Under the Constitution and
Restrictive Rules of the Methodist Episcopal Church are
women eligible as lay delegates in this General Conference? If they are, then this substitute offered by Dr.
Moore does them an injustice, because it puts a cloud upon their right and title to seats upon this floor. If they
are not, then this body would be in part an unconstitu-
tional body if they are admitted.

It follows that whoever supports this substitute either
wrongs the elect ladies or violates the Constitution. If
they are constitutionally a part of this body, seat them;
if they are not, vote down this substitute, and adopt the
report of the committee, with the amendment of Dr.
Neely, and then let them in four years hence in the constitutional way.

After the most careful study of the vital question in the light of history, ecclesiastical, common, and constitutional law, it is my solemn and deliberate judgment that women are not eligible as lay delegates in this body.

Facts, records, and testimonials conclusively prove that in 1868, when the General Conference submitted the matter of lay delegation to the entire membership of the Church, the idea of women being eligible was not the intent. The intent was to bring into the General Conference a large number of men of business experience, who could render service by their knowledge and experience touching the temporal affairs of the Church. When the principle of admitting lay delegates was voted upon by the laity, this idea, and no other, was intended. When the Annual Conferences voted for the principle and the plan, this and this only was their intent.

When the General Conference, by the constitutional majority, acted in favor of admitting the lay delegates provisionally elected, this idea, and none other, actuated them. It was not the intent then to admit women, but to admit men only, and the intent must govern in construing a Constitution.

Dr. Fisk said Judge Cooley is a high authority on constitutional law. I admit it, and am happy to say that I was a student of his over a quarter of a century ago, and ever since then have studied and practised constitutional law, and I am not here to stultify my judgment by allowing sentiment and impulse to influence my decision.

Those opposing the report of the committee, with few exceptions, admit that it was not the intent and purpose, when the Constitution and Restrictive Rules were amended, to admit women as lay delegates. They claim, however, that times have changed, and now propose to force a construction upon the language not intended by the laity, the Annual Conferences, or the General Conference at the time of the amendment. Can this be done without an utter violation of law? I answer, No.

In the able address read by Bishop Merrill, containing the views of the Board of Bishops, he says:

" For the first time in our history several ' elect ladies ' appear, regularly certified from Electoral Conferences, as lay delegates to this body. In taking the action which necessitates the consideration of the question of their eligibility, the Electoral Conferences did not consult the Bishops as to the law in the case, nor do we understand it to be our duty to define the law for these Conferences ; neither does it appear that any one is authorized to decide questions of law in them. The Electoral Conferences simply assumed the lawfulness of this action, being guided, as we are informed, by a declarative resolution of the General Conference of 1872, defining the scope of the word ' laymen,' in answer to a question touching the classification and rights of ordained local and located ministers. Of course, the language of that resolution is carried beyond its original design when applied to a subject not before the body when it was adopted, and not necessarily involved in the language itself. This also should be understood, that no definition of the word ' laymen' settles the question of eligibility as to any class of persons, for many are classed as laymen for the purposes of lay representation, and have to do with it officially as laymen, who are themselves not eligible as delegates. Even laymen who are confessedly ineligible, who are not old enough to be delegates, or have not been members long enough, may be stewards, class-leaders, trustees, local preachers and exhorters, and, as such, be members of the Quarterly Conference, and vote for delegates to the Electoral Conference without themselves being eligible.

" The constitutional qualifications for eligibility cannot be modified by a resolution of the General Conference, however sweeping, nor can the original meaning of the language be enlarged. If women were included in the original constitutional provision for lay delegates, they are here by constitutional right. If they were not so included, it is beyond the power of this body to give them membership lawfully, except by the formal amendment of the Constitution, which cannot be effected without the consent of the Annual Conferences. In extending to women the highest spiritual privileges, in recognizing their gifts, and in providing for them spheres of Christian activity, as well as in advancing them to positions of official responsibility, ours has been a leader of the Churches, and gratefully do we acknowledge the good results shown in their enlarged usefulness, and in the wonderful developments of their power to work for God, which we take as evidences of the divine approval of the high ground taken. In all reformatory and benevolent enterprises, especially in the Temperance, Missionary, and Sunday-school departments of Church-work, their success is marvellous, and challenges our highest admiration. Happily no question of competency or worthiness is involved in the question of their eligibility as delegates. Hitherto the assumption underlying the legislation of the Church has been that they were ineligible to official positions, except by special provision of law. In harmony with this assumption, they have been made eligible, by special enactment, to the offices of steward, class-leader, and Sunday-school superintendent, and naturally the question arises as to whether the necessity for special legislation, in order to their eligibility to those specified offices, does not indicate similar necessity for special provision in order to their eligibility as delegates, and if so it is further to be considered that the offices of steward, class-leader, and Sunday-school superintendent may be created and filled by simple enactments of the General Conference itself ; but to enter the General Conference, and form part of the law-making body of the Church, requires special provision in the Constitution, and, therefore, such provision as the General Conference alone cannot make."

Now, sir, this language moves forward with a grasp of logic akin to that used by Chief Justice Marshall, or that eminent jurist, Cooley, from whom I beg leave to quote. Cooley, in his great work on "Constitutional Limitations," says :

"A Constitution is not made to mean one thing at one time, and another at some subsequent time, when the circumstances may have changed as perhaps to make a different rule in the case seem desirable. A principal share of the benefit expected from written Constitutions would be lost, if the rules they establish were so flexible as to bend to circumstances, or be modified by public opinion.

" The meaning of the Constitution is fixed when it is adopted, and is not different at any subsequent time."

This same great author says :

" Intent governs. The object of construction applied to a written constitution is to give effect to the intent of the people in adopting it. In the case of written laws it is the intent of the lawgiver that is to be enforced.

" But it must not be forgotten in construing our constitutions that in many particulars they are but the legitimate successors of the great charters of English liberty whose provisions declaratory of the rights of the subject have acquired a well understood meaning which the people must be supposed to have had in view in adopting them. We cannot understand these unless we understand their history.

" It is also a very reasonable rule that a State Constitution shall be understood and construed in the light, and by the assistance of the common law, and with the fact in view that its rules are still in force.

＊　＊　＊　＊　＊　＊　＊　＊　＊　＊　＊　＊

" It is a maxim with the Courts that statutes in derogation of the common law shall be construed strictly."

Here, sir, we have the language of Judge Cooley himself. It is as clear as the noonday's sun, and he utterly repudiates the pernicious doctrine that the Constitution can grow and develop so as to mean one thing when it is adopted, and something else at another time. You can never inject anything into a Constitution by construction which was not in it when adopted. And you are bound, according to all rules of construction, to give it the construction which was intended when adopted. No man of common honesty and common sense dares to assert on this floor that it was the intent when the Constitution was amended to admit women as lay delegates. It follows inevitably that they are not constitutionally eligible, and to admit them is to violate the Constitution of the Church, which, as a Court, we are in honor bound not to do.

It has been asserted with gravity that the right to vote for a person for office carries with it the right to be voted for unless prohibited by positive enactment. This proposition is not true, and never has been. We have seen, when the Constitution and Restrictive Rules were amended, the intent was to admit men only as lay delegates. No General Conference can, by resolution or decision, change the Constitution and Restrictive Rules. Grant, if you please, that the General Conference, by its action in 1880, had power to make women eligible in the Quarterly Conference as stewards and class-leaders, this could not qualify her to become a lay delegate in the law-making body of the Church. The qualifications of lay delegates to this body must inhere in the Constitution and Restrictive Rules, according to their intent and meaning when adopted. It is fundamental law that where general disabilities exist, not simply by statute, but by common law, the removal of lesser disabilities does not carry with it the removal of the greater ones.

Legislation qualifying women to vote in Wyoming and elsewhere had to be coupled also with positive enactments qualifying her to be voted for, otherwise she would have been ineligible to office. This is so, and I defy any lawyer to show the contrary.

§ 3, Article 1, Constitution of the United States, reads:

" The Senate of the United States shall be composed of two Senators from each State, chosen by the Legislature thereof for six years. No person shall be a Senator who shall not have attained to the age of thirty years, and been nine years a citizen of the United States, and who shall not, when elected, be an inhabitant of the State for which he shall be chosen."

These and no other qualifications are worded or found in the Constitution of the United States touching the qualification of Senators. Is there a layman on this floor who will dare assert that under the Constitution of the United States women are eligible as Representatives or Senators? Words of common gender are exclusively used as applied to the qualification of Senators. The words persons and citizens include women the same as they include men. Nevertheless, in the light of the past, I am bold to assert, that any man who would dare stand in the Senate of the United States, and contend that women are eligible to the office of United States Senators, would be regarded by the civilized world as a person of gush and void of judgment.

Article 14, United States Constitution, §1 :

" All persons born or naturalized in the United States and subject to the jurisdiction thereof, are citizens of the United States, wherein they reside. No State shall make or enforce any law which shall abridge the *privileges* or *immunities* of citizens of the United States ; nor shall any State deprive any person of life, liberty, or property without due process of law, *nor deny to any person within its jurisdiction the equal protection of the laws.*"

(Tax case and what was decided.) (Mrs. Minor *vs.* Judges of Election. 53 Mo. 68.)

The first case indicates that the word citizen when affecting property rights includes corporations.

The second, that the word person, when it relates to

the woman claiming the right to vote, does not confer upon her that right.

The language is: No State shall make or enforce any law which shall abridge the privileges or immunities of any citizen of the United States. Nevertheless, a Republican Circuit Judge held this language did not entitle Mrs. Minor to vote. A democratic Supreme Court of Missouri held the same, and the Supreme Court of the United States, in an able opinion written by men known as the friends of women, conclusively demonstrated that these constitutional guarantees did not confer upon woman the right to vote. Why? Because, from time immemorial, this right had not obtained in favor of woman, and these words of common gender should not be so construed as to confer this right, since it was not intended when made to affect their status in this regard.